unravel me

SPECIAL EDITION

JENN PLUMMER

Wildflower

Unravel Me

Aspen Ridge, Book One

Published by Wild Lupine Books LLC

Editing by Katie Ducharme - Between The Covers Editorial

Cover Art by Qamber Designs

contents

join jenn plummer's readers' group

Stay up to date with Jenn Plummer by joining her Facebook readers' group, Jenn's Harlots. Ask questions, get first looks at new books/series, and have fun with other book lovers!

https://www.facebook.com/groups/jennsharlots/

a note from the author

Dear readers,

Welcome to Aspen Ridge. Unravel Me is book one in a five book, interconnected standalone series. You do not have to read them in order but for the best experience, I recommend that you do.

Themes include: explicit language, sexually explicit scenes, discussion of depression, anxiety, panic attacks, parental death (off-page), stalking (not by MC), attempted SA (not by MC).

Please read responsibly. If you have any questions about this list please don't hesitate to reach out to me directly.

Sending you all love.

playlist

Let Her Go - Passenger
I Fall Apart - Post Malone
Audience of One (Ghost Note Symphonies) - Rise Against
Heartbeat Slowing Down - The All-American Rejects
Power Over Me - Dermot Kennedy
All on Me - Devin Dawson
Mercy - Shawn Mendes
Enough is Enough - Post Malone
Here is Gone - The Goo Goo Dolls
Lights - Ellie Goulding
Lose Control - Teddy Swims
Feel So Close - Calvin Harris
Come a Little Closer - Dierks Bentley
Stay - Justin Bieber & The Kid LAROI
Beautiful Things - Benson Boone
Don't Let Me Down - The Chainsmokers
Thinking Out Loud - Ed Sheeran

For my sweet husband, Michael.

You are the only man who has ever known and loved all of me. Crazy and all. Thank you for always encouraging me to do whatever makes me happy. This wouldn't have been possible without you. I love you.

ivy

"THAT STUPID MOTHERFUCKER!"

"I'll drink to that."

Picking up my next shot of tequila, I gently knock it against my best friend's before tossing it back. Wincing, I reach for the lime and press it between my lips, sucking the crisp tartness into my mouth.

"How is this my life? Honestly, Zoe, what the fuck am I going to do now? I can't afford rent in Seattle on my own." My voice leaks with desperation and I cringe. I need to be stronger than this if I'm going to keep it together.

Today I walked in on my semi-long-term boyfriend railing the bikini barista from the coffee stand down the street, doggy style, in our bed. As if that wasn't bad enough, the asshole glared at me like *I* had done something wrong. He didn't look shocked that I had come home early, no, his face reddened in anger and frustration that his orgasm was interrupted. You can't make this shit up. As the severity of my situation sinks in, I drop my forehead down on the cold bar top.

The worst part? Because trust me, it gets worse. Not only is it his apartment that I was living in, but the restaurant I'm the sous chef for? His parents own it.

Yep. Let that settle in. Luckily my natural flight response kicked in—something I've become somewhat of a pro at—and I ran off to Zoe's apartment to figure things out and process the dumpster fire that has become my life.

The alternative would have been to bash his head in with a table lamp, which was a thought that crossed my mind while watching him rut into the rando. Even though I'm fairly sure that'd be considered a crime of passion, I couldn't take my chances. So, here I am sitting at a bar in Downtown Seattle with my best friend, slinging back shots like we're twenty-one again. It's this or jail time. I may project that I'm tough and can handle a whole hell of a lot, but that's all a carefully built façade, and I know I'm not cut out for jail.

"Well. I was thinking . . ."

"That's never a good thing for me, Zo . . ."

"Don't kill me, but, you could always move back home? Like, to Aspen Ridge. You've got your parents' house just sitting there empty," she suggests sheepishly.

"Ha. You're kidding, right? I'd rather take my chances on the street. I have no interest in ever facing the ghosts that fill that house or live in that town."

"Ivy. Listen. I get it. I know your heart and I hear you."

I go to interrupt, and she puts her hands up to stop me.

"I know what you're going to say. It's the memories. It's what the house represents. I get it, babe. I do. But it's an entire house just sitting there. You sell that fucker and your situation would change drastically. I don't want you to move for any amount of time, but damn. If it was me, I'd be pouncing all over that opportunity. How many people get left a paid-off house for fuck's sake?"

I'm not hearing any of it. My parents got pregnant with me when my mom was nineteen and my dad was thirty-four. It was a huge scandal in town and caused serious heartache for the grandparents I never had the chance to meet. They cut my mom off when she chose my dad, completely ashamed of her decisions and unwilling to support her. Not long after, they moved out of state, and I've never had contact with them.

When I was a little girl, my mom used to tell me her dreams of becoming a writer who traveled all over the world and wrote about her experiences. She gave up the life she had dreamed for herself to be with my dad because she believed in the fairytale of it all, believed in him and his pretty words.

My childhood was spent being told how important it was for me to grow up and leave Aspen Ridge, to go into the world on my own and make something of myself. My mom was a dreamer and wanted to see me live the life she never got to. As I got older I watched her wither away, losing her dreams and the love she traded them for.

Once upon a time she happily changed the course of her life to be with my dad. She was in love. But he was rarely home, and when he was, I never saw them be affectionate with one another, never saw my dad show her love or support. He feigned indifference to both of us. Her heartbreak became more and more evident as the years passed and she sank further into depression. I thought that my parents had a fairytale love story when I was little, but the hard truth of it was that my father preyed on and exploited my mother and her naivety. She may have loved him, but he just wanted to own her. His something young and pretty that he kept at home, locked in her gilded cage. She never had the opportunity to build her own life. She was simply embedded into his already existing one.

My parents were killed in a car accident fifteen months ago and my mom never left Washington. While I work hard to keep the promises I made to my mother—that I would leave Aspen Ridge and create a life on my own—it's hard not to ask myself if this is what *I* really wanted to begin with.

After all, I was happy in Aspen Ridge . . . at one point.

"It's my dad's house, Zo. I don't want anything from him. He's given me enough and I have the therapy bills to prove it. End of discussion."

"Okay, okay, point made. You know you can couch surf at my place for as long as you need, we'll make it work until you're on your feet again."

"I love you for it." I drop my head back and take a deep inhale. "Why's it so difficult to not stick your dick in things that you shouldn't? Is monogamy really that hard?"

"Seeing as how I don't have a dick, I'm really not sure. Brooks is an asshole, Ivy. But tonight we're going to forget about that cheating fuckface and party like the confident, gorgeous, badass women we are. We'll face this shitstorm tomorrow."

I give her a halfhearted smile. I loathe going out. It's never been my scene. I'm much more a "grab a beer and sit on the bed of a truck and watch a bonfire" kinda girl. But I love her for trying.

"Can't we go back to your place, order a pizza, and binge on some trashy tv?"

"Uh. No. You need to get out and be out of your head."

"You're the worst."

"But you love me." She waves the bartender down, who she's been checking out since we got here.

"Hey, what can I get you?"

"Hmm. I'm in the mood for a screaming orgasm if you can manage," she says with a flirty wink.

The bartender's eyebrows shoot to his forehead at her bluntness, and I let loose a nervous laugh.

"Don't mind her. She's absolutely insane. She means the shot, not her. Vodka, Kahlua, Irish cream, and amaretto, I think." Quickly trying to recall her go-to shot.

As he walks down the bar away from us, she smacks me on the arm.

"You're such a buzzkill."

"We're nursing my shitty life tonight, just like you said, not hooking up with bartenders, no matter how hot they are."

"Hey, there's an idea. You could always pick up some bartending shifts for extra cash. That's an option!"

I groan. Loudly.

"I can't go back to bartending, Zo, c'mon. That would be like going backward in my career. Actually, it is going backward in my career. Chef by day, bartender by night? No thanks. Plus, the men are such pigs."

Add bartending to the list of things I'd rather not be doing. The tips were incredible at the restaurant I used to work at, but it was a taxing job in an environment that made me want to crawl out of my skin.

"It's 'cause you're such a smoke show, babe. They can't help but want a piece of you."

"You keep thinking that," I say, rolling my eyes at her.

"If I didn't think it'd ruin our relationship, I'd be trying to get a lick for myself."

I toss my head back in a deep laugh.

When I say my best friend is crazy, I mean it. Her audacity knows no bounds. She is the quintessential life of the party. We met in California during our college days while working at the same bar. When I wanted to move back to Washington, she was down to stick with me. Our relationship was that insta-connection kind of friendship. We're the epitome of opposites attract, though, and it's obnoxiously obvious in most situations.

She has gorgeous ice-blonde hair that she keeps in a stylish bob, whereas mine is midnight-black and down to my waist. She's loud, where I'm more quiet. She's a vivacious extrovert, while I'm a textbook introvert. My circle contains her. If it wasn't for her forcing me around others, I would be at home reading. She has made my life immensely better since she came into it and as cliché as it may be, I'd be lost without her. Craziness and all. She's my ride or die.

My phone goes off for the tenth time in the last thirty minutes. Pulling it out of my purse, I slide it across the bar in Zoe's direction, laying my forehead back on the bar top with a groan.

"Your turn. It's him again, isn't it?"

Zoe picks up my phone and glances over the texts before turning it to face me so I can read them.

"Man, he went from pompous dickwad to full-on maniacal overlord in the span of an hour. Fuck, Ivy."

I read over the slew of texts that get progressively more intense.

> Brooks: We need to talk about this. Come home and we will get through it.
>
> Brooks: Ivy. You don't want to do this.
>
> Brooks: Answer your goddamn phone. I swear to fucking God Ivy don't ignore me.

I push the phone back to her, unable to focus on any of it. I can't let this get to me.

"Just put it away. Turn it off. Throw it out the fucking window for all I care. He's just pissed he was caught." I sit up and twist my hands together in my lap before shaking them out at my sides, doing my best to control my breathing. This will not get under my skin. The last thing I need today is a panic attack in the middle of a bar.

"C'mon then, my girl, let's get you drunk and have some fun!"

We spend the next two hours sipping on drinks and dancing on the dance floor. Zoe does everything she can to help me forget the day and enjoy the moment, but my mind continues to flood with anxiety over how to move forward.

We take an Uber back to Zoe's studio apartment around midnight and I fall onto her couch to hopefully get some sleep. Zoe's suggestion that I move back home has been on constant repeat throughout the night. That damn house really is just sitting there. I lay awake in the dark room, doing my best to work through every scenario. I have some savings that can get me through for a while, but not if I want to stay in Seattle. With the cost of rent, I would plow through it too quickly. But maybe if I moved back to Aspen Ridge temporarily and sold my parents' house, this could set up my life and give me the boost I desperately need. As I envision what it would be like to be back in my hometown for the first time in ten years, my mind drifts to thoughts of the boy whose heart I shattered by leaving. The boy who loved me so fiercely. Who planned our life together.

And I ran. Hard and fast and never looked back.

Until now.

CHAPTER 2

Sawyer

"Does it look like I give a shit how you get it done? Because I don't. Just get it fucking done."

"Yes, Mr. Hayes," my brother says in his signature sarcastic tone.

"Don't be a dickhead, Dallas."

"So, do you only cuss out the employees you're related to or is this the way you're going to run the distillery now? Man. I don't remember Dad cussin' on the job." He looks off into the distance, pondering his question in an annoyingly patronizing way.

"Dallas," I say, barely holding my shit together, "hire someone. I don't care if you agree with it or not, but we are moving forward with hosting events here. It will benefit the company and the community. You've managed to toss out every single application we've received thus far. Do I need to task someone else to get it done?"

"You're the boss, Sawyer. I'll get it done. But I don't agree with this, and I think we're opening ourselves up to a shit show. We aren't a vineyard, we don't need to open house and welcome everyone and their mother in to see what we're doing."

"Point noted. Are we done here?"

"Yep. I'll keep you updated. Boss." He mock salutes me like

the dickhead he is and leaves my office, shutting the door behind him.

I lean back in my chair and roll up the sleeves of my shirt. Becoming CEO of Aspen Ridge Distillery was always the plan for me. My great-grandfather started the company and it's been passed down through four generations. When my father was ready, I knew it would be passed to me. Did I expect it to happen at twenty-nine? No. But six months ago my father suffered a series of strokes that left him with physical and cognitive challenges that made running a company difficult. So here I am, running our family's business.

With my asshole brothers.

My phone vibrates on my desk with an incoming text. Unfortunately, my siblings and I are extremely close and none of them have boundaries when it comes to communication. We have a sibling group chat, and my phone is usually going off multiple times a day with a message from one of them.

Dallas: Better watch your backs. CEO Shithead Sawyer is on the warpath

Liam: Fucking hell. What'd you do to piss him off?

Me: You know I'm on this text thread right?

Dallas: Yup. Just don't give a fuck.

Me: Yeah? You tell them your new nickname?

Kinsey: Ooo! I love updated nicknames. Spill it

Carter: So Dumbass Dallas is out

Me: Dickhead Dallas is in

Kinsey: Ah ha ha

Liam: Okay that's pretty good.

Dallas: Fuck you all

Kinsey: Can't say I disagree. Sorry big brother

Carter: Sorry man it works

Dallas: How'd this turn into bashing ME?
Sawyer's the one being a dick throwing his
weight around.

Carter: Walking into a meeting and am
silencing you immature fucks.

Dallas: If by meeting he means going to
Ruby's to pick up someone to warm his bed
tonight

Kinsey: Eww! Carter haven't you slept with
everyone in AR already? There can't be
anyone left for you to bang.

Dallas: I think the only free females left are
Ms. Nettie and Ruby herself and neither would
touch him.

They're not completely wrong. Carter is a notorious playboy and
has left a slew of broken hearts in his wake. Except, of course, the
seventy-something-year-old Ms. Nettie and fifty-year-old Ruby.
Ruby owns the only bar in Aspen Ridge, The Night Owl, and
Carter frequents the place like he works there instead of the
distillery.

Carter: Fuck you dickhead. Those old women
would be happy to have me in their beds

He's probably not wrong. I roll my eyes.

> Kinsey: Gross Carter
>
> Liam: Wtf is wrong with all of you?
>
> Dallas: Can we get back to shithead being a shithead?
>
> > Me: Just get your head out of your ass dickhead and we won't have issues
>
> Dallas: Bite me Sawyer you grumpy mofo
>
> > Me: Let's go a few rounds at the gym this week huh? Might do you some good to have your ass handed to you again
>
> Kinsey: Do you two ever stop?
>
> Dallas: Bring it big bro. 🥊
>
> Liam: Don't worry about them, Kins. You know they just need to get it out of their system. I'll be there.

I run my hands through the short hairs of my beard and set my phone back on my desk, done with the conversation. My brother Dallas is two minutes younger than me and believe it or not, we are the closest relationship out of the five of us. We're as thick as thieves, but driving each other fucking crazy has always been the norm. We're fraternal twins, both of us have a short fuse and take no shit, but that's where our similarities end. In our early teens, one heated argument got physical and we each walked away from it with black eyes, split lips, and Dallas with a chipped tooth. Surprisingly enough, our dad signed us up for boxing lessons. He said it would give us a safe outlet for our aggression and we'd learn some discipline. Now we're nearing thirty and still knocking each other around the ring as a de-stressor and workout. Our dad called it "controlled violence." Whatever it is, it works for us.

Being the oldest of five kids isn't easy, especially when four of us work together at our family's distillery. Dallas is my right-hand man at work and we go head-to-head most days. Since we're twins, it started as a discussion about which one of us was going to take the CEO position from our father. It wasn't much of one, though, because Dallas made it clear he didn't want the pressure, even though he has fought me on every goddamn decision I've made over the last six months.

Liam works as our lead in quality control and carries a ton of pressure. He's the mad scientist behind the scenes. Carter is the youngest son. It shows. Once the company boomed under our father, he created Carter's position as a college graduation gift. Brand Ambassador. He lives for the spotlight that the rest of us can't fucking stand.

Our family wouldn't be complete without the youngest, though. Our sister, Kinsey, wanted nothing to do with the family business and just started her first year as a kindergarten teacher at the elementary school in town. She may be the smartest one of all for getting out and not working day in and day out with us clowns.

I check my watch and note that it's already 7 p.m. Deciding that I've overstayed at work long enough, I pack up and finally head home to relax for the night. I was prepared to work long hours when I took over this position, and since no one's at home waiting for me, I don't mind them. It keeps me busy, and I enjoy the work.

I back my truck—a red 1990 Ford F150 that I've been driving since I was a teenager—into my detached garage and park it next to my motorcycle. The truck was handed down to me by my grandfather the day I got my license. It's complete with rusted cab corners and a pretty little dent on the right side of the bed from a run-in with a mailbox when I was sixteen. With the money I'm making running the distillery, I could easily replace it, but I'm attached.

I close up the garage for the night and walk across my gravel driveway, eager to get inside. After kicking off my boots in the mudroom, I beeline straight to the kitchen to grab a beer and head for the back patio. Despite growing up in a distillery and appreciating what we create there, I'm a beer guy, and only reach for the whiskey when it's been a shit day.

I drop down on my outdoor couch and take a long pull from the frosty beer. I relish the quiet and love late summers in Washington as the temperatures start to dip but it isn't quite chilly yet. The piece of land that sits behind my house was one of the reasons I purchased this place. I built the wraparound porch myself to spend as much time as I could spare out here. There's a breathtaking view of the Olympic mountains and the tall forests that lay at their feet. While the evenings are quiet and dark, it's the mornings that I enjoy the most. Thick fog settles across the landscape, the only real sound, the rustling of trees and wildlife. When I found this house, sitting on five acres just on the edge of Aspen Ridge, I knew it was perfect.

It's the first home I've ever purchased and when I saw it, I couldn't help but feel disappointed that I didn't have a wife by my side. There was even a time when I was convinced I knew who that woman was, but she left me a long time ago. I know without a shadow of a doubt that she was the one, and the reason I'm still single. I've slept around here and there but I've never wanted a relationship, none of them were Ivy.

While we went to school together our entire lives, we didn't get to know each other until the sixth grade. She was late for the first day of school and walked into Mrs. Murray's class wearing a dress that came down to her thighs, paired with leggings, ankle boots, and a thin little black tattoo choker around her dainty neck. Black hair was piled on top of her head, held by a crown of mini butterfly clips. She nervously stood at the door rubbing her hands together, unsure of where to go. Mrs. Murray directed her to the only open seat available. Right next to me.

She joined me at our desk, and I watched as she got settled with her backpack, notebooks, and colorful pencils.

"Hi, butterfly."

"Hi. butterfly? It's Ivy. I'm Ivy. Ivy Turner," she stuttered nervously. I chuckled at her. She was so cute. I looked back up at all the little butterfly clips in her hair. For a reason I couldn't understand, they suited her.

"Hmm. I like butterfly better. I'm Sawyer Hayes."

I went back to Mrs. Murray my senior year of high school and thanked her for sitting my future wife next to me that day. She didn't remember doing that of course, but I never forgot it. She sat us together and changed my life for the better. Or so I had thought.

As I sit here alone as dusk draws in, with no one but myself for company, I can't help but wonder about her. In the decade since I've seen her, I've never been able to completely let her go. One way or another she always slips back into my thoughts.

A month after we graduated high school, her phone was shut off when I tried to call. My heart began to race and I knew something was very, very wrong. Dallas and I drove over to her house and her mom met us at the door.

"Hey, Ms. Jane, is Ivy home? Her phone says it's been disconnected and it's worrying me."

"Sawyer, Dallas. Ivy left last night."

I take a step back from the door, unsure what her statement means. Ivy wouldn't just leave without telling me. Her phone is off, that's it. My brother looks me over, concern etched into his face. What the hell is going on?

"I don't understand. What do you mean she left? Where did she go?"

"She left, Sawyer. She doesn't live here anymore. I can't tell you where she is, but she won't be coming back."

Her words pierce me like a thousand shards of glass. I rub the spot on my chest where my heart is supposed to sit, before falling onto my knees.

"Shit. Sawyer. Are you okay?" my brother says as he reaches for me.

"I need more information, please. What are you talking about? Ivy wouldn't leave me. What do you mean she's never coming back? Please, Ms. Jane. Tell me."

I'm desperate. I have to understand what's going on and where my girl is. She wouldn't do this.

"I don't owe you an explanation, Sawyer. Look, I appreciate you being good to my daughter all these years, but now it's time for her to live her own life. She's left Aspen Ridge and she won't ever return. This is childhood love. You'll move on from her."

I watch as Ivy's cold, emotionless mother turns and shuts the door in my face as my world crashes down around me, the weight crushing my existence and everything I thought was real.

Agony. That's what this feeling is.

I can't breathe. This can't be real. This has to be a nightmare.

I vaguely hear Dallas, but his voice is muffled like he's under water.

Grasping at my brother's arm, I frantically lift myself to stand. I stumble forward, banging my fist on the front door.

"Ms. Jane! You can't do this to me! Please! I need to know if she's okay. I need to know where she is! Please!!"

"Sawyer, come on, let's go talk to Dad. Dad will help. We'll figure this out."

"I can't. Ms. Jane! Open the door! Please! Dallas, I can't live

without her. Where the fuck is she? I need her, Dallas. I love her. Tell me where the fuck she is!"

"I know. Let's get to Dad. Get to the car. I've got you."

Dallas drags me to the car, taking the majority of my weight. My legs don't work the way they're supposed to. I sit in the passenger seat of my truck and am engulfed in her scent. She's in this truck as much as I am. I rub my fist hard against my chest again, knowing that if there's no Ivy, there's no heart behind my ribs.

I did everything I could to look for her after she left, but I haven't been able to find her. And I've really tried. My parents got involved and I begged her mother to tell me where she was so many times that she threatened my father she'd call the police if he didn't get me under control.

She took Ivy's secret to her grave.

When her parents passed away fifteen months ago, I waited with bated breath for her to come back. I thought for sure she would at least attend their funeral. The day of, I made myself physically sick with nerves waiting for her to show her face. When she didn't attend the service, I slept in my car at the cemetery because I couldn't take the chance of missing her sneaking in to say her goodbyes.

She never showed.

My best friend Reid's dad handled the estate, and Ivy's contact information was luckily in her parents' will. He notified her of their passing and her inheritance of the house. But he refused to give me the information for privacy reasons. I was furious. I drank myself into an angry stupor the day after the funeral. Reid and Dallas had to forcibly drive my ass home and put me to bed after I showed up drunk to Reid's dad's hotel room demanding he give me her number and tell me where she was.

She has no social media and I've never been able to find her online. I considered hiring a PI on more than one occasion, especially because we've got one living in AR, but there's a part of me that accepts that she doesn't want to be found. That part wars with the other side of me that's furious at her still.

She left me.

I toss back the remainder of my drink, lock up my house, and head to take a long shower to wash the day away. After stripping and tossing my clothes into the laundry bin, I walk into my massive stone shower and let the hot water spray over me, rinsing the stress of the day and my shitty feelings down the drain.

My mind chooses torture and stays on Ivy. All glossy black hair and emerald eyes. I try to imagine what she'd look like today, what makes her smile, what makes her feel good. I picture her sweet, plump lips and remember what it felt like to kiss them. The way her body would mold to mine anytime I put my arms around her. The physical chemistry between us was too strong to ignore. We were drawn to each other like two magnets, unable to resist the pull.

Feeling my cock pulse with need against my lower abdomen, begging for attention, I brace my hand on the shower wall, letting the water beat down on my back, and grab it firmly in my fist. I lose myself picturing what she would look like laying naked on my bed. Her raven hair sprawled out in a wild mess on my white sheets. I'd drag her ass to the edge of the bed, settle on my knees between her thighs, part her lips with my thumbs, and drag the flat of my tongue from her center up to her clit. I'd eat her until she was a squirming mess beneath me. I'd find her limit, seeing how many times I could get her to come on my tongue.

I never got to taste her like that and it's a regret I have to live with.

I stroke myself brutally, my fist pumping up and down, imagining my tongue swirling over her slick center. I'd lick her until her hips bucked wildly, until she came undone under me, soaking my face, her sweetness dripping down my chin, my name on her lips as she screams out in pleasure.

Fuuck. I grip my cock tighter as I come harder than I have in months, hot ribbons of cum pulsing out of me and onto the shower floor. The calm that usually washes over me after an orgasm doesn't arrive. Instead, I'm slammed with anger.

"FUCK!" I roar in frustration. I slam my hand against the shower wall, welcoming the sting of pain I get in return. "Fuck! Fuck!"

Feeling less clear-headed than before, my emotions go from anger to anguish and back again. I rinse my body and turn the shower off. Wrapping a towel around my waist, I brace my hands on the bathroom counter and stare at myself in the mirror, hating that she still has control over me.

Hating that even after a fucking decade apart, I still can't get over her.

The ugly truth of it, though? She didn't just leave me behind in Aspen Ridge when she ran off, she took my goddamn heart with her, and I've been fucking empty ever since.

ivy

EVER BEEN JOLTED AWAKE BY A BLENDER CRUSHING frozen fruit ten feet from where you're sleeping? 0/10. Do not recommend. After a fitful night of sleep on Zoe's couch rethinking every decision I've ever made, I'm woken up with a jolt by my best friend making a smoothie at the ass crack of dawn.

"Zo! What the hell?"

"Sorry!" she screams over the noise.

I clutch a pillow over my head and wait for her to silence the jet engine crashing through the kitchen.

"Okay, Okay! I'm sorry, Iv. I'm done!"

"You're good. But Jesus, what are you blending that needs that much power?"

"Uhm. A lot of stuff. You probably don't want to know what I put in these things. Better to just drink it up and know it'll make your body happy, especially after drowning ourselves in tequila last night."

She fills a smoothie bowl, places sliced bananas on top, and sprinkles it with some seeds. My best friend, a walking contradiction. Has no problem drowning herself in alcohol, but god forbid she misses her morning garden smoothie.

She calls it balance.

I call it insanity.

"It's green, Zo. And surprisingly thick. I'll stick to coffee. You have at it."

"Soooo. What are your plans for the day?" she asks.

"Well, I need to face the rat bastard at some point. Gotta pack up all my clothes and things from the apartment. It should be quick, it's not like I have a lot of personal items anyway. Just my clothes, toiletries, and a few essentials. Everything else is his, Zo."

Groaning, I drop my head into my hands and take a few deep breaths, refusing to cry. I know better than to tangle my life up with someone so tightly. When I was eighteen, my mom drilled it in to me to never be so consumed with a man that I lost myself to him. She made me promise to never give up myself so wholly that I would be reduced to nothing in the wake of his inevitable betrayal.

So to sit here now, knowing that I know better? It's crushing. I failed myself and my mom and I'll be damned if it ever happens again. I have to stay strong. It's my only option.

I met Brooks a year ago when I applied to be a chef at his family's restaurant. He came on strong and I was swept up in the whirlwind of his pomp and circumstance. He was ridiculously handsome, with styled blond hair and an athletic build. But what I was drawn to the most? He was into me without suffocating me. He chased me just enough that I knew I was wanted, but not so much that I felt I needed to run away. In hindsight, I see that his lack of giving a damn about my whereabouts most likely means that he's been sticking his dick in a lot more than the bikini barista I caught him with. The coffee sours in my stomach at the thought. Thank the gods above I always made that weasel wrap it up.

"You've got this, babe. Remember how strong you are. Don't take any shit."

"Love you bad, my ZoZo."

I shower and get dressed in some clothes I borrowed from Zoe's closet; a cute cream sweater that hangs off of one shoulder, and a pair of high-waisted leggings. I pull on my booties from last night and glance at myself in the mirror, trying to manifest the bravado I need to face the day. I've got this.

Brooks' apartment building sits in one of the premier areas of Seattle. It has views of the city and water and screams luxury with its sleek modern design and furnishings. It also screams Mommy and Daddy's money. I use my keycard to access the elevator and my skin starts to itch as it slowly rises upward to his floor. Wringing my hands in front of me, I take a deep steadying breath, doing my best to calm the panic clawing its way up my chest before opening the apartment door as quietly as I can. As much as I need to face Brooks and collect my personal things, I really don't need any more visions of him rutting sloppily into another random partner.

"Ivy? Is that you?"

Is he for real right now? Who else could it be, dumbass?

I walk into the open living room as Brooks leaves the bedroom in a pair of dress pants, barefoot, electric razor in hand. God forbid he's anything but perfectly clean-shaven. Bile rises up in my throat at the thought of his smooth skin on mine. What did I ever see in him?

Maybe it's the September Virgo in me, but when I'm done with someone, especially if they do me wrong, I am completely done.

Queen of Detachment.

Goddess of Dissociation.

Empress of Indifference.

All emotions are gone and I feel nothing at all. My withdrawal game is so strong it's like he never existed at all.

"I knew you'd come back to me, darling."

Darling? I hold back a dry heave. He starts to approach, and I put a hand out to stop him from coming any closer.

"Nope. Fuck nope, Brooks. I'm here to get my things. That's it."

"You can't be serious, Ivy. Don't be a bitch about this. We're going to work through it."

"Don't be a bitch about what exactly? The fact that I walked in on you fucking someone else? How long have you been sticking it in other people? You know what? Never mind. I don't want to know."

But his face confirms everything I already assumed. I thought I had decent people-reading skills, but damn if I didn't miss some red flags on this one.

"Just let me get my things, Brooks, and I'll be out of your way."

I move farther into the apartment and collect two duffel bags from the storage closet before heading into the master bedroom, my boots clicking hard on the wood floors. Brooks watches me the entire time, making my skin crawl. His eyes wander all over my body and a smirk spreads across his smug face.

I rip open the drawers of our shared dresser and shove my panties and bras into the bag, making sure to grab my vibrator that's hidden under it all, before moving into the walk-in closet to collect the rest of my clothes. I pull everything off the hangers, not particularly caring how I'm packing, just making sure I get it all so there's no need to ever step foot here again.

I return to the bedroom where Brooks is sitting on the edge of the king-sized bed with his hands pressed in front of him. Ignoring him, I scoot into the bathroom when I hear his steps follow. A shiver runs down my spine as he walks up behind me and places a hand at my hip and his other on my exposed shoulder. I shrug him off, but with him behind me, I'm squashed against the bathroom counter. He pushes his hard dick into my ass, forcing the marble edge of the counter to dig into my hips. My heart rate starts to pick up as fear and panic start to take over. I close my eyes for a split second and take a deep breath to hold on to the control.

"Don't fucking touch me, Brooks. Give me some space to pack."

"You love it and you know it. Don't make this difficult. We're going to work through this and move on. You're fucking *mine*. We work because we give each other space. But you know who you belong to at the end of the day. I may fuck other people from time to time, but you're who I want to be with. We can have makeup sex and everything can go back to how it was before. Don't pretend like you don't love when I fuck you."

Whipping around to face this arrogant asshole, I give his chest a push to put some space between us. Call it courage, fear, or stupidity, I can't take any more of this.

"Do I love it, though? Do I? Aaaah. Ohhh, Brooks! Yes! Yes! Aah," I moan, and I watch as his face transforms from blissful, cocky arrogance to pure anger. "Sound familiar, dickwad? You *never* got me off. And I mean *never*. Not once. I waited for you to go into the bathroom and made myself come.

Every.

Single.

Time.

And the bikini barista you were shagging? She was faking it too. She looked bored, you dumbass. As far as the other shit you spewed? I'm not even going to dignify it with a response. Now get out of my way so I can pack the rest of my things and leave you in Mommy and Daddy's apartment to do whatever the fuck it is you want to do."

I toss everything in my bag and rush out of the bathroom.

"You stupid bitch! You're not leaving me!" he yells.

"Yep, you've said that already. Fuck off, Brooks."

"You think you can just leave me, Ivy? Where ya going to go, huh? Zoe's couch? You think you can do better than me? No one's going to love you. You're a closed-off fucking ice queen. Why do you think I was fucking other people? You're just some-thing pretty to keep and have on my arm. You fit a fucking check box. That's all. You aren't fucking leaving me, Ivy."

He managed to hit a nerve after all. A deep one. I'll be damned if I end up like my fucking mother.

While I'm frozen in place, he takes the opportunity to approach, grabbing my face and kissing me hard. He holds me firmly between his hands and forces his tongue past my lips and into my mouth. The smell and taste of old coffee mixed with the smooth skin of his mouth pulls the dry heave I was holding back up my throat, and a nasty-sounding gag comes from deep within me. He jerks his face back in fear of being puked on, and I use that free moment to drop my bag and grab both of his shoulders. I bring my knee up between his legs as hard as I can, relishing in the feel of his balls being crushed between his body and my knee. I've always wanted to do that, and as the pain contorts his face, he yells.

"Damnit! Ivy, you bitch!" He releases me and immediately drops to the floor, clutching his crotch.

I shake my hands at my sides, quickly stepping away from him.

"This isn't over, Ivy!" he yells through his agony, his face crimson, eyebrows knitted together in pain. While I want to forget him entirely, I hope I remember the look on his face for eternity.

I grab my bags and hustle out of the apartment, letting the door slam behind me. Once I get to my jeep, I throw everything in and settle into my seat.

"Goddamn it to fucking hell!" I scream. "This will not break me. You will not break, Ivy. You can handle anything," I repeat to myself.

I pull out my phone to text Zoe and update her while my body comes down from the shitstorm that just went down.

Me: I'm omw back. It's over.

Zoe: How'd it go?

Me: Nightmare. He came on to me, forced a kiss on me and got my knee to his ball sack.

Me: Dropped like a sack of potatoes and let out a cry like a tiny child. It was glorious.

Zoe: Holy shit you're a goddess. I wish I could have seen it.

Me: I'm glad it's over. We'll talk later.

I take a few moments to steady my breathing and recenter myself. I've never seen him behave like that. He was aggressive, pushy, and demanding. Was I blind? I throw my busted-up jeep into drive, hightailing it out of the parking garage, and drive back to Zoe's. My phone goes off a few times, but I wait until I get into her house before digging it back out of my purse.

Plopping down on Zoe's couch, I pull a pillow into my chest, hugging it.

I have a missed text from Zoe telling me she loves me, six from Brooks, and one from Brooks' mother. I open up his texts first to see what angry garbage he's decided to throw my way.

Brooks: This isn't over Ivy. You're mine and you can't leave me. I won't let you.

Brooks: Everything I've done has been to make sure you're mine. How do you think you ended up moving in with me so quickly?

My stomach cartwheeled at that one. Did he have something to do with us getting evicted? There's no way.

Brooks: You can have tonight but then I expect you home. You have no one and nowhere to go. You need me. See what happens when you mess with me Ivy.

The rest is more of the same and gives me a terrifying glimpse into the life I could have had with him if I hadn't caught him cheating. How did I miss so much? I open his mom's text next and my heart sinks into my stomach. While I didn't expect to keep my job, I didn't imagine it would end this way.

Tina: Ivy, we are disappointed to hear that you and Brooks are no longer together but given the circumstances, we understand why he ended things and support his decision. Due to your indiscretions, we have deemed you untrustworthy and no longer a good fit for our restaurant. Your employment with us is terminated effective immediately.

Well, isn't that just fucking lovely. Psycho ex-boyfriend, homeless, and unemployed. I clasp my hands together so tightly my nails leave half-moon imprints and I struggle to catch my breath. I close my eyes and inhale deeply, filling my lungs and holding it.

One. Two. Three. Four. Five.

I release and count to five again before repeating the process until I feel my heart rate slow and the pain in my chest subside.

Fuck.

This will not break me.

Will it?

CHAPTER 4

Sawyer

THE WEEK PASSES IN A BLUR OF MEETINGS AND PUTTING out fires. By the time Friday rolls around, I'm in desperate need of letting off some steam. Pulling out my phone, I bring up my sibling group chat.

Me: Need to release some energy. Gym tonight?

Dallas: Always down for kicking your ass shithead. 7?

Liam: I'm in

Carter: You know there's other ways you can release some energy that are more fun?

Kinsey: No one listen to Carter and his playboy ways. Sawyer, beat the shit out of something. Don't be like Carter!

Ignoring my siblings and pocketing my phone, content with their agreement that we'd meet up later, I settle into the workday and start by checking emails. I lose track of time until my first meeting of the day knocks on my door.

"Hello, Mr. Hayes? I have an interview with you, my name is Blaire Hollis. HR sent me over."

She holds her hand out to shake mine. I grasp her palm and welcome her into my office. Her professional photo online doesn't do her justice. She's a beautiful woman. Her red hair is curly in a tamed way and hangs down past her shoulders. She holds herself with confidence and doesn't seem the tiniest bit nervous.

"Please, have a seat, Ms. Hollis."

"Please, call me Blaire. Ms. Hollis seems so formal and makes me think of my mother."

"Blaire, then. Well, let's get right to it. As you are aware, you are more than qualified for the position we are looking to fill. Your degrees combined with your experience are ideal and exactly what we're looking for."

"Thank you. I'm happy to be considered."

"My first question, though, why the move from Florida to Aspen Ridge?"

"Well, my parents are actually from Washington. My dad was in the military, so I grew up all over the world. When he retired, we were stationed in Florida and ended up staying there since I was already attending college. We lived in Japan and Alaska for a while, and I fell in love with the cold. I'm a winter girl through and through, though, and knew I wanted to live somewhere with four distinct seasons. So here I am. I moved here last month and am staying with my grandparents at the moment. Sorry, I realize that was a long-winded answer."

"You're fine, we're pretty lax around here. Welcome to Washington. I can't imagine living anywhere but here and I hope you enjoy it and come to love it. Back to the job, you understand that this position is new to our company? That we are looking for someone to create, implement, and host events and tours at Aspen Ridge Distillery? You would be working closely with my brother, Dallas, who is my COO, and sometimes meeting with our Brand Ambassador."

"Thank you for clarifying that for me. As you saw, I hold a bachelor's in hospitality management and a certification in project management. As much as I would love to walk into a position that has already ironed out the wrinkles, I love challenges more, and am very excited about the prospect of this role."

"That's all I needed to hear. Your resume, along with your portfolio, speak for themselves."

"Than—"

Blaire is interrupted as Dallas swings my office door open and waltzes in like he owns the place.

"Sawyer, your damn phone is going straight to voicemail!"

"That's because I'm in a meeting. As you can see."

He finally notices the redhead in front of me when she turns in her seat to greet him. I grin wildly, knowing I'm about to piss him the fuck off. He peruses over her body quickly but unashamedly and I know he likes what he sees. That's all about to change.

"Dallas, meet our newest employee, Blaire. She'll be working with you as our Events Coordinator. Blaire, my brother, and COO, Dallas."

Dallas doesn't take his eyes off of her as they squint to slits. The energy in the room shifts as I feel the irritation roll from him in waves. Blaire doesn't so much as squirm in her seat, but chooses to break the silence between them.

"Nice to meet you, Dallas. I'm looking forward to working with you."

"For."

"Excuse me?" she asks, tilting her head to the side.

"Working *for* me."

"Ahh. Well that remains to be seen," she quips.

Dallas jerks his head from Blaire to me and snaps, "Good luck tonight, Sawyer. You're going to need it," as he storms out of my office. Blaire shifts back to face me and places her hands neatly in her lap as she gives me a bright, devious smile.

"I hope now that you've met my brother, you will still accept the position?"

"Oh, no worries there. Like I said, I love challenges." Her face is downright sinister. She's perfect for this role.

If his unprofessionalism and attitude didn't scare her off, then I know I've made the right decision. I just hope she drives him fucking insane in the process.

I get Blaire set up with HR and move on to the rest of my tasks for the day. It's already getting dark outside by the time I finally close my laptop and rub my burning eyes. Days that are spent in front of my computer drain the life out of me. Glancing at my watch and realizing it's a hell of a lot later than I thought, I grab my keys and helmet and head out, tossing my leather jacket on as I go. Luckily, I know better and always keep a change of workout clothes in a locker at the gym. My motorcycle purrs to life under me and I take off to meet my brothers.

By the time I walk onto the floor of the gym, my brothers and my best friend, Reid, are taping each other up and getting their gloves on. I hurry to the locker rooms to change, adrenaline and excitement starting to flow through my veins. I make my way back to the floor when Dallas sees me coming and nods before climbing into the ring. I ignore him and go check in with the other three.

"Hey, man. You ready for this? He's pretty worked up today. What'd you do to him?" Liam asks, ever the mediator.

"He did it to himself. And the question is, is he ready for me? Been a long-ass week and I'm ready to go rounds with him."

Reid tapes up my hands and wrists and I get my gloves on before joining my dickhead brother in the ring. Energy is coursing through me, and I stretch my neck from side to side. We meet in the middle and touch gloves before stepping apart, and then we begin our dance. I fucking love fighting in the ring. If I hadn't had my life planned out for me, this is what I'd do.

"You wanna tell me why *you* hired our event coordinator, shithead?"

"Easy, dumbass. I told *you* to do it and you didn't. You kept coming up with reasons why they weren't a good fit. Well guess what? I found a good fit. Did you forget who now runs this company? Have fun working *with* her."

"Like fuck I will." He swings at me hard and fast. I expected it so I duck under and use the time to land a hook to his ribs. He groans and stumbles to the side but is quick to recover.

I barely have a moment to straighten before he jabs at me again. This time I barely dodge it and his glove nicks the side of my head. I chuckle at him.

"That all you got?" I know I'm egging him on, but I want him to unleash. I'd feel bad for pummeling him like I need to if he isn't giving me his all. I want to feel his hits as bad as I need to throw them, and I know he needs it too.

"Fuck you," he snarls as he bounces on the balls of his feet. He comes at me with a right hook that I duck under just as his left comes up and I take an uppercut under my chin. I give him a toothy smile as my mouth fills with tangy iron.

"There we go, buddy. That wasn't so hard was it?" I shake out my arms at my sides, move my jaw around, readjust my mouth guard, and then pounce, landing two quick jabs to his face and another to his ribs before he grabs around my head with his gloves and holds me in a clinch. I take two blows from his knee to my stomach and ribs before I can shove him off and land a hook right under his eye, hard enough to make him wince. We lose all our grace and finesse after that and grapple with one another, it goes on and on as we let out our frustration with our fists before Liam and Carter yank us apart, leaving us both panting.

"Jesus, break it up," Carter spits at us.

Carter and Liam share a look.

"Animals. Our brothers are fucking animals."

"Never woulda guessed these two shared a womb."

I look at Dallas, his nose is bleeding, and he's got a small cut under his eye. I know based on how I'm feeling that I'm looking similar. I walk up to my brother, grab him roughly around the neck, and pull his head into mine, forehead to forehead.

"We good?"

"Always, asshole."

"Good." I tap the back of his head with my glove and head to the locker room to catch my breath and clean myself up. I'm quick to rinse my body off in the shower and get dressed before returning to my family.

"You want to go down to The Night Owl for a drink after this?" Reid asks when he sees me approach.

"Nah, raincheck. I'm beat. Family dinner on Sunday, though, yeah? You know my mom loves to see you. Hey boys, I'm heading out."

"Such an old motherfucker. You really can't hang anymore can you?" Carter teases.

"Oh, I can. I just don't want to hang with you lame assholes," I yell over my shoulder as I walk away and leave the gym.

I approach my motorcycle, a beautiful 2016 Harley Davidson Sportster, and swing my leg over, ready to head home and leave the day behind me. I live for the feeling of being on my bike, the connection I have with it—just me and the road. Riding takes all my focus, consuming all of my senses, and allows me to be completely lost in the moment but intensely alive all at once. As the wind hits me, the engine purrs under me and I'm flying over the pavement, my mind completely free of everything except this.

The only other time my mind has ever emptied is when I was with Ivy. When I was near her, I was pulled into her orbit.

Consumed.

Obsessed.

Lost to everything that was *her*. Even though we were kids, I knew it was more than that. I always knew. She was made for me.

Anger is still coursing through my bloodstream as I anticipate getting the fuck out of downtown and into the open space that will allow me to push myself and my bike to the limit.

The moment I get to the edge of town where everything opens up, I fucking gun it.

ivy

MY PHONE RINGS NEXT TO ME FOR THE MILLIONTH TIME since I left Brooks' apartment on Friday. Even though I'm 99 percent sure it's him again, my fingers itch to flip it over and check on the off chance it's Zoe or one of the dozen places I've applied at this week. Brooks has been incessant in his pursuit to talk to me. His phone calls and texts have been getting progressively more demanding and psychotic. After the barrage of phone calls and text messages the night I left him, I blocked his number. Now he just calls me from various work numbers and leaves voicemails. Giving in to the need to know who it is, I pick up my phone.

Missed Call
   Unknown Number

Lovely. My phone chimes in my hand with an incoming text.

Unknown Number: You're mine Ivy.

. . .

No the fuck I am not. How the knee to his undercarriage and me moving out of his apartment wasn't a bright, flashing neon sign for this asshole is beyond me. Clearly he is absolutely delusional. At least he hasn't shown up at Zoe's. It would be hard not to reconsider beating him with a table lamp if that were the case.

Blocking the new number and putting my phone back down, I return to the computer to continue my job search. I've applied at every restaurant in the Downtown Seattle area whether they're hiring or not, and I'm about to expand my search. I'm desperate. I know it's only been a week, but I haven't had any luck. I've worked so hard and love cooking so much. I really don't want to have to go back to bartending. I want to run a kitchen. Needing to take a break, I pull up the fake social media account that I keep for random times I need to cyberstalk people.

Hello, Nora, no profile picture, thirty years old, from Ogunquit, Maine. I place my cursor in the search bar and hesitate. Do I really want to go down this rabbit hole? While I've stalked people for Zoe and myself before potential dates, mostly for her, I've never searched for anyone from Aspen Ridge. Leaving home was the hardest thing I've ever had to do. The pain of Sawyer's betrayal, of leaving him and everything I've ever known, was too much to bear, and I haven't been able to bring myself to look anyone up. Leaving Aspen Ridge right after I graduated high school changed me. All of the plans and dreams that were crushed in the wake changed the course of more than just my life. The pain was suffocating.

Like every day over the last two weeks, I raced home to check the mail. Admission letters were going out and I was still expecting letters from several schools. Sawyer had already been accepted to the University of Washington, his first choice. Which makes sense since it's his parents' alma mater. The look on his face was pure joy when he opened his acceptance, and then per usual, his focus shifted from himself to me.

"I know you'll get in too. Then after our freshman year we'll look for a little apartment together close to campus. I can't wait to live with you, Ivy. Wake up to you every single day. We'll finally be able to start our lives together."

"I hope so. All of this hinges on me actually getting in, though."

"You will. They'll be lucky to have you. You worked hard."

"I just want to be together."

And I did. Sawyer was all I knew from the time I was eleven. When I was with him, nothing else in the world mattered. He was endgame for me. But that day, I received two admission letters. One to the University of Washington, and one to my dream culinary school in California. That was the first event that triggered the rapid spiral that led to me leaving Aspen Ridge for good.

I hover my cursor over the search bar, torn between curiosity and apprehension.

What if he's married?

What if he has a family of his own?

My heart sinks into the acidic depths of my stomach, nausea rolling through me in waves.

I quickly slam my laptop shut and shove it to the side. Pulling my legs to my chest and dropping my head back onto the couch, I accept defeat. I don't want to know. Call me a coward, but survival will make you do crazy things. And I've been in survival mode since the day I got on an airplane at SeaTac. Brooks was right about one thing, I am an ice queen. The pain would have swallowed me whole if I hadn't shut off completely. If I can just hold it at bay and not allow myself the time to think, then I will be okay.

Because if I face it?

It will surely break me.

Needing to get out of Zoe's apartment, I decide to walk around downtown and get a coffee. I thrived working the long hours that were required of me as a bartender, and then a chef. It kept my thoughts muted while I functioned in the hustle and bustle. Having nothing to keep me busy has given space to the unwanted thoughts that plague me.

I walk into the busy coffee shop and get in line. Even though I've lived in Seattle for the last six years, the city is suffocating. Compared to the open spaces, country dirt roads, and mountain air of Aspen Ridge, Seattle feels like a concrete wasteland that's slowly caving in on me. It has its perks, sure. There's always some place open to grab a bite to eat, coffee shops on every corner, vibrant culture, beautiful parks, buildings, and museums. But the past week, everything around me is getting louder and louder and I find myself craving the comfort of my old home.

I'm jerked from my thoughts when a firm hand slides around my waist and pulls me flush against a hard body.

"Don't make a scene." Brooks' voice rings through my ears as he leans down and rubs his face into my hair. I cringe and do my best to step out of his space, but his hold around my waist is brutally tight. Alarm bells go off in my head.

"Let me go, Brooks," I say through gritted teeth. I try to elbow him in the side as discreetly as possible.

"I told you already, my darling, never. Now let's get some coffee and go home."

"I'm not leaving with you, Brooks. Get. Your. Hands. Off. Me." I enunciate every word as I do my best to squirm from his hold, but it only seems to strengthen him.

I start to panic and frantically look around the busy store. Everyone is looking down at their fucking phones, too busy wrapped up on their devices to notice that I'm right here being strongarmed into leaving with my possessive ex. Do I yell? Scream? What the fuck do I do?

The line moves forward and Brooks shuffles us ahead. I use his movement to my advantage and step down hard on his foot. His grip around my waist loosens just enough that I lurch myself forward into the customer ahead of me. We stumble a few paces and it gets me just far enough away from Brooks that he would have to forcibly remove me at this point. I'm not going to make this easy on him.

"I'm so sorry! I wasn't paying attention and the man behind me bumped into me. I have a thing about men in my personal space and I pulled away too abruptly. Are you alright?" I say, my voice dripping with sweetness but laced with a twinge of fear.

The woman I bumped into looks old enough to be my mother. She scowls at Brooks before turning back to face me.

"It happens and I completely understand. Why don't you go ahead of me and order and then we'll sit together until you feel comfortable to leave."

My face beams with gratitude. Thank you to the powers that be that this woman would understand. I chance a look back at Brooks and there is no hiding the furious look on his face. Fuck. I may have just pissed off the devil in disguise. Who is this man? When we were together he didn't give off these psycho possessive vibes. I continue to be shocked that I was so blinded.

I order my coffee and offer to purchase my savior's as well. I watch as Brooks leaves the shop and climbs into his car before speeding off.

As I'm waiting for our coffee order, my phone vibrates in my purse. I pull it out to more texts from Brooks.

Unknown: You'll pay for that little stunt Ivy

Unknown: Think about embarrassing me again and I'll make sure you regret it

Unknown: Come home.

. . .

The woman next to me lightly touches my arm to get my attention and I startle slightly, still shaken up.

"What's your name, honey?" she asks me.

"Ivy."

"Beautiful name for a beautiful girl. I'm Mabel. He wasn't a stranger was he?"

We find our seats by a window looking out at the busy Seattle streets. I place my coffee down on the table before wringing my hands together in my lap nervously.

"No, ma'am. He's my ex. I left him after he cheated on me and he is not happy, nor is he ready to let me go."

"You did the right thing. Are you alright now? Do you need help or have someplace safe to go?"

Her words slice me open. Someplace safe to go. God, I've been holding it together for so long that I don't know what that truly feels like anymore. The first thing that comes to mind is Aspen Ridge.

The next is Sawyer.

I have Zoe and I'm always welcome at her apartment, but I don't want to make her uncomfortable or put her in an unsafe position. And I can't stay there much longer, sleeping on her couch and taking over her space.

Someplace *safe*.

"Yes. I do. I'm spending the night with a friend tonight and tomorrow I am heading home. I'm safe there."

"Good. Remember that you're stronger than him. Women always are. We're underestimated, but that just gives us an edge."

Decision made, I thank her and go back to Zoe's to break the news to my best friend that we'll be spending some time apart while I go hide out in Aspen Ridge, lick my wounds in the fresh mountain air, and hopefully change my circumstances.

I just hope that I survive returning home.

brooks

I SIT IN MY CAR AND WATCH IVY THROUGH THE window of Zoe's first-floor apartment. Even though I'm angry with her after the stunt she pulled at the coffee shop earlier, I know I have to make her come home. I will make it better. She'll see.

From the moment I saw her I knew she was perfect for me. She's everything I want in a wife. Gorgeous, stopping every man in their tracks when she walks into a room. Quiet, doesn't ask questions, and a pussy I love to fuck. And she's all mine. No one else can fucking touch her.

I convinced my parents to hire her, I didn't give a fuck if she burnt toast or was a Michelin Star chef. She was going to be my wife, and after I married her, she wouldn't be working anyway.

The next step was a cakewalk. It wasn't difficult to convince my grandfather to purchase the building she lived in with those losers she called roommates. She belonged at my condo with me. I gave her a week to stay with her friend before I swooped in and saved the day. She agreed to move in with me over a few glasses of wine and some slices of cheesecake. Fucking child's play.

If she had waited just a moment longer before she busted into our bedroom, it would have looked like I was fucking Zoe. It was my one fuckup. I shouldn't have had her bent over facing the door.

Fucking idiot!

I smack myself in the head with my palm until I feel a dull ache.

It took me fucking weeks to find someone who looked just like her best friend. I would have played the victim. Coming up with a story about how Zoe had been trying to hookup with me for months, seduced me, and fucked everything up. I'd beg for her forgiveness, but that friendship would be ruined.

She'd be all fucking mine.

I'll fix it. I'm coming for her.

She'll come back to me even if I have to lock her up and throw away the key.

She's all mine.

CHAPTER 7

Sawyer

MONDAY CAME HARD AND FAST AND I WAS DESPERATE for more caffeine if I was going to survive the day. Last night was our weekly family dinner at my parents' house and it went much later than I wanted it to. Since the clouds promised rain, I took my truck and pulled up in front of Bean Haven for a cup of coffee before heading into the office. Hopping out of my truck, I round the front and spot Ms. Nettie sitting outside with her tiny dog in her lap, as usual.

Nettie Haven is an older woman in her seventies who owns the only coffee shop and bakery in town. She opened it with her husband forty-something years ago and it's been a town staple ever since. Her granddaughter, Hannah, has been taking things over and has worked hard to liven the place up. Ms. Nettie is a busybody through and through and she has been sitting outside watching the comings and goings of the town on Main Street for as long as I can remember.

As I get closer, the dog jumps out of her lap and runs up to my ankles, yapping and growling the entire way. It looks more like a rat than a dog. This is the last thing I want to deal with this morning. Hate me all you want, but I can't stand tiny dogs. They're ballsy little shits with bad attitudes.

"Good morning, Ms. Nettie," I greet her, irritation leaking into my tone. "You really need to put your ankle biter on a leash so she doesn't run away from you." I swoop up the pup by her stomach and drop it back in Ms. Nettie's lap as it rears back and attempts to bite at my hands, making vicious sounds and baring her teeth. Jesus. This is normal behavior for this little pest. I've never seen a large dog act this way unless provoked.

"Morning, Sawyer. Winnie doesn't like a leash, it irritates her skin."

"Ahh. Yes. I remember now. Hannah inside?"

"Who else would be in there runnin' the place if I'm out here?"

"Alright. Thanks, Ms. Nettie. Nice chat."

I open the shop door and the bell chimes above my head. A few people are having coffee and pastries at the tables that line the wall across from the display case. Hannah leans over the counter as she chats up my brother, Liam. The two of them have been best friends since grade school and are still inseparable. The entire town always thought they'd end up together, but three years ago Hannah got pregnant and has been trying to work things out with her daughter's father since. Even though the asshole is never around. He's my age and the two of us never got along. He bailed on Hannah the moment she found out she was expecting, and he's been in and out since. Liam never left her side and has been in Charlotte's life since the day she was born. Still leaves me wondering, but I'm not one to push.

"Hey, asshat, don't you have work to do?" I say as I pat my brother on the back.

"I could say the same to you."

"Yeah, but didn't you hear? I'm the boss." I give him a wink and he punches my arm. "Hey, Hannah. How are you?"

"Hey, punk. I'm good. You here for coffee? I have extra apple cinnamon muffins in the back if you want one."

My order's been the same for a decade. Black coffee and an

apple cinnamon muffin. Truth be told, I fucking hate the muffins. Can't stand apples. Or cinnamon. They were Ivy's favorite, and I would surprise her with them any time she was having a bad day. Or a good day. Or just anytime I wanted to see her smile.

I started ordering them shortly after she left and it just stuck. No one knows but me.

"Same as always, Han. All to-go. Unlike this jerk, I've got things to do this morning."

"I'll get it all packed up for you. No worries."

Hannah leaves us to pour my coffee in a to-go cup and pack up the breakfast I'll force myself to choke down later.

"I expected your face to look worse after that beating you and Dallas gave each other. Haven't seen Dallas all weekend so I don't know how he fared."

"My face is fine, it's my ribs that took the beating. You hanging out with Hannah and Charlie tonight?"

"Nah. Levi is supposed to be coming in for a few days to see Charlie so she's going to be with him," he says reluctantly. Liam does what he needs to do to keep the peace between him and Charlotte's dad, but I know deep down he hates the fucker more than I do.

"Alright. You okay?"

"Yep. All good."

Hannah walks back up to the counter and hands me my coffee and muffin.

"Alright, Sawyer! Here you go."

"Thanks, Han. Rickhouse later today?" I ask my brother.

"Yep. I'll text you."

"Sounds good."

I grab my things and head outside, where I'm immediately attacked by the tiny, sorry excuse of a dog, again. I shake my leg gently to get her to let go of my pants, but she keeps a death grip on them with her sharp little teeth.

"Ms. Nettie. C'mon," I say, exasperated. "Control your

animal. I've got places to be and preferably with my pants not ripped to shreds."

"Oh get over yourself, Sawyer. Maybe if you weren't such a grump she'd actually like you and then she wouldn't come atcha."

"I'm sure that's exactly it. Now please grab her so I can go to work. Or I can call Mr. Hopkins down at the station and have him come talk to you about the leash law?"

"Sawyer Hayes, don't you dare threaten me or I will call your mother right now."

"My apologies, Ms. Nettie. I am limited on time and need to get to work. Could you please pick up Minnie so I can go?"

"It's Winnie."

"Yes, Winnie. Could you please pick up Winnie? I'd like to get to work," I say through gritted teeth and a fake smile.

Finally, she leans down and picks up the little rat and I'm able to head to my truck.

Aspen Ridge Distillery supplies traditional American whiskey to Washington and Oregon, and all operations take place here. Our main building is a large warehouse that looks more like a log barndominium than it does an office space. Floor-to-ceiling windows line the length of the front of the building with large, wide glass doors that open up the space to a huge deck. Inside, is a massive open floor plan with two sets of stairs on either side of the room leading to a U-shaped loft, which flows around the perimeter and hosts our offices. The ceiling boasts exposed logs and industrial pipes, the floor, a smooth poured cement. My mother's touch is everywhere. There's a coffee bar on the bottom floor and potted plants scattered throughout. Large, framed photos of my family through the generations line the walls, and it reminds me of the hard work that paved the way before me.

I pull open the door to my office, revealing a stark contrast from the rest of the furnished building. My office is bare and sterile. I take a seat at my desk, dropping my food down and booting up my computer. Windows line both sides of the room, the side behind me giving views of the rolling mountains, the other, a straight vantage point of the hallway and stairs, allowing me to see who's coming my way when the privacy smart film is off. I sip my coffee and choke down the muffin as I go through my morning routine: check my calendar, email, and make plans for the day ahead. A little before lunch I decide to make my rounds and check on things with Dallas, before meeting with Liam and Carter to tour one of the rickhouses. I jog down the stairs where I hear Dallas and Blaire in a heated argument. Rounding the corner, I find the two of them standing in front of a wall that houses shelves with various bottles of whiskey. I lean against the wall and cross my arms, hoping to witness Dallas being owned by this fiery woman.

Blaire has a hand on her hip and her other is whipping around animatedly as she snaps at my brother. While I know I shouldn't condone this kind of behavior in the workplace, it's a family business, and I know my brother is more than difficult to work with. I'd bet my savings he deserves everything she throws his way.

"You're being ridiculously unreasonable and making doing my job impossible, Dallas."

"Need I remind you that you work for me? You can't make changes like this. You can request them. And then I can veto them. Then you deal with it and move on. It's not happening. Figure something else out, princess."

"*With* you. Your brother was pretty clear and concise about that. We're supposed to be working *together* and you're being stubborn. Why are you so against this?"

"It's unnecessary. *You're* unnecessary. This is a sham and a waste of time. What even is an event planner? Do you honestly think that's a job?"

"Coordinator. There's a difference, but I don't expect a thick-headed, pompous overlord like yourself to know that. And it got me hired here, *Dallas*, so whether you like it or not, you're stuck with me."

Well damn. She's fierce and can definitely hold her own against him. Good. She's going to need thick skin if she's going to survive working with my dickhead brother. Having enough eavesdropping, I walk up to them.

"Hey, Dallas. Blaire. Problem here? Maybe I can help."

Blaire shifts to face me and does her best to mask her irritation. My brother on the other hand, sees me and gets more worked up. That old saying, "pick your battles," yeah, Dallas picks every single one.

"There's no problem here. I've got it handled. We just happen to have a difficult employee who is insistent on making changes without my consent," Dallas says, not holding back.

"Ahh. I can see how that would frustrate a control freak like yourself," I retort, and he shoots daggers at me with his eyes. Blaire covers a chuckle behind a fake cough. "Blaire, what seems to be the issue?"

"We need a place to begin and end tours. We also need a place for tasting menus and for people to gather and order flights. I suggested we put a bar in. Here," she says as she motions to the wall in front of us. I can see her point and the potential of the area she chose. "The wall already holds shelves and the space in front of it is empty and close to the large bay doors and that gorgeous wraparound porch, which gives plenty of room for extra seating."

It makes sense and I see the value in it. It's a good suggestion. I don't understand why Dallas wouldn't go for it. Other than the simple fact that he likes to make things as difficult as possible.

"You have the proposal?" I ask her.

"Of course. I sent it to Dallas over the weekend. He 'vetoed' it." She makes air quotes with her fingers while looking directly at him.

Of course he did.

"Send it to me and I'll look it over this afternoon. I like the idea and think it could work. Good work, Blaire."

"Thank you, Sawyer. I'm happy to see one of you is logical."

"You aren't serious right now?" my brother says to me, turning away from Blaire.

My phone chimes in my hand with an incoming text.

Liam: Rickhouse B

"We need to meet with Liam and Carter before lunch. Walk with me, Dallas." I nod at my brother.

Dallas and I walk in silence until we get outside and round the corner to head to the other side of our property that hosts our rickhouses.

"She's the fucking devil, Sawyer. What were you thinking hiring her?"

"She's overqualified, dickhead."

"Wrong."

"Thought she'd be a good fit for the team."

"Fucking wrong again."

"She's sweet."

"Abso-fucking-lutely wrong."

"I knew she'd get under your skin and drive you crazy."

"And there the fuck it is. You asshole."

"Dallas you just gotta work with her, man. She's going to do a good job here. Did you learn nothing from Dad? An ounce of decorum and professionalism maybe?"

"Have you met me?"

We reach the front of the building where Liam and Carter are waiting for us. Our rickhouses are enormous buildings that hold all of our barrels through the aging process. Each row and place of the barrel changes the outcome of the spirit. We're entering Liam's wheelhouse now, the part that he lives for.

We enter the building and I'm engulfed in the smell of oak

and charred sugar. I love it. Today we're checking on a few barrels of the same mash bill that have been aging for different amounts of time. While all of us grew up here and love different parts of the whiskey business, Liam is the only one of us who has a love for the recipes and the process. He's passionate about it in a way that the rest of us only appreciate it. We spend the next hour talking and tasting from two barrels before closing up for lunch, knowing we're running slightly behind to meet our sister. Her school is closed today for a waiver day, and we promised we'd have lunch with her at her favorite place. Like clockwork, all of our phones go off with an incoming text alert as we walk the long gravel drive to the staff parking lot.

"Kins?" I ask, not bothering to pull my phone from my pocket since Carter is already holding his.

"Yep. She says, 'where are you fools? I swear to God you had better not be ditching me or I will murder you all in your sleep,'" he reads in his best Kinsey impression.

We all laugh. Our sister is a tiny pixie of a thing, but tough as nails. I guess she'd have to be after growing up with four older brothers. We didn't take it easy on her just because she's a girl, and she certainly doesn't have a princess complex because of it. She can handle herself on the worst of days and we're all proud of her for making her own way in the world.

"We had better hurry up in case she wants to see her threat through," Carter says as he fakes a fearful shiver. We all pile into my truck. Since I only sipped enough to taste today, I drive by default, which is our normal now that I think about it. When I drink, I typically only do so in the comfort of my own home. I like to be in constant control and when I give that up, I need to know I'm not going to fuck things up.

We arrive ten minutes later at Barrel House to see our smiling sister waiting for us at a table.

"Miss us?" Carter asks as he plants a kiss on our sister's cheek. Liam, Dallas, and I follow suit. She may not be a princess, but we'll be damned if she doesn't feel an equal amount of our love with all the shit we give her.

"Never. But god, were you guys in a freaking rickhouse? You smell so good! Tasting without me?"

"Hey now, don't be mad. Business has gotta run while you're out there wiping noses and singing the ABCs."

As expected, Kinsey reaches out and smacks Dallas right in the chest.

"That's not all I do and you know it!" She looks at me before continuing, "Dickhead Dallas was a perfect new nickname by the way. We're keeping this one for a while."

We all laugh in agreement.

"Alright! Fill me in! What is going on with you all?" she says.

We make small talk before the waitress comes over to take our orders.

"Hey, Hayes bunch. I just want to let you know that our menu is actually really small at the moment. Hendrix had a family emergency in Utah, and we aren't sure when he'll be back. Our line cooks are fantastic, but we had to shorten the menu and take off the more complex items."

"No worries, Luna. I hope everything is okay with his family," I reassure her.

"I'll pass that along when I talk to him. Can I get you all something to drink?"

We place our orders and spend the next hour talking and eating burgers and fries before saying goodbye to Kinsey and loading back up in my truck to head back to the distillery.

After separating from my brothers, I settle back in at my office. Already having the plans from Blaire in my inbox, I spend some time reviewing the proposal and decide to call them both to come see me in an hour. I make some phone calls to potential buyers and review production costs for this quarter, with just enough time to down a protein shake before my meeting.

I only just sit back in my chair when Dallas walks in.

"Haven't you seen enough of me today?" he says.

"Have a seat. Try not to be a dickhead."

Blaire knocks on my door and Dallas whips his head around in her direction. He groans dramatically, loud enough for her to hear, and I shoot him a warning glance that he ignores.

"Thanks for coming, Blaire. Have a seat."

"Of course, Sawyer. What can I do for you?" she says, all smiles, bright eyes, and cheerful. I hold back a laugh. She's all sunshine and roses while my brother is storm clouds and weeds. But man does she rise to each one of his challenges.

"I looked over your proposal, Blaire. I'd like to move forward with the plans. I think it will add value and it makes sense. If you could have some design mock-ups made and send that over with the financials to Dallas we'll get it in the works."

Blaire smiles brightly while Dallas crosses his arms and shakes his head slowly. I feel his tension and I know he's ready to pop.

"Thank you. I'll get right on that."

"One more thing. It seems that you two are having issues working together. Is this something HR needs to get involved in?"

Dallas' head snaps up and he gives me one of his "you aren't fucking serious" looks.

I'm not. But he doesn't need to know that.

"I'll be honest. It's been a difficult first week," she states flatly. Dallas rolls his eyes, but I feel the tension coming off of him in waves. His fists clench and unclench on the armrests, and he sits up taller in his seat. "But I really want this job and I would love nothing more than to make it work here," she pauses and shifts in her seat before continuing, "I just have one stipulation, if that's okay, Sawyer?"

Aaand POP.

Dallas cocks his head to the side and begins to turn in her direction in a move that reminds me of one of those horror movie dolls whose heads slowly rotate all the way around. It's eerie as fuck and I have to hold back a shiver. Blaire is undeterred and holds her ground.

"And you feel that during your first week of work, you're in a position to put stipulations in place for your employment? Who do you think you are?" Dallas' voice is calm and controlled, but the deep, menacing way he delivers it matches his creepy as fuck facial expression.

I'm debating excusing Blaire from the room for her protection while I get an exorcism performed on my twin before she replies to him. I sit back and cross my arms over my chest deciding I'd rather see how this plays out.

"I do. Because the CEO thinks I'm a worthy member of this team and I was hired to fill a need. I'm good at what I do and I know I can add value to this place, but I also need this job. It seems to me like we both need each other. So, yes. I think I am in a position where I can put a stipulation for me to stay since *you* are creating a toxic work environment."

"Dallas," I warn. I watch my brother closely as he shuts his eyes and inhales. His hands white knuckle the armrests as he struggles for composure. He slowly opens his eyes and looks at Blaire.

"Fine. What's your one stipulation?" The coldness of his voice is replaced with condescension.

"Honestly, it's nothing major, but I think it's important so that we clear up any lingering confusion. I want you to admit that we work *together* and move forward as a *team*." Quick and straight to the point. Dallas delivers a short-lived, menacing laugh.

"No can do, princess. Just stay out of my way."

He stands and then storms out of my office like a toddler who was told no.

"I don't make it a habit of apologizing for my brother's behavior, but I am sorry in this case. I'll talk to him. It'll be fine and I'll make sure moving forward that he isn't disrespectful. Get the proposals to him and cc me on everything."

"Thank you, Sawyer. I promise I'm not a difficult person to work with. He brings out a side of me I don't recognize. I'm not sure why he dislikes me so much. People usually love me."

"I'm not worried about it, Blaire, and you shouldn't be either. It'll be okay and he'll come around."

She nods before grabbing her notebook and leaving me to my empty office.

Maybe I should reconsider sending his ass to HR.

CHAPTER 8

ivy

THE DRIVE FROM SEATTLE TO ASPEN RIDGE WILL TAKE me almost four hours at this point. I wish I could blame the traffic, and I could until I got out of the city, but there are so many scenic lookout points that I have to keep pulling over to marvel at them. Sure, on some clear days we get an amazing view of Mount Rainier, and I love it when my mountain comes out and shows off. But this? Snow-tipped mountains in the distance cast a magnificent shadow over the lush forest below them, the crystal lakes spread out at their feet. Overcast days like today are my favorite, when everything is blanketed in cloud cover and a light mist travels along in the breeze. It's enchanting and mystical and I forgot how much it gave me life. These scenic views that Washington holds have so much beauty that it takes your breath away. I have to ask myself how I ever lived in a city. I'm sure it aided in my lack of thriving there.

I stocked up on my favorite snack food and have been blaring the music to pass the time. As I reach into the bag of Chex Mix, I sigh in frustration as I only pull out rye chips, having done all I could to pick around them without Zoe here. I hit the speed dial on my phone to call her.

"Are you there yet?" Her chirpy tone fills the car, bringing a huge smile to my face.

"I miss you already, ZoZo!" I whine.

"The rye chips are in your way aren't they?"

She knows me so well.

"Ugh. Yes. And I'm driving and I can't pick around them anymore. They're so gross. I honestly don't know how you love those things."

"Can't help ya, babe. Maybe you should just start eating them like a normal person?"

"Nope. Can't do it."

"Can't or won't?"

"Both."

"How far out are you? You've got to be getting close, right?"

"Uhm. GPS says another hour. I'll text you when I get there."

"K. Drive safe."

"Love you."

My belly is full of butterflies as it hits me that I'm almost to Aspen Ridge. The nervous ones, not the fluttery excited ones. I can't believe I'm really driving back to my hometown. I'm fine until I think about it, then I start to feel so anxious that I could throw up. The butterflies quickly change to an angry swarm of hornets as an overwhelming terror starts to take root at the prospect of running into people that I used to know. The people that I used to love and never said goodbye to. That self-loathing part of my brain creeps in and tells me that I wasn't all that memorable to begin with and they've all moved on with their lives just fine without me present.

I know I'm overthinking all of it, but why would they welcome back someone who caused harm to their loved ones? Again, the negative thoughts balance the optimistic ones. Maybe I didn't cause any harm at all. Maybe I did everyone a favor by leaving. And by everyone, I mean one boy in particular. Maybe he felt trapped by me and is much better off without having to focus on me like he always had. My thoughts and feelings war with themselves for the rest of the trip until I take the exit for my hometown.

Aspen Ridge is a small town that hides away west of Olympic National Forest. Tucked away and hidden from the rest of the world, it's a gem if you love the outdoors, nosey neighbors, and one restaurant option. The air is different here. Cleaner. Fresher. It makes your body hum with liveliness, but also coats you in a comfortable peace. I blame the constant cloud cover that blankets it, the mountains that cocoon it, and the coast it backs up to.

I pull the Boston Bruins hat down that I impulsively stole from Zoe in hopes of looking more like an out-of-towner, and sink deeper into the driver's seat as I slow my speed and approach downtown. I use the term downtown loosely. It's a two-lane road with brick buildings lining the street on cobblestone sidewalks. Beautiful flower baskets hang from every streetlamp, shop windows are decorated with lively displays. I can't help but wonder if Ms. Nettie still sits outside of her coffee shop and reports speeders to the police station. Bean Haven made the best apple cinnamon muffins and my mouth waters at the thought of them. They were my favorite thing on earth. I tried to recreate them on more than one occasion, but could never get the recipe perfect. I keep my head low, maintain my speed, and pass through the strip unscathed. I release the breath I was holding and continue to drive to the other side of town.

Pulling onto Lupine Lane, a long gravel drive that leads to a small cul-de-sac, I easily navigate toward my childhood home on autopilot. My hands shake as I drive down the long dirt road and pull into the driveway of the old house, overwhelmed with nostalgia.

And not the good kind.

Rather, nightmares that escaped from the depths of hell to haunt me.

Memories that I've long since buried.

Even though I haven't returned to this place since I was a teenager, somehow it's managed to remain the same, only older. The cul-de-sac still sits with one house on either side of the circle and miles of woods behind them both. The picket fence that frames the front yard is whitewashed and aging, the paint peeling and chipping away due to the changes in weather and neglect. The house is a large arts and crafts style home that's usually found in this part of the Pacific Northwest. It's simple but charming.

In an eerie kind of way.

I put my perfect beater of a jeep in park and take a moment to gather my thoughts.

It's just a house.

It's just a house.

It's just a house.

It shouldn't matter that it was really more like a cage.

Or that it's the place where my mother spent my entire childhood depressed and alone, grieving the life she gave up and the love she never got in return.

Some days I wished that I had been enough for her. But I realize now that it's hard to trade the life you dreamed of for yourself for something else and be grateful for it when what you have is actually all smoke and mirrors. She was okay giving up everything she wanted for herself to have a fairytale life with the man she fell in love with. But she didn't have that. And it killed her long before the car accident did. My heart hurts at the reminder.

My phone buzzing in the seat next to me pulls me out of my head. I pick it up only to be greeted with my best friend's face.

"Calm down, Zo. I literally just pulled into the damn driveway," I say, not bothering with greetings.

"Babe, you should have called me the moment you arrived in that town! I worry about you."

"I told you I was fine. I can do this."

It's just a house, I mutter to myself again. I climb out of my jeep, trying to balance my phone between my cheek and shoulder while simultaneously grabbing my purse to dig out the house keys the estate lawyer mailed to me. I look up at the aging house and really take it in.

Shit.

Was this place always this creepy looking? Walking up the rocky gravel entryway, I notice the wild lupines that grow in this part of Washington are still everywhere you look. Their vibrant blues, pinks, and purples breathe life into the otherwise dark landscape. Without them, this place would look like somewhere Hansel and Gretel would go to disappear deep in a haunted wood.

I approach the same yellow door that I had so many times before. What was once bright and cheery, masking the shitty memories inside, is now faded and chipping, much like the rest of the place, and matches the memories much better.

"Ivy! Are you even listening to me?" Zoe's yell pulls me back into the present.

"Yeah. Of course I am. I'm just trying to get into the house with all my shit and talk to you at the same time. Calm yourself down, hussy."

"Okay, so I've been thinking."

"That's never a good thing."

"Hear me out, dammit."

"Spill."

"You need to find a hot fling while you're there to help distract you from the crash and burn of your life. It would do you some damn good to be railed by some smoking fine piece of ass while you're holed up selling that place. Your vagina probably doesn't even work anymore."

My mind flicks back to one man in particular that I'm positive I could get lost in.

The one man I'm avoiding.

The one man I don't want to face.

I push the key into the lock, but it doesn't click over. Lovely. It's already unlocked. Fan-freaking-tastic.

The front door creaks and groans as I push it open and take

my first steps into what is going to be home for the next few months. It's eerie being here completely alone and my skin breaks out in goosebumps.

"Ivy Paige!"

"God, Zoe!" I practically yell. "My vagina is just fine, thank you for your concern."

"They'll need the jaws of life to pry you open for insertion, Iv. That thing hasn't been entered in how long now? Shit-for-Brains and his needle dick don't count."

"My pink vibrating best friend has been getting the job done nicely, actually. Guaranteed orgasm, and who needs a man when I can get myself there without all the fuss? I'm not about to start complaining about the much easier cleanup either. And you know what? I don't have to worry about being fucking cheated on by it," I rant.

I drop my bags onto the tiled entryway floor and take in the large open area in front of me. Everything looks like it was left the same way my parents had it, but is covered in a thick layer of dust. I guess I inherited all the shit in this place too. Maybe I can pay someone a fee to have an estate sale for me to get the place emptied and more cash in my pocket.

I walk through the open entryway and into the expanse of the living room, looking over everything as I go. As I near the hallway that leads to the stairs, I find myself face to face with a very large, very muscular beast of a man heading my way.

I scream as I stumble back, dropping my phone in the process.

"Holy shit balls! What the fuck? Who are you? How did you get in here?"

Goddammit, the front door was unlocked. Fucking great. First moments back in this town and I'm going to die at the hands of Hottie Hulk here. And of course I dropped my phone. Christ, Ivy. Guess calling 911 isn't a quick option, and it's not like anyone on the outskirts of town will hear my screams while I'm butchered into tiny pieces or stuffed in a freezer for him to do god knows what to later. I should probably lay off the true crime shows. Going to need to dissect that later if I survive this.

"Are you okay? Jesus," the beast says in the huskiest male voice I've ever heard. He holds his hands out, grabbing my forearms to help steady me.

"You're not in danger." He releases my arms and puts his in the air, palms facing me in the universal sign of surrender. That does nothing to curb my fear given that he is standing in my house.

In the dark.

Alone.

Even if it has been abandoned for a year and a half. Maybe he's a squatter. Fuck. That's probably it. Now I've got to figure out how to remove a sexy as fuck homeless squatter from my dead father's nightmare shack and figure out where I'm going to sleep in this town without announcing that I'm back. I don't know how yet, but I'm determined to stay way under everyone's radar.

In and out. Fix it up, sell it, get on with my life.

"I asked you a question first, fucker. Now who are you and how did you get in here?" I back further into the main living space where there's more light.

"Reid. I live next door. I check on things around here from time to time."

"Suuuure you do. Right. And I'm Megan Fox. Who asked you to do that?"

"My parents. They knew the owner, Brian Turner. My dad handled his estate after he passed away. Now who are you? This place has been empty for well over a year." His voice may be deep, but you can't miss the softness in it.

Reid steps into the large living room and paces closer to me. Okay, so I was right about the beast thing. He has to be well over six feet and he's packing some serious Khal Drogo muscles. Fucking. Hell. How?

His tan skin is covered in tattoos from his fingers and up both arms, disappearing under the pushed-up sleeves of a hoodie. It's formfitting for a sweatshirt and leaves little to the imagination. He's in amazing shape and I can't help my mouth from falling open slightly while I gape at him.

Fucking hell is right. Where do men like him come from? They're made in a lab, aren't they? Surely they don't come out looking like this perfect Greek god. I can't imagine what his parents look like. Lawyer my ass. They have to be models. Or Olympus' twelve descendants at a minimum.

I grasp my hands in front of my stomach and twist them together.

Focus, Ivy.

"Oh. Uh. Okay. That makes some sense. I wasn't expecting anyone to be here. You scared the shit out of me," I say, more than a little exasperated, unsure whether it's from the fright of my life or the Adonis in my space.

"Sorry 'bout that. I wasn't expecting you either. Total coincidence to be here at the same time. And as much as I was enjoying listening to you convince yourself that your, what did you call it? Your 'pink vibrating best friend?' was better than a man, I couldn't stay here all day . . ." He pauses and slowly peruses my body from bottom to top before meeting my eyes again. "Unless you want me to convince you that you're wrong?" he says with a smirk. "You still haven't told me who *you* are."

A nervous laugh escapes me. Is he seriously hitting on me right now? I'm suddenly self-conscious of my holey black leggings and baggy, oversized sweatshirt. I absentmindedly rub my hand through my hair and tuck it behind my ear. He has to be fucking with me. This kind of shit only happens to Zoe.

"Shit! Zoe!" Scurrying to pick up my phone, I'm greeted with a rainbow of expletives from my best friend's colorful vocabulary.

"Zo, I'm fine. It's okay. A neighbor is here and I was obviously expecting the house to be humanless." I punctuate the last word and toss a glare at him.

"Are you sure? Should I call the police? Are you okay? You just scared the shit out of me, Ivy!"

"Breathe, psycho. I think I'm fine. I'll call you tonight, I promise." Hanging up the phone on my best friend, I return to find my muscular guest leaning up against the wall with a shit-eating grin on his face.

"Okay, Drogo. Here's how this is going to go. I'm 1 and 0 for making men drop to the floor due to my knee to their balls this month and I'd happily make it 2 for 0. So, I'm going to ignore your witty remarks about being able to take over the job of my vibrator, not gonna happen. If you're done here, I'm assuming you remember where the door is?" I make a shoo motion at him.

"Drogo, huh?"

My mouth drops open.

"That's what you took from what I just said?" Fucking men.

He sets his eyes on me and takes a few steps forward as I match them to step back. We pace until I'm backed right against the wall. Fucking genius, Ivy. Because that's exactly what you want to do when alone with a stranger. Become the victim!

Reid stops with us toe-to-toe and places a hand next to my head, semi-caging me in.

Holy hell.

His muscles flex next to me and I can't help but look at the tattoos that run along his veiny forearm.

"How 'bout we start over, huh, sweetheart? Who are you?" he says in a husky whisper as he brushes some rogue hair out of my face and tucks it behind my ear. He's standing so close that I can smell the mint gum he's chewing, coupled with some clean and masculine goodness.

I take a steadying breath and chance looking up at this massive man crowding my space. His deep-green eyes meeting mine hitches my attempt at steady breathing. My god he is gorgeous. His long, dark chocolate-brown hair is secured in a low ponytail, pieces have come loose and fall into his face as he peers down at me. My pussy responds in kind by throbbing. I can feel the wetness pooling between my legs and I feel unsteady. Okay, so maybe it's been a little too long since I've felt a man, even longer since I've been with one who knows what he's doing. I hate to stereotype people, but damn does this man look like he knows exactly how to make a woman feel good.

"Alright, smooth talker." I chuckle as I make mistake number three thousand in the last five minutes; placing my hands flat open on his chest in an attempt to push him away. I'm met with such solid male perfection that I don't actually push him away at all. Instead, my traitorous bitch of a body decides that's its cue to release an appreciative moan that unfortunately doesn't go unnoticed by the beast crowding my personal space. I immediately retreat and place my hands behind me, dropping my gaze from his.

"Fuck. Tell me what I have to do to pull more sounds like that out of you," he whispers as he places his fingers under my chin and forces my face to meet his again. My heart is about to beat out of my fucking chest. Is this happening right now? This can't be seriously happening.

"Do we have to talk so close to each other?" I ask. His fingers are still lifting my chin, his thumb aimlessly rubbing back and forth.

"I'm rather enjoying it. But if space is what you want . . ." he says. Before releasing my chin, he cups my cheek, dwarfing it in his large hand and letting it drop as he takes a single step back. I immediately feel the loss of him.

"Better?"

"I mean, I can definitely think more clearly without you that close to me," I huff. "Ivy. My name is Ivy," I stutter like an idiot. His head rears back like I slapped him and his eyes squint as he cocks his head to the side and studies me.

"Ivy," he repeats in a statement.

The way my name rolls off this man's tongue just sounds too good. He drops his head more and shakes it slightly as if coming to a realization and he needs to pull himself together. I mean, I'm a goddamn stranger for fuck's sake. Reel it in, buddy!

He mutters something under his breath that sounds like "of course" and takes a few large steps back from me.

"Ahh. The daughter. This is your place. That makes more sense."

"How did you know that?"

"I told you, my father and his firm handled the estate. Since you never came to claim the place and I live next door, he asks me to check on it. I'm aware of who you are, Ivy. I just didn't expect you."

"Oh-Okay. Yes. You did say that. Sorry. I spoke to him last year after my parents passed." My heart picks up pace and this time I know for certain it's not because of hottie Reid in front of me. It's fear of him telling *anyone* that I'm back in Aspen Ridge.

"As much as I'm enjoying this little meeting, I am sorry for scaring you. I really wasn't expecting you. I stop by once a month to make sure everything is okay with the place. Make sure no teenagers are breaking in, that kinda thing."

I take a moment to stare up at him. His eyes are still heavily lidded, but they look sincere and full of kindness. Maybe he's telling the truth.

Maybe.

Possibly.

"Yeah. So, you're right, I'm the daughter that inherited this place. I'll be living on the property for a few months."

"Just a few months?"

"Well . . . I plan to spend the time fixing up the place, I figured it would need some sprucing up, and then selling it so I can move back to . . . home."

"Hmm," is his only response.

"Hmm? What's hmm?"

"I think you should keep the place."

"Well. You don't know me or what's best for me so, sorry to tell ya, but your opinion is moot," I say with a bit more attitude than intended.

He turns and heads for the front door. "We'll see about that."

Fear squeezes my heart again and has me moving after him. I reach out and grab his wrist, pulling him to a stop and demanding his attention. His eyebrows raise in question.

"Hey, uhm. I know we just met and all, but is there any chance that maybe you could keep it to yourself that I'm here?"

He stares into my eyes for several moments before he nods once and pulls away. I try to stay confident, but I know my face is giving the desperation and fear away.

"Enjoy the rest of your day, Ivy. I'll be seeing you."

Reid pulls the door shut behind him, leaving me alone with my head spinning as I slide down the wall until my bottom hits the hardwood floor. Bringing my knees up to my chest, I fold in on myself, my mind lost to the bizarre interaction and the fear of people finding out I'm here. Before I know it, the lonely memories that haunt this house invade me once again.

<hr>

After having a mini pity party, I pull myself together, grab one of my bags, and head to my old room. The old, wood stairs creak and whine under the weight of each of my steps. I pass by my parents' closed bedroom door and continue to the very end of the hallway. Opening my bedroom door, nostalgia slams into me. The large window at the end of the room casts shadows across the space that hasn't changed since the day I left. A twin bed sits in the center, my desk across from it. I float over to the desk and look at the pushpin board hanging above it that I left filled with photos, running my fingertips across the faces of friends I left behind. Us at homecoming junior year, a Goo Goo Dolls concert we drove all the way to Emerald Queen Casino for, wearing wetsuits and learning to surf at Grace Beach. I pull a pin out of a photo and bring it closer. It's me at senior prom. I'm wearing a deep-red gown that hugs me perfectly, my dark black hair in ringlets and half up, but it's the boy next to me that I can't look away from. I'm looking at the camera, a smile on my face, but he's looking down at me like I'm the most perfect thing in the entire world. He's wearing a black tux, his arm wrapped around my waist possessively. He was always possessive and brutally protective. Not in an abusive way, in a, "I know I'm the only one who's ever loved and touched her" kind of way. I was his. Sawyer was my first and only love. The one person in the world who knew all of me and still loved me. From the time we met in the sixth grade he was convinced we would be together forever, and he reminded me of it every chance he could. No alternative existed for him.

Tapping my pencil aimlessly on my desk while I sit in Mrs. Pierce's English 4 class and try to follow along with her lesson on The Tempest, my eyes linger for a moment on the closed classroom door. Sawyer stands in the hallway, off to the side of the window, and cocks his head to the side, ushering me to follow him. I hesitate only briefly before I raise my hand and ask for a hall pass to the girls' bathroom. Once outside the classroom with the door pulled closed behind me, I look up and down the empty hallway to see that Sawyer is nowhere to be found. Chancing a solid guess at where he's waiting, I walk the hallway until I'm forced to turn into the stairwell where his firm hand grabs my wrist, yanking me further in, and pushing me up against the wall.

"Hi, butterfly," he whispers with a devilish smirk as his hands snake up my arms, shoulders, neck, and then find their home grasping my face. His thumb brushes lightly across my lower lip as he hums.

"Hi, Sawyer."

"I've missed you, Iv. So much," he whispers as he snuggles his face into my neck.

"You just saw me this morning, dork."

"Don't you know by now that even a minute without you is too long?"

"Mmhm. I missed you too, you know."

"I know, baby."

His eyes flicker back and forth between my lips and eyes as one of his hands presses into my waist, pushing me flush against the cold brick wall. Goosebumps break out over my body.

"Can I kiss you now?"

I nod my reply as his lips crash down on mine a split second later.

It goes from zero to sixty in hardly a moment. It's always been this way between us. This tether exists that keeps us connected. His touch lights me up like fire. I couldn't fight it if I tried.

His hand roams my waist until his fingertips meet my skin. He slides them under my shirt confidently, knowing I won't push him away. His fingers tug gently on my navel ring before slipping around to my lower back, holding me close. His tongue meets mine in a tangle as we pull at each other to get closer, my hands grabbing fistfuls of his shirt, holding him hostage, never wanting this to end. I could do this forever and it would be all I need to make me happy for the rest of my life. I need him like I need air, like nothing else matters. I feel it in the depths of my bones. Our makeout session slows until our lips break apart. Sawyer continues to lean against my small frame and rests his forehead on mine.

"I love you, Ivy, don't ever forget that."

"I won't. I love you too."

Needing to clear my mind, I do the same thing I've done the majority of my life when the pressure gets to be too heavy. I change into a pair of running leggings, throw on my favorite sweatshirt, pull on my hat, and lace up my shoes. Here's to hoping no one recognizes me.

I head outside as dark clouds move across the sky and block the sun's warm rays. I take a deep breath of fresh air and risk a glance over at Reid's house. He's jogging down the path in gym shorts and an athletic shirt that clings to his ripped body like a second skin, carrying a sweatshirt in his hand.

You've got to be fucking kidding me. Turns out luck really isn't on my fucking side lately. Did I kill a fairy?

Maybe I should burn some sage.

Hire a priest.

Toss some salt over my shoulder.

Buy some crystals.

I clearly need to get straight with the universe, 'cause she is continuing to bring her wrath to my doorstep.

"Really?" I dramatically ask the sky.

"I was thinking the same thing," his gruff voice grates on me.

"I see your body looks exactly as I expected it to, Drogo. Jesus. I need to know, you were made in a lab right?" I motion my hand up and down his body.

"What?" His eyebrows arch in question.

"Never mind. You're a runner?"

"Yup. Stress reliever."

"Ugh. Annoying. Same."

"Well, we can go our separate ways here or we can both be adults and just go for a run. I can go at a slower pace if you want to run together."

I can't tell if he's just trying to rile me up or if he's being serious. I'm going to go with the latter.

"Really. Wow. What kind of backhanded suggestion is that? And what are you trying to say? Just because I'm a woman I can't keep up with your masculine pace? Fuck you, buddy. I've been running my entire life by myself. I don't need you now."

"Easy there, sweetheart. I was saying it because you're a tiny little thing and I'm . . ." He repeats my earlier hand motion up and down his body. "My strides are longer. But by all means, let's go. Show me what you've got."

I give him a dramatic eye roll as he throws on his hoodie and stretches his legs.

We take off and he lets me set our pace for the first mile. I keep my head down and my hat low as we wind our way out of the long gravel lane. Luckily, my parents' house sits near the border of

Aspen Ridge, away from other houses, and not remotely close to the downtown area.

"So, Daddy's a lawyer, huh? What is it that you do, Drogo?"

"That's right. He has his own firm in the city. I'm a bit of a disappointment to him, though. I'm actually a tattoo artist."

"Wow. I didn't expect that, but now that I know, it fits. Did you do any of your own tattoos?"

"Interesting question. But yeah. Practiced a bit on my leg when I was an apprentice and then once I got good I did the design on my left wrist. It's more difficult. And I appreciate others' work, so the rest have been done by other artists. You got any?"

I can't help the grin that spreads across my face. "Nope. Virgin skin," I say just to taunt him.

"Fucking hell, Ivy," he groans. "Let me know if you'd like to give me that privilege, I'd be more than happy to be your first."

"Is that right?"

"Mmm," is all he responds with. "So, what about you? What do you do?"

Nope. Not going there. I should have known better than to ask questions and not expect them in return.

"How'd you end up in Aspen Ridge?"

He chuckles, clearly amused by my lack of clever avoidance. He hesitates on his answer, thinking it through.

"Uh, an ex-girlfriend actually. Didn't work out."

"Ahh. Sorry."

Lies. He just pulled that out of his ass. He has a story, but I don't want to dig further and give him an opening to do the same.

We continue in silence for a few more blocks and before we reach the town I turn to jog down the trail that leads to Grace Beach without much thought. My body relies on muscle memory and takes me exactly where it needs to go. After a mile of woodsy terrain, the trees open up to the rocky coastline. I jog over the driftwood and rock-covered shore, pebbles and sea glass crunching under my sneakers until I'm standing right in front of the violent crashing waves. The little beach sits on the rocky, coastal edge of Aspen Ridge, nestled by large Sitka spruce trees.

Surprisingly, our town was named after the founding family, not Aspen trees.

Thick fog hides most of the rock formations that rest out in the water by themselves. Clouds cover the beach, casting a gray, moody feeling that has always whispered promises of peace and tranquility to me. I feel the first drops of rain touch my body in a welcoming caress. This. This is what coming home is supposed to feel like. For the first time in many, many years, I feel safe and whole. I take a deep breath of the fresh salty air, filling my lungs with the crispness that is so specific to this very spot. This tiny part of the world was always my safe place, the one place on earth where the rawness is pulled from me, unforgiving and ruthless, much like the waves of the ocean in front of me. My heart rate steadily increases until it's pounding against my ribcage and all of the tension and stress I've been carrying courses through my bloodstream at once, adrenaline slamming into me with a force so hard I stagger on my feet. I lean against a large piece of driftwood, the cold, rough bark against my palm doing nothing to ground me. I'm consumed with all of the emotions I've kept locked up. For so long I've had to be strong and independent. I've kept it all hidden behind thick walls because it was my only option. I've done everything I was supposed to do, only to end up right back here.

I watch the waves rise and crash as emotions and unwanted thoughts wreak havoc on my body. My head tilts back to face the dreary skies as the clouds open up and rain crashes down.

I break.

A bloodcurdling scream rips from my throat as I fist my hands tightly, my nails breaking the skin on the inside of my hand. "Fuuuuuuuuuuck!"

My body collapses onto the rocky shore and I pull my knees up to my chest. The tears cascade down my cheeks, mixing with the rain. "Goddammit!" I yell to no one in particular. My heart shatters and I can't control the tears now that they've started. The waves of sadness and anger crash over me.

Lost in my turmoil, I don't notice my running companion sit next to me and cocoon me in his large arms, pulling me effortlessly into his lap.

"Hey, hey. Shhh. It's okay. Whatever it is. It's okay."

I want to recoil from his hold and take a seat next to him, but my body sinks into his instead, needing comfort, no matter how foreign it feels. He wraps his arms around me in a reassuring hold and I breathe him in. He smells of sweat, salt air, and cedar.

"Shh. I promise, you're okay." Reid rubs one of his hands up and down my back as he lulls me in a soothing tone. I haven't been held like this in so long, and it adds to the ache in my chest.

The rain slows to a steady drizzle while Reid holds me on the damp beach ground, surrounded by nothing but the Sitka trees and the ocean. The waves continue to crash, water lapping at the shoreline in front of us. I work to steady my breathing and wait for my tears to dissipate, along with my anger, disappointment, and sadness.

"Thank you," I whisper as I sniffle through my breakdown.

"You don't have to thank me, sweetheart. Glad I was here. No one should be alone when they're this upset."

Unsure of what to say in return, I sit in silence while he half holds me until my tears run completely dry and I feel like I have more control over myself.

"Will you tell me what's wrong? I hate to see anyone cry."

I lean back to study him for a moment. He is such an enigma. This huge, tattooed, burly man is so soft and tender. He hasn't shown me anything but kindness.

I take a few cleansing breaths and dry my face on the sleeve of my sweatshirt, even though the rain makes the effort futile. He waits patiently for me to talk, and I realize he's not expecting me to at all.

"I equally loathe and love this place. I haven't been back since I left here at eighteen. I had a really hard time at home, didn't have the best parents, and emotions weren't really tolerated. This beach was my safe place and I'd always let it all out here and feel better. I guess my body just knew I was safe, and after holding my shit together for the last ten years, I needed the release." Reid just looks at me and lets me talk. He's so patient and easygoing, I decide to give him just a little more.

"I've been too scared to ever come back here. To Aspen Ridge, I think. But . . . my life went to total shit and I had no other options. So here I am, back at the beginning and starting over with absolutely nothing to show for the time I was away. I don't belong anywhere. I've been walking aimlessly through a life I never wanted and now I'm back and I don't even have anything here, either."

"I'm sorry. For whatever caused you pain, Ivy. But everything will be okay. You need to believe that."

"I don't know about that. But thanks. I'm glad I ran into you and not anyone else. I don't know how I'm going to live in this town and not face everyone."

"I haven't lived here nearly as long as the rest of the people, but not much seems to change. I'm sure everyone will welcome you back just fine and be happy to see you again."

I let the silence stretch between us before whispering so low that I'm not sure he even heard it.

"Not everyone."

reid

I drop Ivy off at her house and jog across our lawns and into my own. I make it into the entryway before stripping out of all my wet clothes and heading straight to the shower. I'm so torn between what to do that I feel sick. Ivy is so goddamn beautiful, and fuck if she isn't breaking my goddamn heart. I've never seen someone in so much emotional pain. Whatever brought her back here coupled with the fact that she's back at all, has really done a number on her. I know that I need to tell Sawyer that she's here. But at what cost? I don't know if I can handle causing someone else more pain.

Fuck.

The way she looked at me when she asked me to keep her secret. The way her body relaxed into mine when I held her through her breakdown. The way she felt in my arms, even if she was crying, just felt too good. I'm obviously very attracted to her, and there's a clear connection there, but if anyone in the world is off-limits to me, it's Ivy. It figures that the first girl that stirs something inside me is my best friend's long-lost love. Sawyer has seen me through some rough times with my family and he's been a brother to me. I'd never cross a line that would jeopardize our friendship. But if I can't explore what I felt from the moment I saw that girl, I at least want to be her friend. Especially since it's clear she needs one right now.

I wash my body quickly and throw on some clothes, knowing that I'm heading to Sawyers' to face him. I know the damage I've already caused by not telling him as soon as I knew she was here, I'll be damned if I make it worse by keeping it from him any longer.

I just hope Ivy forgives me.

Sawyer

FEELING DRAINED FROM THE LONGEST FUCKING DAY, the moment I'm home I head straight to my bar to pour a drink of whiskey, tossing back the alcohol and enjoying the burn. I pour another two fingers and take a seat on my leather couch, drink in hand, when the doorbell rings. A frustrated sigh escapes me, and I hope like hell whoever it is will just go away. Resting my head on the back of the couch and closing my eyes, my effort to relax is futile as whoever it is just keeps rapidly ringing the bell and following it by pounding a fist on the door. I begrudgingly drag my feet toward the door, heading to greet the asshole when my best friend's voice bellows from the other side.

"Open the door, Sawyer, I know you're in there." I whip it open, surprised to see Reid looking rumpled as fuck, but after the long day I've had, I'm really in no mood for whatever he's got planned.

"Hey, man, didn't expect you. Been a long-ass day, not really in the mood for company tonight."

"We gotta talk." He seems agitated as he walks past me, ignoring my attempt to get him to leave. I push the door shut and follow him into my living area where I find him pacing. Something isn't right. My shitty mood retreats and I go into concern mode.

"What's up, man, you okay?" I ask, not sure what the fuck is going on. He looks at me, his face only giving away how torn up he feels. He rubs his hands through his hair and closes his eyes for a second longer than a blink.

"Reid . . ."

"It's Ivy."

Two words.

That's all it takes for my world to flip upside down. My body is frozen to the spot. My brain takes a full minute to process his words. Shocked, I gape at him as confusion fills my head. I know that Reid knows about Ivy because we've been best friends since college, but he's never met her. He knows what she meant to me all those years ago. He was also there when I fell apart last year after her parents' funeral and she didn't show up like she damn well should have. But what the fuck is he talking about right now that has him all worked up like this?

"I'm going to need you to repeat that for me, Reid. What's Ivy?"

"Sawyer . . . She's here. I met her. Today."

Reid continues to pace, his voice shaky, while I stand stock fucking still. I feel like I just took the hardest punch of my life to my chest, all the air forced from my lungs, and I forget how to breathe.

"Gonna need you to give me more information than that, man." I absentmindedly rub my knuckles into my chest over the spot where my heart used to be, and wait.

"I went over to her parents' place to make sure everything was good, like I do every month, and she walked right into the house."

My shock is starting to wear off and a multitude of emotions start to take over.

"The fuck do you mean she walked into the house, Reid?"

"She just walked right in. I left the door unlocked and did a quick walk-through of the main floor like usual, she walked in, and I scared the shit out of her. She's feisty as fuck, Sawyer . . . and just . . ." his voice trails off as he drops his head back and groans.

"And then what happened?" Not liking his reaction to meeting her one bit, a multitude of scenarios start running through my head and none of them are good.

"Uh, I explained why I was there and who I was and asked the same of her and it took a bit of me pressing before she'd even tell me her name. It was so unexpected, and from what you told me, I thought . . . I don't know what I thought. I just didn't expect it to be *her*." Reid keeps pacing and running his hands nervously through his hair. He's clearly not telling me everything.

"That all?"

He stops pacing and looks at me dejectedly.

"Sawyer. I don't know what the fuck happened. She is gorgeous, man. Like knock you flat on your ass pretty. And witty. And sassy. And fuck if she isn't just . . . Look, she caught me off guard." He groans again before he says words that have me seeing red. "I may or may not have come on to her. I think. I don't even fucking know, man. My head was totally lost. My brain stopped working around her. I'm sorry. Nothing happened, I swear."

My hands curl into fists but I stay rooted to the floor. We have years of history but fuck if I don't want to drive my fist through his face right now.

"What the fuck did you just say to me?"

Reid puts his hands up defensively. He's got a solid five inches on me in height, and I know he's got me in weight, but right now I want to revel in the feeling of his bones crunching under my fists.

"How the fuck did you come on to her? You said you just met her!"

"I told you! I don't fucking know! She was on the phone with some chick, talking about how her vibrator is better than a man. Next thing I knew I was prowling her up against a wall and asking if I could prove her wrong. Christ. That sounds so messed up.

What the fuck is wrong with me? Sawyer, you know me. I don't do that. But that's where it ended."

"Reid . . ." Yeah, crushing the bones in his face against my fist sounds really good right about now.

"The moment she said her name I backed the fuck off, Sawyer. But as I was leaving she begged me not to tell anyone she was here. She was really worried about it, or I would have called you right after I left. I was really fucking torn man, you've gotta understand that. If you saw the way she looked at me when she asked me to not tell anyone, you'd understand my position. I went home and changed for a run to clear my head."

I've never seen Reid so flustered before and it's his saving grace, the only reason his nose isn't broken yet. He's usually so calm and collected. He may be a giant, but he's usually a big softy. Whatever transpired between them clearly worked him up. But I'm freaking the fuck out and need him to hurry up with his story so I can go find my girl.

"Continue, Reid. 'Cause that had to have been hours ago. I'm losing my patience here."

"I left for a run and she was heading out her door at the same time."

"So you went for a run. Instead of immediately fucking calling me!"

"She uh, she went for one too. She said she's been running her entire life. It was another coincidence," he rushes out. "Listen, none of that even matters. She's in rough shape, Sawyer. I knew I needed to tell you she was in AR and that's why I'm here. But you need to listen to me. She's in *rough* shape. Whatever she's been going through, she's back here and it doesn't seem like she had much of a choice in the matter. I think you should wait before you see her."

"I should wait," I repeat, eerily calm, but my fists clench and unclench at my sides.

"She ran straight to the beach. We were talking and she seemed fine. Then she went completely quiet as she turned off the main road and onto the trail. I fell back and gave her plenty of space, but once she got to the beach she let out an angry scream and then just sat down and bawled her eyes out."

"She was *crying*?" The pain laced in my voice as I yell causes him to wince.

"Yeah. She was crying . . . I told you, she's in rough shape."

Body on autopilot, I rush to the front door, I've already wasted precious time letting Reid explain. I bend to pull on my shoes as Reid reaches for my arm, stopping me.

"Don't, Sawyer. Trust me. She said she's struggling being back here. She looked heartbroken. I know this isn't easy to hear, but seeing you is going to make that ten times harder right now. Give her a few days to reacclimate and work through her shit."

"I've given her ten fucking years, Reid!" I scream. "Ten! And you're telling me that right now she's down the road from me and she's *hurting*? I'm not going to sit here and fucking wait. No."

"Make sure you know what you're doing, man," he says solemnly and releases my arm.

"I do."

I grab my helmet and hop on my bike. Before I even realize, I'm pushing 100 on the back roads. The ride to her parents' house goes by in a blur. It takes me less than ten minutes of pure turmoil, and before I know it, I'm racing up the steps of Ivy's childhood home. Fear rips through me over the possibility of her not being inside as I whip open the door. It bounces off the wall with a bang as I bust inside, not bothering to kick it shut behind me. I register her scream and it's music to my ears.

She's here. My Ivy.

I take a few long strides into the house before I find her standing in the middle of the living room, frozen, staring out at the open space with a fire poker lifted in her arms like a baseball bat.

As soon as she sees me she staggers back a step, the poker falling from her hands and clattering to the hardwood floor. I watch her face transform from blotchy pink to pale white and her perfect, plump lips part slightly, forming an "o". Her beautiful green eyes are red and puffy, evidence that she's been crying. She's just as goddamn beautiful as I remembered, even more so. The hole in my chest begins to ache at the sight of her and I rub the spot with my knuckles.

I take a confident step toward her, even though I feel anything but. My mind reeling with shock and uncertainty. I can't believe she's really here.

"Hi, butterfly."

Her breath comes out in a rough exhale as her eyes close and slowly open to peer at me.

"Hi."

And then I'm moving. I grab her around the waist and haul her to me, one hand grabbing around her head, threading my fingers through her long, silky hair as I hold her to my chest. Both of our breaths are heaving, and I feel her body tremble against mine as tears soak my shirt. I press my face to the top of her head, breathing her scent deeply into my lungs. She smells of the salt air, a reminder that she's been to her safe place today, and of cherries and almonds. Fucking sweet perfection.

"Fuck. Ivy. My god. I can't believe it."

She wraps her shaky arms tightly around my waist, holding me with the same desperation that I feel as her body lets go and relaxes into me, allowing my body to mold around hers. I can't believe she's in my arms right now. My Ivy.

"You're really here, Sawyer?" she sobs.

"Yeah, baby. It's me. I've got you."

I reach down and pick her up by the back of her thighs, her long, lithe legs wrapping around my waist. She hunches over me, her face pressed into my neck, and her arms wrapped around me like a little koala. I hold her up by her ass and take in my surroundings before moving toward the couch.

Ivy has a sleeping bag laid out on top of it with a pillow, a Kindle, and a glass of red wine sitting on the end table.

"Baby, why are you sleeping on the couch?" I sit down, keeping her straddled across my lap, not wanting any space between us. She sits up straight and looks at me, her eyes dancing all over my face, shock etched into her features that surely matches my own.

I move my hands to her beautiful face, my thumbs brushing against her soft, tear-stricken skin before moving down to settle on her waist. She's wearing a crop top, and my hands heat on contact with her bare skin. Just like they always did. My eyes roam, taking as much of her in as I can, noting every change and difference the last ten years have made.

"My god, Ivy, you're so fucking beautiful, look at you." She's always been the most beautiful girl I've ever seen, but now?

Fuck.

Now she's all woman. She wears her raven-black hair long, reaching her waist. She's filled out in the best places, and I can't help but want to touch her all over, explore her body like it's the first time all over again. Because that's exactly what it would feel like. I want to see every change in her body, every mark, scar, every inch and beautiful piece of her. But now we're adults and not fumbling teenagers. Now I know to take my time and learn exactly how to make her feel good. I want to commit this new Ivy to memory to keep her with me for the rest of my life. Her shock morphs to panic as her eyes continue to glass over with tears, her chest rapidly rising and falling as she kneads her hands together between us.

"Is this real? I'm not dreaming? You're being so kind, Sawyer. I thought you'd hate me. You must hate me."

I take her hands in mine and lay them flat over my chest, letting us both feel the rapid beating of the heart she just returned to me.

"It's real. I'm real." Ignoring the last part of what she said, I change the subject, not ready to confront her about what she did to me. The pain she caused. I choose to focus on now and every-thing else can wait. Like why she's suddenly back in Aspen Ridge.

"Now tell me why you're sleeping on the couch and not in one of the beds."

"I just . . . can't be here."

Everything Reid told me flashes back and mixes with every-thing that I already know about Ivy and her parents. This is the same woman who left her home at eighteen without telling anyone but her mother, and didn't even return after the death of her parents. Of course she doesn't want to be in this house now. She didn't even want to be here when she was growing up.

"Then you're coming back to my place."

"Why are you here? How are you here? I thought you would hate me . . ." her voice breaks and her eyelashes flutter as she looks at me through gorgeous, watery eyes. There's a sharp pain in my chest, the ache she caused forever present.

"Baby. Right now, I'm holding you in my arms. Something I always hoped I would have the privilege of doing again. Trust me, there will be plenty of time to talk."

She gives me a partial smile, her lips turning up on just one side as she shrugs her shoulders. My heart and mind are racing to keep up with the situation. I can't help but rub my hands up the length of her arms and over her shoulders until I'm cupping her face, just like I used to.

"I mean it, Ivy." I pull her face toward mine and she follows, her eyes glancing down at my lips. Her breath hitches right before I press against her soft, supple lips. I kiss her tenderly, just lips, but the heat is still a raging inferno between us and pleasure races down my spine. I don't linger, I just need to feel her again. I break away before I'm ready to, knowing that this heating up isn't what either one of us needs right now. Nor do I know if she even wants me like that. She could have a husband for all I know. But I'm a selfish bastard and I needed to feel her again.

She rests her forehead against mine and we sit in silence, sharing air.

"You aren't staying here, Ivy. Not if you don't want to."

"I don't have a choice, Sawyer. There's . . . a lot. I . . . I'm fine. Okay? I'm fine. Just have a lot to deal with. And the house. I just, I hate it here."

She starts to climb off of me and I'm not having any of that shit. I hold her firmly in place by her thighs and then gently grab her chin, forcing her to look at me. Her eyes are filled with unshed tears and whatever part of my heart was just returned to me fucking breaks.

"I don't care. Not about what you've done, where you've been, or what's going on. Right now, all I care about is that you're here and that you're hurting and alone. If you think I'm going to walk away and leave you sleeping in an empty house, in a sleeping bag on a couch, you are sorely mistaken."

I wait patiently while she considers her options. She pulls her bottom lip into her mouth and bites down, making my cock twitch under her. Fuck. I can't help this pull between us. Her every move, every breath, is like a thousand arrows piercing my heart. It's foreign, after going so long feeling empty. Releasing her chin, I swipe my thumb against her sweet lip, setting it free from the hold between her teeth. A part of me knows I should resist, fight against these overwhelming emotions to protect what pieces of myself I have left, but I can't. She's the only one in the world who can make me feel alive, make me forget about everything else but us. I selfishly want to be with her, to hold her close and never let her go. The fear that my undying love for this woman will only lead to pain again is drowned out by the desire to do everything I can to see her smile. I can't help but be drawn to her, like a moth to a fucking flame.

ivy

My brain hasn't caught up to what's happening. Sawyer is *here*. My Sawyer.

At first I thought I was hallucinating. The sound of the door banging against the wall and quick footsteps heading in my direction still ring in my ears as the fear ebbs away. I assumed the worst since Reid and Zoe are the only ones who know I'm here. Nothing could have prepared me to see Sawyer standing in front of me, his face just as shocked as mine. The air left my lungs at the sight of him.

"Hi, butterfly." His deep voice and his name for me replay on a loop.

I shake my head and look into his gorgeous eyes. He's changed so much, but his eyes are still those deep crystal-blue I used to get lost in. His rich brown hair is trimmed close at the sides and styled longer on top. He has facial hair that's kept short, and his body has gone from that of an athletic, skinny teenager to a very fit, muscular man. He looks so different, but it's those gorgeous eyes that stayed the same, only sadder, almost lost.

"We're going. Now," he declares.

Sawyer stands while still holding me firmly to his body. My legs wrap around his waist, and I collapse again into his chest and shoulder, taking a deep inhale. He smells like fire, cedar and something slightly sweet, it's a comforting caress as I fill my lungs with him. It reminds me of safety, comfort, and love. The things that are so very specific to *him.* Things I haven't felt in another person in so long.

He holds me with one arm wrapped around my bottom and bends to grab my phone and purse before heading to the front of the house. He walks us into the evening and shuts the door.

"As much as I enjoy carrying you, you need to get a helmet on." He slides me down his body when I realize we're standing in front of a gorgeous motorcycle. I don't know anything about them, but it's beautiful. The boy I knew had an adventurous side. He loved to snowboard all winter long and surfed in the summer. The motorcycle fits him perfectly.

He grabs the helmet that's sitting on the seat and puts it on my head before adjusting the clasp and securing it.

"A bit big, but we'll get you your own. This'll do for now."

I watch as he swings his leg over the monstrosity. He sits on the bike, kicks up the stand, and gets comfortable before looking at me. Even through the haze of my emotions, the sight of him sitting on it does something to me. Warmth trickles down my spine and my traitorous pussy is screaming at me in remembrance of him. Our height difference puts us about eye to eye now and I must look like a fool just staring numbly at him. At least he has no idea how wet he just made me. The simple act of him sitting on a motorcycle does more to light up my body than anything else in the last decade. Except for maybe this afternoon when I met Reid.

Because, of fucking course.

"Get on the bike, Ivy."

I glance up at the house and know that I don't want to go back in. The lonely memories of growing up there are too thick.

Of watching my mother wilt at the hands of my father.

Her words of advice to me to never sacrifice my dreams for a man.

Of knowing that she had to grow up too young and died before she ever got the chance to really live.

I look back at Sawyer, my mother's voice raging in my head, telling me not to leave with him. The boy who was so sure our lives were meant to be spent together. The boy who would have done anything to keep me. The look written all over his face confirms he knows the battle raging inside my head. Like he's waiting for me to choose.

I nod before I climb on the motorcycle behind him, keeping my hands pressed against my thighs, unsure what to do with them. Sawyer reaches back and grabs my wrists, pulling my stomach and chest flush against his back, wrapping my hands around his waist.

"Feet on the pegs, sit still, lean with me. Got it, baby?"

"I think so."

"Hold on tight," he says right before starting it up. The rumble of the engine vibrates through me and he slowly pulls us out of the long driveway before increasing our speed. I instinctually lean in closer and grip harder around his stomach. Fuck, he feels so toned everywhere. He mumbles something that sounds like "that's my girl," but I can't be sure over the noise from the bike and wind. I watch the trees speed by, listen to the rumble of the bike, and lay my head on his back, completely lost in the moment.

I don't even know how much time passes as we ride to his house. Who knew being on the back of a motorcycle would feel so freeing?

We arrive on the other side of town and take a long dirt road until we reach a beautiful log cabin. Sawyer removes the helmet from me as Reid is jogging down the steps of Sawyer's porch.

I should have guessed. Traitor.

"Ivy . . ." he says as he continues to walk toward me.

Sawyer steps between us.

"Why the fuck are you still here?"

Reid approaches Sawyer and I take a nervous step back.

Sawyer is a big guy, but Reid is massive. When I said Hulk, I fucking meant it.

"I know you have shit to talk about and work through, but I'm not okay with hurting her. So get the fuck out of my way, Sawyer, and let me apologize."

Sawyer makes a guttural sound and I decide to step around them both before this escalates.

"Sawyer, it's okay." I place my hand on his chest over his leather jacket and he covers it with his own, holding it to him but never taking his eyes off Reid.

"Ivy. Heard you met Reid already. My asshole best friend."

That stuns me a bit. Clearly they were close enough for Reid to be standing outside of his house, but best friends? The asshole must have run right over here to tell him. The sting of betrayal that I wasn't owed by a stranger who showed me kindness is a painful misplaced ache. I turn to face Reid, my back to Sawyer.

"Best friend, huh? So I never stood a chance at hiding out here. Fucking figures," I say to Reid, that misplaced hurt feeling a whole lot like rage right now. "Did you know? The whole time. Did you know who I was, who I really was and who I used to be to him?"

"Ivy. Please . . ."

"Answer her," Sawyer says through gritted teeth.

"I didn't at first. But after you said your name, it clicked. Yes. I know more about you than just that you inherited that house. I had to tell him. Please believe me, I'm sorry, sweetheart."

"What the fuck did you just call her? Sweetheart? Is there more you're keeping from me?"

Sawyer spins on Reid and I quickly shuffle to stay between them.

"STOP! Fucking stop! I don't give a shit. About any of this. Please, Sawyer, just let me go to bed and tomorrow I will figure everything else out. On my own. So both of you, just please. Shut. Up!" I scream.

Both men freeze and look at me. Their faces mirroring each other, a mix of sympathy, concern, and anguish.

"You're right. Let's get inside," Sawyer says.

"I'm so sorry, Ivy." Reid's voice is laced with regret and hurt.

"Show me where I'm sleeping, please. I just want to go to bed and deal with this mess later."

"I'll head home. I know you've got this, I just wanted to apologize. Let me know if you need anything, yeah? I'm sorry again, Ivy. Truly."

"Yeah. Sure," I say.

Reid hesitates but then leans in to give Sawyer a half man-hug thing. The two are obviously close. Fucking figures, huh? Here I was thinking the universe had given me a friend in AR who didn't know me previously. Of course he's best friends with the one man I wanted to hide from. Thank you, Universe, you evil bitch.

I follow Sawyer into his house, too tired to even pay attention to the space or how he lives. The adrenaline has worn off and numbness settles in its place.

"You're in here." Sawyer opens up a set of French doors into a huge bedroom on the main floor. I take a hesitant step into the room and am consumed by the smell of cedar and what I'm now sure is maple. The same smell I inhaled while he held me at my parents' house. It's all him. I turn to face where he's leaning against the door frame, running his hand back and forth across his short beard.

"This is your room," I deadpan.

"Smart girl."

"Funny. I can't take your room, Sawyer."

"You can and you will. There isn't anywhere else you belong. At least for tonight."

My shoulders sag in defeat. Not having any more energy to fight him on it, resigned, I turn back to the room and take it all in. A king-size sleigh bed in rich cherry wood sits in the center with a dark gray blanket and crisp white sheets covering it. Matching bedside tables sit on either side and a large window gives a beautiful view of the night sky.

I hear the click as Sawyer shuts the door behind him, leaving me to myself.

Noting that I didn't actually pack a bag like he told me to, I help myself to a shirt from his dresser. I strip down to my panties and decide to lose the bra as well. I put on Sawyer's shirt, climb into his enormous bed, and curl up on my side. Fuck nighttime routine, I just need to sleep this day away. I lay my head against his pillow and pull the blankets up past my shoulders. The smell of him engulfs my senses. He smells more like a man now, but he's still all him. I close my eyes and am flooded with memories.

Sitting on a log at Grace Beach watching the flames in the bonfire, Sawyer grabs my hand and pulls me to stand. "C'mon. Follow me."

I tighten my fingers around his and let him lead me from our senior class to the other end of the beach where his truck is parked. He pulls open the tailgate and I smile at the sight. He's filled the bed of his truck with blankets and pillows. He lifts me around the waist and sets me inside before climbing up and joining me, pulling the tailgate closed behind him. We lay down next to each other and stare up at the dark sky filled with stars, our hands clasped tightly between us.

"Oh my god, Sawyer! Did you see it? I just saw a shooting star!"

"Better make a wish."

I close my eyes and wish for the first thing that comes to mind.

That this boy will love me forever.

I roll to my side to gaze at his gorgeous face.

"What'd you wish for?"

"I can't tell you or it won't come true! You know the rules of wishing."

"I keep all your secrets. Tell me."

He brushes my hair from my face before yanking me by the waist closer to him.

"Tell me, Ivy."

"I wished that you would never stop loving me. That you'd love me forever."

His face lights up with the biggest smile.

"Easy, baby. Wish granted."

He leans in and takes my mouth with his before pushing me onto my back and laying his body on top of mine. My legs fall open to make room for him. Our kissing heats up quickly and as clothes are removed and our bodies join each other, he tells me. Through every moment we're with each other, under the stars at my favorite place in the world, he tells me. With every touch, every kiss, and every word.

"I love you."

I wake up alone in Sawyer's bed, my heart heavy and a knot in my stomach. It's pitch black outside his bedroom window, but I don't care to check the time. I know I need to talk with him, but the thought makes me want to stay huddled in his bed and hide under the warm blankets. So much has changed since we last saw each other and it terrifies me to face him. Will he understand why I had to disappear? Knowing that I've done enough damage by running and that avoiding the inevitable is only going to make things worse, I leave the comfort of his bed and the safety of his bedroom. I walk aimlessly through his dark, quiet house, the wood floor cool under my feet, until I see a flickering light from a small fire through a set of large windows at the back of the living room. My emotions are all over the place. I just hope I can find the strength to say what I need to say and that he'll be willing to hear me out. I give the glass a gentle knock before sliding open the door and stepping out. He's sitting on a long, plush patio couch, a glass of bourbon in his hand, watching the fire.

"Can I join you?"

"Of course you can. You don't have to ask." His voice is calm and my nerves settle slightly. I take a seat on the far side of the couch and watch the little embers float away from the fire into the night.

"It's beautiful here, Sawyer. You've made a beautiful home for yourself. Do you . . ." I lose my nerve to ask. I know he put me in his bed and kissed me earlier, but that could all be explained and justified, we were both in shock. We were each other's first loves. But part of me just wants to know before I'm surprised.

"Do I what, Ivy? Just ask."

"Do you have anyone you share it with?"

He laughs. Actually laughs.

"No. No, I don't have anyone to share it with. What about you? Do I even want to know?"

"There's no one." And isn't that the truth. The only person I have left in the world is Zoe.

Silence stretches between us as we sit in the glow of the fire.

"Sawyer, I know I don't have any right to ask you anything, I don't even have the right to ask you about your life, but I'm going to anyway. I just need to know. Do you . . . hate me? For what I did."

His breath hitches and he leans forward to set his glass down on the edge of the stone firepit before standing and moving closer. He sits facing me, our thighs pressed together, his body turned toward mine as his eyes study my face. I'm not sure what to expect, but my eyes flutter closed as he moves to hold my face in his hands. I open them slowly and my heart shatters all over again. His perfect blue eyes are a storm of emotions, filled with tears ready to spill over. If possible, even after all the turmoil I've experienced, my heart breaks at the sight.

"Do you really think you could do anything to make me *hate* you? Do you think I could share my life with anyone but you after what we had? Do you think any amount of time apart could change how I feel about you, butterfly?"

I choke on a sob as the dam breaks and both of us let the tears we were holding back flow freely. He pulls me into him, holding me against his chest as we both cry.

"I'm so sorry, Sawyer. I'm sorry."

"Me too, baby. But now I have a question for you that I need answered."

"Ask. Ask anything, please." Desperate to comfort this man, I know I would give him whatever he needed in this moment to feel better, to fix the hurt that I inflicted.

"Why?"

Insecurity, vulnerability, and heartbreak are etched into his beautiful features and my heart aches for the pain I caused this man. I knew this was coming. I knew I would have to answer that question someday and that it would bleed me dry when it came time to explain the decisions that affected more than just myself. I sit up taller on the couch, putting some space between us so that I can look at him when I speak.

"There's no simple answer. It was a multitude of things that contributed to me leaving," I answer him truthfully. "You got into the University of Washington, and we were waiting for my acceptance letter. You had made all of these plans for us, and I wanted them too. But what I didn't tell you is that I also applied to culinary school in California. As much as I wanted to go to California, I was willing to give up that dream to be with you and stay here, together."

"Ivy . . ."

"Just listen. I won't be able to get through this twice, Sawyer. It's killing me," I beg. "I hid the admission letter in my room because I was so happy that I actually got in and wanted to keep it as a memento. In June, right before our high school graduation . . ." I take a moment to pause, so desperately unsure how he is going to react to this next part. I wring my fingers in my lap nervously and look him in the eyes before continuing, "I had a pregnancy scare." His face pales and he reaches for me, placing his hands on my thighs.

"What did you just say? Ivy, were you? Were we? We were so careful, baby."

"I wasn't. I wasn't, I promise," I quickly continue. "But my mom found the pregnancy test box and she was so heartbroken, Sawyer. She was already so sad. She said it would kill her to watch me go through what she went through. Even though we were together all those years, there was a lot I kept hidden from you that went on at home. I had this incredible mother when I was little, and by the time I was in high school, all of that light she used to have was gone. My dad slowly let her just disappear, Sawyer. He was supposed to love her and she gave up everything for him. She just withered away after. She didn't want that for me. She was convinced I was blinded by you, by young teenage love, and making decisions that would change my life forever before I was ready to. She made me promise that I would never build my life around you or any man. That I would stand on my own before I settled down. Thinking I could be pregnant scared me. As much as I've always wanted to be a mom, I couldn't have handled that. My mom added fuel to the fire. I should have gone to you. I know that. But she was in my head. I didn't want to end up like her."

Deciding not to bring up his part in manipulating me right now, I chose to focus on my part in all of it.

"Before I knew it, she had helped me pull my acceptance from UW and made phone calls on my behalf to the Culinary Institute. I didn't know what to do. She made me question everything, Sawyer. I was just . . . numb."

"So you left. You just ran away. The week you left you were so off. I couldn't figure out why."

"I'm sorry, Sawyer. I wanted to talk to you, I just didn't know how. There was a lot going on. I was so scared, and I know I took the cowardly way out. I planned to reach out to you after I got settled, but I was just so afraid of your reaction that time kept moving on, and then before I knew it, four years had gone by and

I knew my window had passed to explain and be forgiven. I didn't know how to do this." I motion my hand between us. "I didn't know how to explain."

"Do you know what happened after you left, Ivy?" No longer able to look him in the eyes, I watch as he bounces one of his legs nervously.

"No . . ."

"I was so heartbroken I had to defer my admission for a year. I took a year off, barely left my bedroom, and hardly ate. I just couldn't function. No one would tell me where you went or why you were gone. My parents forced me to go to therapy. You broke me, Ivy. You left and you took my fucking heart with you. I haven't been fucking whole since!"

He stands swiftly now, pacing in front of me, his voice slowly getting louder. "There was no closure, no answers. Just this abyss of fucking nothing inside me." He points to his chest with his fingers, roughly pushing them into himself. "So in your attempt to preserve yourself and your life, you destroyed me. And now you're telling me that the reason you left was because your mom thought that we were like them? That somehow the love I gave you for seven fucking years would dry up and you'd be left an empty shell of a woman like your mother? That's what you're saying, Ivy?" He runs his hands through his thick hair and turns to stare out into the darkness in front of us. Unsure of what to say, I start apologizing.

"Sawyer, I'm sorry. I was barely eighteen. We were kids!"

He whips his head in my direction, pointing a finger at me.

"Don't. Don't you dare downplay what we had. You know damn well it was fucking different. You felt it, Ivy. I felt it! In every single look, in every touch, every kiss, every time I was inside you! So don't say that again." The venom lacing his words hits its mark and I can't help but wince, my broken heart shattering into tiny pieces at the pain I've caused him. How many times can a heart break before it dies altogether?

I watch as Sawyer wipes the tears from his face.
I know he's right.
I felt it.
And I fucking ruined it.

CHAPTER 12

Sawyer

I THOUGHT I HAD FELT PAIN WHEN IVY LEFT ME AT eighteen.

I thought I had felt it again when I waited for her to show up last year.

I was wrong.

Hearing why she left me is worse. Even so, it doesn't feel right seeing her close in on herself, crying, hurting, gasping for air. None of it fucking matters anymore. I can't change a fucking thing that's happened before this moment. But I can have a say in how we move forward.

"I need to know, Ivy. Just please don't lie to me. Not now. Not ever. Do you understand? I only want the truth from your lips."

She hiccups through her tears but nods her head.

"Words, Ivy."

"Ye-yes."

"Are you happy? With your life? I don't even know why the fuck you're back all of a sudden. But are you happier? Without me and Aspen Ridge?" She freezes, eyes locked on mine, her plump bottom lip quivering. It's fucking destroying me not to comfort her.

"No, Sawyer. I'm not happy."

My body deflates and I sit back down next to her, running my hands through my hair. I don't know what I wanted to hear. That she's happy and has been living her life fully and fulfilled without me or that she's been unhappy and living a life that she never truly wanted. But at least now I know my way forward.

I nod once before leaning in and scooping her body into my arms, standing, and walking us through the house. Her face is a blotchy mess and contorts into confusion as I drop her onto my bed. I leave her sitting, puzzled, and walk to the bathroom to retrieve a box of tissues that both of us need.

Returning quickly, I take a seat in front of her. I blot her skin, wiping away the tears and letting her blow her nose while I do the same.

"I never could stand to see your tears. Seems like they still hold power over me after all this time."

She at least chuckles lightly before apologizing again.

"You want to tell me why you're suddenly back?"

She pulls her knees up to her chest and rests against the head-board, clearly forgetting that she's only wearing one of my T-shirts and a skimpy pair of panties. The shift in position gives me a perfect view of her bare ass in a thong. I reach behind me, pull up the throw blanket from the foot of the bed, and wrap it around her legs. I don't need any distractions. And based on my cock lengthening in my jeans, she's still just as distracting as she always was, despite this heavy conversation.

"The last ten years have been hard, Sawyer. And over the last few weeks it crashed and burned. I made some bad decisions and there was a ripple effect."

"We've got all night, baby. Fill in the blanks for me."

"Uhh. I did go to the Culinary Institute, I'm a chef now and it was the right choice for me. I feel alive in the kitchen. I worked as a bartender through school, which I hated, then worked as a line cook for a few years. I finally got my first job as a sous chef at this incredibly prestigious restaurant. But . . . promise you'll be an adult about the next part?"

"No promises when it comes to you. But I'll stay calm. Keep going."

"Not long after I was hired, I started dating the owner's son like an idiot. Mistake number one. Mistake number two, we were only dating for a few months before I moved in with him. I had an apartment with two roommates, and it was working fine, but then our building was sold and we had to move. I wasn't exactly friends with them, so we just went our separate ways. I was couch surfing at my best friend Zoe's condo, and when Brooks found out, he told me to just move in with him. So I did."

"Fucking hell." I try to hold back my anger. I figured she would have moved on with other men, but the confirmation that someone else touched her and slept next to her every night has me feeling possessive anger, jealous rage, and more crushing pain.

"We weren't serious-serious, but I thought it worked well enough, I guess. In hindsight, I think I was just swept up in all of it and trying to force myself to keep moving forward with my life. Well, a few weeks ago, I came home early and found him fucking someone else."

I shoot to my feet and drag my hand through my hair. What kind of piece of shit was she seeing? Who the fuck would cheat on her? How could anyone hurt this woman?

"It gets worse, unfortunately . . ."

"Holy shit, Ivy. I don't even know what to say right now," I tell her truthfully.

"I went back the next day to pack my stuff, and not only did he try to force himself on me but—"

"What? Tell me he didn't . . ." I fall to my knees in front of her at the edge of the bed, my shaky hands pushing her legs down and sliding tightly around her waist, pulling her to me, terrified of her answer.

"I fought him off, Sawyer. I'm tougher than I look. It was terrifying, but he'll be lucky if he can procreate someday."

"That's my girl," I say, relieved that she wasn't assaulted, but I make a mental note to look further into this Brooks guy. Piece of shit was lucky to breathe the same air as her. I stay crouched on the floor beside the bed, my hands on her waist, looking up at her while she continues.

"He was pissed and must have called his parents right after he recovered because his mom sent me a text terminating my employment because *I* cheated on *him,* which forced him to end his relationship with me. He made himself out to be the victim and sullied my name and my reputation. I've worked so fucking hard, Sawyer. And I've been all alone while I do it. I have my best friend, Zoe, but he ruined everything I worked so hard for. And I just let him. It was like all my mom's words came rushing back over me. Men would always disappoint me, and I should never wrap my life up in one so tightly that they could destroy it. And look at me now. I'm not even upset that he cheated, or that it's over! I'm just disappointed in myself." Her eyes fill with tears again and they start to trickle down her face.

"I've been staying at Zoe's and applying everywhere I can, but I just haven't been lucky. So I thought if I snuck back here and fixed up my parents' house I could sell it, and I would be in a much better position financially than I currently am."

"Butterfly . . ."

Her eyes flutter closed at the term of endearment.

"He's pretty scorned for whatever the reason. He's been calling and texting me from different numbers constantly. I've ignored every attempt, but it's still unnerving that he won't just let me go. It definitely aided in my decision to come back here. He's gotten very possessive of me. So here I am."

"Are you worried about him hurting you? Or coming after you?" I have to ask. I need to know what she's facing here with this douche. I plan to find out everything I can and pay him a little visit.

"I don't know. He scared me. I thought I knew him well enough. I definitely didn't expect any of this. But I can't say that it doesn't make me nervous. Especially after his behavior when I picked up my things, and then another time at a coffee shop."

"What happened at a coffee shop?" The fear is holding me in a vise grip and won't let up.

"That was kinda the last straw. He came up behind me and told me not to make a scene, then tried to force me to leave with him. I let myself fall into the customer ahead of me and thankfully she picked up on the situation and helped to get me out of it. But she asked me if I had anywhere safe to go, and the first place I thought of was . . . here."

Good girl.

"Let me know next time he reaches out, okay? You don't have to face things alone anymore. I'm not going to let anyone hurt you, Ivy," I promise.

Her shoulders shrug like she doesn't quite know what to make of that. She's been on her own for so long that it's hardened her. I wonder how much contact she had with her mother after she left, or if that relationship was abandoned along with the rest of them.

"Thanks, Sawyer. I'll probably just report him to the police if he doesn't stop soon. I need to focus on selling that house. I was going to try to fly under the radar. Probably out of the question now, huh?"

"You didn't think people would find out you are here?" I'm a little shocked by this. She grew up in AR and knows what a close-knit small town it is. Even if people don't know our story, everyone knows me and my family. Word would have gotten back to one of us.

"I was honestly going to try to keep it that way. I practically begged Reid to keep it a secret. I had no idea who he was. Pretty shocked to find out the first person I run into here is your best friend."

"Ivy, I would have found out eventually. You know that."

"Yeah." She closes her eyes and lets her head fall back against the headboard in a sigh.

"So, what now? You're just going to fix up the place, sell it, and then go back to wherever you came from? I don't even know where that is."

"Seattle."

I freeze, letting the word hit me like a blow to the face. I stand and pace in front of the bed. I can't believe she's been this close the entire time and I had no idea.

"Seattle? Fucking hell, Iv. You've been a few hours away all these years?"

"I didn't want to face you, Sawyer. I mean, I did at first, but then so much time had passed I didn't know what to fucking say anymore. Hey, remember me? The girl who left without an explanation? Yeah, no. That wouldn't have gone over well."

"How about before that, Ivy? Has that ever crossed your mind? How about, "Hey, Sawyer, I want to go to culinary school in California instead of going to U-Dub and living together. How can we make that work? You didn't even give me a chance!" I know my voice is raising at this point, but fuck. She left me. I know I want to focus on moving past all of this, but damn if it isn't difficult to hear all of it.

"Answer me this then, Ivy. Do you really think I would have done anything but support you? Do you think I would have kept you from reaching any of your dreams?"

"I don't know. We were kids for fuck's sake!"

Wrong answer. This time I lean forward over the bed and grab her face between both of my hands, forcing her to look directly in my eyes.

"What did I tell you about saying that?"

"It's the truth," she spits.

"Don't push me, Ivy. Or I'll be forced to remind you exactly what's always been between us. You think it's just gone? Do you think any amount of time could change our connection? You may be hurting right now, but don't forget that I knew your body first. I see how flushed you are with me this close to you, how your skin just broke out in goosebumps when I touched you, how you shifted your legs closer together."

I lean closer, ghosting my lips over hers before whispering into her ear, "Tell me, butterfly, if I touched your pussy right now, what would I find? Would you be dripping wet for me?"

"Sawyer . . ." she says, barely a whispered breath. Her chest rises and falls while her eyes shoot back and forth between mine.

"That's what I thought. Don't say that shit again or I promise I'll remind you."

ivy

Holy. Shit.

I lift my fingers to my lips, swiping two of them back and forth while I sit on Sawyer's bed, stunned.

"Tell me, butterfly, if I touched your pussy right now, what would I find?"

He strokes his hand across his short beard and ticks his jaw before bringing his eyes back up to mine, as if he were re-hearing the same thing, shocked by his own words. With all the madness of the evening, I haven't properly taken him in. He's changed so much. His rich brown hair is mussed, like running his hands through it is a common occurrence. There is no arguing that he is all man now. His body has filled out in the best places. It's clear that he works hard to stay in shape, I wonder if he's still boxing his brothers. His biceps strain against the navy blue henley that fits his body like a glove, his forearms thick and veiny.

I was always putty in Sawyer's hands. There was something about being swallowed up into his vortex that emptied my brain of all rational thought. All I saw, heard, and felt was him. And now? Hearing the deep timbre of his voice say those filthy words, his warm breath caressing my ear and down my neck, his big hands holding my face exactly where he wants me—my core pulses and throbs in need. I can't deny that he's right. No matter how much time has passed, that pull to be swept up in him hasn't changed. We may be strangers now, but our cores recognize each other as if they are two halves of a whole.

This undeniable connection.

A tether that lights me on fire, a flame that only he can stoke. Even after all this time, just being in close proximity to him makes me feel more than I have in years. It burns brighter the closer he is to me, the longer he looks at me, the more he touches me. It's like I've been asleep and seeing him again has jump-started my heart. How did I walk away from him?

"Get some sleep, Ivy. You've had a long day."

His voice startles me out of my thoughts. I watch him as he walks toward the open door of his bedroom.

"Where are you going?" I ask, slightly confused and not wanting him to leave.

"To the couch."

"Sawyer, you don't have to sleep on the couch."

"But I do. We have a lot to process and we aren't going to do that lying next to each other. The last thing I want is more separation from you, Iv, trust me. But at least this time I'm choosing it and I know where you'll be when I wake up."

His words, although true, sting. Fresh tears prick my eyes and I do my best to blink them away. He walks back over to the side of the bed and pushes my hair behind my ears before grasping my jaw again in his large hands. He tilts my head back so I'm forced to look into his eyes.

"No more tears. Rest. We'll talk more in the morning. You may think that you have to figure everything out on your own, but you don't. You have people here in this town who have always loved you, Ivy. You can have whatever life you want, as long as you're living it for yourself. Not your mother. Not me. Yourself." His voice is gentle, almost pleading with me. As if the way I'm treating myself and the way I've been living all these years is causing him pain. Not pain for how it affects him, but pain seeing me this way.

His words hit home.

He uses the pads of his thumbs to wipe the stray tears from under my eyes before leaning down and pressing his perfectly warm lips to my forehead. I close my eyes and take the first breath of steady air in what feels like an eternity. A calmness washes over me. He releases me before I'm ready and returns to the door. He places his hand on the side of the door frame and drops his chin to his chest for a moment before looking back over his shoulder at me.

"Be here when I wake up, baby. Please."

He leaves me alone in the bedroom, the door shut softly behind him. I listen to his footsteps retreat down the hallway before silence takes root in the empty room.

I nestle into his bed and pull his blanket over my shoulders until it's tucked under my chin. The warmth of it surrounds me and I'm filled with his scent. All woodsy and sweet. It's comfort, and smells like coming home. Despite his request, I cry myself to sleep, the weight of my actions pressing down hard on my heart, his words playing on repeat.

Have I been living the life my mom wanted for me all these years? Or have I been living for myself? My mother never had the chance to experience the world around her. In my attempt to make sure I didn't turn out like her, and experience all that she didn't get to do, I didn't explore what I wanted most of all.

A life spent with Sawyer by my side.

CHAPTER 14

Sawyer

WALKING AWAY FROM HER TAKES THE STRENGTH OF A monk. I walk past my bar and collapse onto the couch, knowing alcohol won't fix anything right now. I'm stuck between two distinct paths, and the thought of choosing one creates a war inside me. My immediate reaction is to be a neanderthal and demand that she admit she's mine and never let her leave me again. But my Ivy instincts know that in order to move forward she needs to make every decision for herself. If she left me because she needed to be independent, then the last thing I should do is force her to stay. I must be crazy to still want this woman after a decade apart, and the mayhem she left in her wake. But seeing her again is like surfacing after being pulled under by a wave. I want the opportunity to know her again. I want to hear every detail of what she's been through, what her life has been like before it crashed and burned. I also want to hunt down the motherfucker that hurt her. It fucking killed me to hear she isn't happy. She may have plans to leave Aspen Ridge, but I'll be damned if she leaves in the same state she arrived.

I want her to be happy.

I want that to be with me.

But Ivy needs to choose me.

I pull out my phone and click on Reid.

Me: You were right. She's in a rough place. I don't like it but I'm glad you were there for her for whatever went down earlier.

Reid: Is this your way of apologizing?

Me: I won't apologize for blowing up on you. She's off limits. That's a hard line. I'm giving you a pass this one time because of our history.

Reid: I didn't mean any harm, brother.

Me: I know

Reid: You handling everything okay?

Me: Fuck no. I want her back, Reid. So fucking bad. But she needs to come to me. I can't force her.

Reid: I don't know her story but you're right, man. You can't force her. It's clear she's got some shit to work through

Does he think I don't fucking know that? I run my hand through my hair before tugging on the ends. Fuck. The power this woman has over me is unreal. I feel unhinged when it comes to her.

Reid and I go way back. We've been friends since college. He had some serious shit go down that brought us even closer when I dropped everything to take care of him. I saw him through his darkest days and he's done the same for me.

I know his heart bleeds nothing but pure love. Yesterday I would have said that nothing could ever come between us, and today I know for a fact I'd put him six feet under without feeling an ounce of remorse if he ever put his hands on Ivy.

Me: She does. We both do.

I close out of my message with Reid and drop my phone on the coffee table.

Fuck. I can't believe Ivy is here. I never lost hope that I'd see her again someday, but fuck if it doesn't gut me to see her in so much pain. She's so goddamn beautiful, though, even with the life dulled behind her gorgeous eyes. My dreams didn't do her justice. I'd do anything to bring that life back to her. I spend the rest of the night tossing and turning, restless on the couch, scared to wake up and find out everything was all a dream, or worse, that she's run again.

I wake with the sun and make my way to the kitchen for coffee. I drop a pod into the Keurig and grab my phone while it brews. My finger hovers over the sibling group chat and I debate whether or not to text them all or just Dallas. I decide word of mouth will eventually spread and they might as well hear it straight from the source.

Me: Taking a few days off. Dallas, you got things covered?

Carter: Jesus, you've never taken time off.

Kins: Everything okay big brother?

Dallas: You know I do. Can't promise the she-devil will be there when you return but I've got it under control. What's up?

Me: Need you all to keep this to yourself. I've got your word?

Liam: You know you do. What's going on?

Kins: Type faster, you're making me so nervous

Me: Ivy's back.

Dallas: What?

Me: I'm not going to get into details right now.

My phone immediately rings, it's Dallas, I pick it up and whisper.

"Hold on, I gotta step outside."

I grab my coffee mug and sneak out to the back porch, closing the door quietly behind me.

"Hey."

"That's some bomb you just dropped, Sawyer. Considering you just snuck your ass outside, I'm assuming she's at your place?"

"You'd assume right. But it isn't what it sounds like."

"Then what is it? Cause I've got my keys in my hand and ready to head to your place. Give me something."

"I'm fine. Stay where you're at. I need you to handle things at work for the rest of the week. She just showed up out of the blue."

"At your place?"

"No. Her parents', hiding out like a little criminal. Reid ran into her, that's a story for another day. But then he told me she was in town, and I stormed over there and hauled her ass over to my house like a caveman."

"How'd that go over?"

"She didn't put up a fight, actually. She's been through some shit. She's pretty defeated. There's no light behind her eyes anymore."

"Fuck, man. And how are you doing?"

"Shocked. Processing. The adrenaline of everything coming together last night has worn off and I feel pretty numb right now. I don't know her plan, but I'm going to do whatever I can to figure it out."

"You want her to stay?"

"You know the answer to that, Dallas."

"Look, I'm not happy with her. It's going to take a hell of a lot more than just her showing back up in town and waking up in your bed for me to forgive her. Whatever happens between you two, you're going to have to give the rest of us time. You know that right?"

"I get it. And I didn't say I forgave her. But I'm going to figure this shit out and move forward. Whatever happens, at least I'll get closure this time."

"No matter what, you got us. I'll hold down the fort."

"Don't burn everything to the ground in my absence, please. And for fuck's sake don't fire Blaire. I don't know if anyone else would put up with you."

"No promises."

We hang up and I read the ten missed texts from the group chat.

Kins: Holy. Shit.

Carter: Are you fucking with us?

Kins: Omg. Wait, are you serious?

Liam: Wtf. Are you okay?

Carter: She's back for good?

Kins: Sawyer!

Liam: He's probably talking to Dallas

Carter: That's bullshit. Sawyer, wtf man

Kins: Come on. You can't drop that bomb and then forget about us. Wtf?

Me: Dallas called me

Kins: Of fucking course he did, while the rest of us are forced to wait. Can you please fill us in now?

Me: I said I wasn't going into details right now. Ivy is back in town. I don't know her plans. I don't know what it means. She's just here right now.

Kins: Like here as in AR or here as in your house?

Me: Both

Kins: Sawyer please be careful. I know I was too young to fully understand but I don't want you to get hurt.

Me: I'll fill you guys in later. Keep it to yourselves and for the love of God don't tell Mom and Dad.

I pocket my phone before opening the glass door and sneaking back into the house. The sight in my kitchen stops me in my tracks, coffee mug halfway to my mouth. Ivy is wearing nothing but one of my T-shirts. Her back is to me, and she's on her bare tiptoes as she reaches, searching the cabinets, presumably for a coffee mug. Her long, lithe legs are on display, and her ass peeks out of the bottom of my T-shirt. I groan and cover it with a cough. She spins to face me, leaning against the counter, and places one of her hands over her heart.

"Jesus, Sawyer. You scared the shit out of me."

"Sorry. Morning. Get any sleep?"

"Uhm, kind of, I guess. Thank you. Mugs?"

"How about we go get some coffee and breakfast out?"

She fidgets with her hands and shifts from foot to foot. I didn't realize my plan until I said it. I know she doesn't want anyone in town to know she's here, but she can't stay locked up like a hermit forever.

I'm going to show her what life could have looked like here with me.

"C'mon. I'll drive you back over to your parents' so you can change, and we'll go get some breakfast."

"I don't know, Sawyer. I don't think anyone wants to see me."

"You won't know until you show your face again. Stop being so mean to yourself."

Her hands move to the hem of my shirt and she plays with it between her fingers while biting her bottom lip before meeting my eyes again.

"Okay."

"Yeah?"

"Yeah. Let me go put my clothes on from last night, I can just wear those and we can go."

She walks to the edge of the room before hesitating and looking back at me sheepishly.

"Can we take your motorcycle?"

I choke on the sip of coffee I had just taken. She wants to be on the back of my bike?

Clearing my throat, I rasp, "Fuck yes we can."

CHAPTER 15

ivy

I JOG DOWN THE HALL INTO SAWYER'S ROOM AND PULL his shirt over my head, leaving it folded on the dresser. I yank on my clothes from last night and sit on the edge of the bed with my phone in hand, waiting for it to power on. I know Zoe will be awake, but I don't have the time to explain everything right now.

My phone comes to life and texts start popping up in rapid succession.

Unknown: You can't ignore me forever.

Unknown: Answer me

Zoe: Brooks seriously showed up at my place. He's looking for you babe.

Zoe: I told him you weren't home right now but he seemed suspicious. Call me. He was acting pretty crazy.

. . .

Unknown: You think I wouldn't figure out you
left town?

Unknown: You can't hide forever Ivy.

Unknown: We belong together. This isn't
fucking over. Not by a long shot.

Dread fills me but I do my best to shake it off. I don't think Brooks will chase me all the way to Aspen Ridge, so I click on Zoe's messages and shoot her a text telling her that I think Brooks will get over it soon, especially since I'm not there anymore, and ask if she's free to video chat tonight. I think within a week Brooks will be over it and onto the next thing.

I hope.

I have no idea what the hell I'm doing going into town with Sawyer. I'm unsure where we stand with each other, but I find myself unable to say no to him despite my hesitation. In less than twenty-four hours, all my plans for returning here have gone up in flames. I owe Sawyer another talk, and if he wants to go get break-fast, that's what we'll do. My nerves are getting the best of me, and dealing with all of this on an empty stomach isn't helping. Since I finger brushed my teeth before going to the kitchen in search of coffee earlier, I'm ready to go, so I turn my phone off—not wanting texts from Brooks to pop up in front of Sawyer—and place it back in my purse.

I find him waiting for me in the entryway wearing a pair of denim jeans, boots, and his jacket, a hand running through his hair as he looks me over.

Holy shit. He's so fucking sexy.

"Hey. Last night I was a little reckless with you, so I want to apologize. My judgment was muddled and it won't happen again.

I'll take you on the back of my bike any time you want, but you're going to have to dress appropriately. I have a spare leather jacket that you're going to wear, as well as a helmet."

He holds a jacket out for me to slip on, and I turn my back to him before putting my arms through the sleeves. I face him again and his eyes meet mine.

"May I?"

I nod my head and watch his face as he zips the jacket up, his eyes following the track. He adjusts the collar before meeting my eyes again, his are filled with mirth and he grins wickedly.

"What?"

"You look good in my jacket."

"Hmm. I'd argue that, since I'm swimming in it."

He cuffs the sleeves twice so my hands are free.

"You ready?"

"No." I laugh.

"What now?"

"I missed that sound."

"My laugh?" I chuckle again.

"Yeah."

"Liar. Everyone makes fun of my laugh. It's obnoxious."

"I always loved it, Ivy. You know that." He gives me the most lethal wink.

"I see you're still a smooth talker." I dramatically roll my eyes. "Let's go. I'm starving and I need caffeine before I get mean."

"After you."

I open the front door and head into the morning air. It's the first week of September and the temperature outside is perfect. It's still warm, but not sweltering like some days in July and August. It's early and the sun has just finished rising. Fog kisses almost everything still and I forgot just how much I love mornings up here in the mountains. I take a brief look around his property and it's clear he found a gem on the outskirts of town.

To the left of his house sits a large four-car garage. The door starts to rise to reveal a truck and his motorcycle, I realize he must have moved it into the garage after I went to bed last night. I look everything over when it hits me.

"Sawyer, is that?" I point to the unmistakable red truck. He looks at it before looking back at me.

"Yep. Same one. Don't have the heart to get rid of her when she still runs great."

"Oh, wow."

"Yeah. Lots of memories in that thing, huh?"

"Yeah. Lots."

One in particular stands out above all the rest. The night we lost our virginity to each other in the bed of it. I shake my head and see him still looking at me. He smiles like he knows exactly what I was remembering.

I watch him kick up the stand of his bike and walk it out before putting the kickstand back down.

"Climb on, baby."

"Before you?"

"I want to see you on it."

"You aren't serious."

"Oh, but I am. Now get on the bike, Ivy."

I swing my leg over and sit back on the seat before giving him a wide, cheeky smile.

"Happy?"

"You have no idea how much." His smile is devilish and so fucking handsome. Butterflies take flight deep in my stomach and goosebumps scatter across my skin as he studies me.

"Now you can get off."

"What? What the fuck was the point of that?"

"I told you. I wanted to see you on it. You should see your smile. Feels good, huh?"

"Oh my word, Sawyer." I climb off the bike and give him an exaggerated eye roll, even though I know the smile hasn't left my face.

He puts the helmet I wore last night on me and buckles it before doing the same with his own before sitting on the bike. I watch as he expertly kicks up the stand and steadies it before he motions to me with his finger.

"Let's go, baby."

I get as comfortable as I can before his hands reach back to grip my thighs and pull me so I'm flush against him again.

"Wrap those thighs and arms around me. No excuses."

My thighs are spread wide to accommodate his muscular frame, but I do my best to tighten them around him before running my palms around his sides and hugging him snugly. Sawyer pulls out of his driveway and the ride is just as good as last night. I relax against his back and watch the world fly past us in a blur.

We pull up to Bean Haven and park a few stalls down on Main Street as the panic starts to rise in my chest. Sawyer pats my leg, signaling it's time for me to climb off this beast. I do my best and stumble a bit, because of course I can't do anything gracefully. He hops off in a much more dignified manner. He reaches his hands up to remove my helmet, but I shake my head out of his reach.

"What's wrong?"

"I don't want to go in, Sawyer. Please. I changed my mind."

"Ivy. Trust me?"

Do I? My immediate reaction is yes. But I know I shouldn't. I can't.

Why did I come here?

Why did I let him take me here?

I can't believe I'm standing on Main Street with Sawyer.

Holy shit. Ms. Nettie is yards away.

I look side to side and see people moving about, opening their shops, kids walking to school with their parents.

I can feel my pulse thrumming throughout my body at a rapid pace as the world closes in on me. My hands start to sweat as I twist and knead them in front of me.

My mind starts to spiral, and I take a step back from him and then another. A car flies by behind me as Sawyer reaches out, his hands grabbing both of my arms and yanking me into his firm chest. The top of the helmet bounces off his chin and he grunts. I gasp for air, the weight of the panic attack suffocating my lungs.

"Fuck, Ivy. Are you okay?"

Sawyer puts enough space between us to reach for the helmet again, and this time I let him remove it. His eyes dart all over my face in search of injuries that aren't there, reading the panic that's raging inside me. I see concern and fear written all over him. His hands reach down to brush the hair out of my face before he pulls me back into his chest.

Air. I need air. I close my eyes to focus on the breathing technique my therapist taught me. Five counts in, hold for five, out for five.

"That's it, baby. Breathe for me. You're okay."

His voice is so calming. I instinctively relax into his chest and rest my head where his heart sits. He threads a hand through my hair, holding me close while the other hand continues to rub up and down my back in firm strokes.

Five in.

Hold for five.

Five out.

He continues to shower me with praise as the world disappears and all that's left is the sound of Sawyer's strong heartbeat, his deep, comforting voice, and the smell of cedar and maple.

"Keep breathing."

"You're doing so well."

"You're safe, I promise."

"I'm so proud of you, baby."

I take one last deep breath before I've composed myself enough to look up at him.

"Thank you."

"You did all of that yourself. I'm proud of you. When did you start having panic attacks?"

"Right after I left."

He cocks his head to the side and studies me for a moment

before accepting my answer and moving on from it. I appreciate him not asking further questions on the matter. I forgot how easy it is to talk to him. I'm fairly positive he could ask me whatever he wants and I wouldn't be able to filter myself if I tried. It was always that way. So effortless.

"If you want to leave, we can. Or you can stay out here and I'll go in and then we can leave. It's up to you."

I shift on my feet and twist my fingers in my hand. Sawyer looks down and watches my nervous habit before reaching for them and dwarfing them in his own.

"I would never do anything to hurt you, nor would I ever allow anything to hurt you. Physically, emotionally, or otherwise. Say the word and we'll leave. But I really want to take you inside for coffee and muffins."

I really do want a muffin. And coffee. I can do this. I was born and raised here. It can't break me if I'm already broken anyway.

"Okay." I take another deep breath. "Let's go."

"That's my girl."

He only releases one of my hands before turning and pulling me onto the cobblestones and walking us toward Bean Haven.

Ms. Nettie is sitting outside with a tiny dog in her lap.

"Quite the little show you two just put on over there. You back for good, Ivy?"

Stunned by her straightforwardness, I freeze and stumble over what to say.

"Good morning to you, too, Ms. Nettie," Sawyer says, greeting her.

As if his voice was a trigger, the little dog jumps down from her lap and starts growling and nipping around Sawyer's feet and ankles.

"Really, Ms. Nettie? Must we do this every time I need a coffee? Minnie belongs on a leash," Sawyer chastises.

"Her name is Winnie, you fool. She doesn't need a leash, she only misbehaves when you come around."

I laugh and Sawyer shoots me a glare. I let go of his hand and kneel down to the little mutt, offering my hand out for her to smell.

"Hi, Winnie. Hi, girl." She trots over to me and sniffs my hand before giving it a few licks, her tail wagging like crazy.

She allows me to scoop her up and pet her as she snuggles into my chest.

"Winnie is very sweet, Ms. Nettie. Here you go." I put her back down in her lap and find Sawyer shaking his head at me.

He opens the door to Bean Haven, and I take in the updated decor as I step over the threshold. It has the cutest bohemian vibe. Three of the walls are painted a creamy off-white, while the fourth is red brick. *Bean Haven* is painted in a gorgeous loopy font above the counter. Live plants hang from the ceiling in some of the corners, while others are in huge wicker baskets. The display case is filled with mouthwatering pastries. This is an entirely different space from what it was when I grew up coming here.

"You're going to need a rabies shot after touching that feral little thing," Sawyer whispers in my ear. I feel the pressure of his hand on the small of my back through the leather jacket and my body hums to life, heat traveling through me like a live wire. I ignore it and smack his chest. "Oh, stop it. It's just a little dog ya big baby."

"Little dogs aren't dogs at all. They're an anomaly, annoying, and that one in particular is a pain in the ass."

"Oh my god, are you serious right now? It's a tiny dog the size of your boot, Sawyer. How big of a pain can she really be?"

"You'd be surprised."

We walk up to the counter and I can't help but salivate as I look over everything in the display case.

"Hey, Sawyer!" a chirpy female voice yells from the back room. My head shoots up to gauge Sawyer's reaction to her. I can't help but feel slightly jealous. Obviously, a man like Sawyer has been with his fair share of women by now, but it doesn't mean I'm ready to face any of them.

"Hey, Han! My usual please, but double it."

"Han?" I look at him quizzically.

"I'll wait until your brain catches up."

"Holy fuck, Han-nah? Hannah Haven?"

"There you go, baby. I knew you'd get it eventually. Took you a minute, but I'm proud of you." He smiles at me and I smack him in the chest again with the back of my hand.

Hannah walks out with a white paper bag and places it on the counter. She's yet to notice me. She has incredible violet-colored hair, styled in loose waves that hang right above her shoulders, and from what I can see, she's a regular at the town's tattoo parlor, as an intricate floral design crawls up her arm.

"Two apple cinnamon muffins! Let me make the coffee real quick."

She turns her back to us and starts the coffee, clearly a bit distracted.

I look up at Sawyer to find him already looking down at me. My hands find each other as they start to wring together. He reaches out to pry them apart and takes one in his.

"Your usual?" I ask.

"Yep."

"Since when do you like apple cinnamon muffins?"

"Since you left."

He leaves it at that as if that's an adequate explanation. I continue to look up at his eyes, trying to figure him out when he leans down to whisper in my ear again, something I'm realizing he likes to do.

"And no one said I like them."

My eyes well with tears, but before they can fall, we're interrupted by Hannah placing our coffees on the counter.

She pauses when her eyes finally meet mine and I straighten as I greet her.

"Hi, Hannah." I give her a soft half-smile, still unsure how I'll be welcomed back in this town. Aspen Ridge is small. Usually, if you hurt one person, you hurt the lot of them.

"Ivy?" Her mouth drops open a bit as she looks to Sawyer for confirmation.

"It's really her, Han. Got here yesterday. She's staying with me for a bit. We're trying to keep it on the down-low, though."

"Oh my god. It's really you."

"Mumma!" a little girl squeals as she patters out from the back room and reaches up for Hannah.

"Mumma? Oh my god, Hannah. You had a baby?"

"A lot has changed around here since you left."

She bends down and scoops up her little girl. My heart melts. She's young, her hair falls around her face in wild, kinky curls. She is the sweetest thing I've ever seen.

"This is Charlotte, but we call her Charlie. She just turned three."

"Congratulations, Hannah. She is so beautiful. So is this place," I say as I look around. "Was this all you?"

"It was. Well, me and Liam. He helped so much and did most of the work to save me money. I love it."

"It's gorgeous. I love the entire boho vibe you've got going."

"Thanks."

Feeling awkward, I look up at Sawyer and give his hand a tight squeeze while I shift on my feet. He gets my hint quickly.

"Alright, Han. Good seeing you and the little one. We're gonna get going."

"It was good to see you again, Hannah. Thank you for the muffins and coffee."

Sawyer drops cash on the counter and reaches forward to squeeze Charlotte's foot playfully.

"Bye, squirt."

She pulls her thumb from her mouth and waves at him.

My ovaries explode.

Sawyer leads me out of Bean Haven where we're greeted by Winnie growling at him. This time, a laugh bursts free from my chest. I grab hold of Sawyer's forearm to stay upright while I laugh at him. This dog really dislikes him.

"For fuck's sake. Can we not do this every single time? Please pull Minnie's teeth from my pants."

"It's WINNIE!" Ms. Nettie and I both yell in unison. I fall into another fit of laughter.

"I always did like you, Ivy Turner."

"Likewise, Ms. Nettie."

Sawyer pulls me down the sidewalk as I hold on to him. He drags me into a narrow alley between two buildings and pushes me against the wall. I sober quickly and take him in. The huge smile on his face reaches his eyes, they squint slightly, crinkling at the corners, and that damn smile makes me weak in the knees. I can't help but smile back. His palm snakes under the jacket I'm wearing and rests against the front of my hip. I can feel his thumb shift back and forth over my jeans.

"God, I've missed you." His voice is huskier, deeper, and passionate. The words are backed by the way he said them, full of conviction.

The mood shifts, the air around us thickening.

"I missed you too," I reply honestly.

"Did you think of me?"

"All the time. Did you think of me?"

"Every. Fucking. Day." He punctuates every word.

His eyes glance down to my lips just as my tongue peeks out to wet them. He watches as my tongue swipes across and I pull my bottom one between my teeth. We're standing so close that the rapid rise and fall of my chest brushes my breasts against him. His hand leaves my hip and comes up to slide against my face. I lean into it and close my eyes. His thumb moves across my lips before pulling my bottom lip free.

I look up at him as his head starts to lean down to mine.

Holy shit he's going to kiss me.

And I want him to.

I want to feel him again.

He inches closer, giving me plenty of time to back out. I close my eyes and wait for the feel of his lips on mine.

My traitorous bitch of a body chooses that moment to make a god-awful loud rumble from my stomach that doesn't go unnoticed in the quiet alley. He drops his forehead down to mine as we both laugh.

"Oh my god! I told you I was fucking hungry, Sawyer! Now feed me that damn muffin!"

"Let's get you fed, baby."

We sit down in the little alley, squeezed together, away from prying eyes, Sawyer looking very out of place squashed between the two brick walls.

My first bite of the warm apple cinnamon muffin is euphoric, the flavors bursting on my tongue.

"Ohmygodsogood."

"I'm glad you're enjoying it."

I take an unladylike large second bite and savor the flavors of warm, crisp apples, cinnamon, and yummy streusel topping.

"This is better than sex. Holy fuck."

Sawyer snorts.

"You're doing it wrong then."

I gasp and inhale bits of muffin, coughing and choking on brown sugar.

"Jesus, are you okay?" He pushes my coffee toward me as I hack up a lung. Real fucking cute, Ivy.

"Fine. I'm fine."

We eat in silence for a few moments, me enjoying every mouthful of my muffin while Sawyer scarfs his in two large bites.

"Did you even taste it?"

"Tried not to."

"Why on earth are you eating them if you don't like them?" Finally asking the question I've been dying to hear the answer to.

"You know why, Ivy."

"I don't know if I do . . ." I don't understand it at least. I don't understand what would possess him to do it. Or why. I wait and study his face. His hand rubs aimlessly across his beard and my hands itch to knock it out of the way and feel the short facial hair against my own palm and fingers.

"They were always your favorite. I went in one day with Liam and when I went to order, that's what I asked for."

"My favorite muffins? That you actually hate."

"Yep. It was a piece of you that was left behind that I got to have anytime I wanted."

I let that sit in the air between us. It's been ten years since we've seen each other. This man never forgot about me and did everything he could to make sure he never did.

"So, Charlotte. Liam's right?" Changing the subject to a safer one seems like the best idea at the moment.

"No, actually."

"Oh, wow."

"Yeah. It was a bit of a shock to everyone. The dad is an asshole and he and I don't get along. Liam has never left Hannah's side, though. They're still best friends and he loves that little girl fiercely."

"That's really sweet, and I'm not surprised, actually. Liam was always a good one. That has to be hard on Hannah, though. But my god is she the cutest thing I've ever seen."

"Surprised you didn't settle down. You used to talk about being a mom."

"Well, my life didn't turn out the way I thought it would have back when we were together. And I know that's my fault. To be honest, I didn't really date. I mean, I dated a little, but there was no way I would have had a baby with the last asshole."

"I'm sorry, Iv."

"It's fine. I'm fine."

Sawyer just nods his head as he sips his coffee.

"How's the rest of the Hayes brood?"

"Kins just graduated from college and is teaching kinder-garten now. She loves it. And me and the boys are all running the distillery together."

"No fucking way! Sawyer!"

"Don't get too excited. It was way earlier than I expected. My dad had a stroke, and he really struggles with communication. He's still up and living his life, but running a business this large was too much stress. I took over as CEO recently, Dallas and I work hand in hand, Liam works the actual creation and quality part, and Carter works branding, PR, and relations. It works until it doesn't, but we get through it."

"I'm sorry about your dad. That's hard. I always adored your parents."

He looks at me then, but doesn't say anything back. I suppose there isn't much to say. I'm sure his parents hate me for hurting their son the way that I did. Deciding to change the topic again, I break the silence.

"You and the boys still beating the shit out of each other in the ring?"

"We'll be doing that until we're old and wrinkly."

"Ha. I'd love to see that now that you're all older."

"I'll make sure you get an invite next time. Actually, it would do you some good to get in the ring and get some of that anger and frustration out."

I think it over for a moment. I definitely have some rage that needs to be expelled. There was a huge part of me that actually wanted to beat the shit out of Brooks with the lamp, and was disappointed that I hadn't when given the opportunity to potentially get away with it.

"That's not the worst idea you've ever had. Running definitely works as a stress reliever, but punching the shit out of something or someone sounds freaking delightful. Actually, you know what? Yes. Yes please. I want to do that! Soon. Can we do that?" My voice climbs higher and higher the more excited I get.

"Settle down, you violent little thing. Yes, I'll take you to punch something. But with all those emotions throttling you right now, I don't think punching someone is the best idea."

I laugh and settle down further against the brick wall, my ass on the dirty pavement, squished in front of Sawyer as we finish our coffees in the quiet of the tiny alley off of Main Street.

I feel at peace.

CHAPTER 16

brooks

Ivy's stupider than I thought she was if she thinks running away is going to keep her from me. I'll chase her across the world and drag her home if I have to. I don't mind the chase. It turns me on and will make forcing her to heel that much more enjoyable. Zoe wouldn't give me information, trying to cover for her pathetic friend. But if she's not here, I know she fled back to her hometown. She can't afford to do anything else. Finding her parents' address was easy, and making the plans to stay one town over, even easier. I pack a week's worth of clothes and toiletries into my luggage and head out in my rented Ford Focus.

I'm coming for you, Ivy.

CHAPTER 17

Sawyer

I left Ivy at her house and walked over to Reid's for a distraction. It's different than leaving her in my bedroom for the night, and I forced myself to go against all of my natural instincts and walk away. I want to be wherever she is. I want to remind her how good we are together, and I can't do that if she isn't with me. There is a huge part of me that is fucking terrified that she'll bolt again, and I want to do everything in my power to prevent that from happening.

I knew I was taking a chance on Reid being home or not, but if he wasn't at Rogue, tattooing, or on a run, he'd be here. I knock once before letting myself in and walking through his house. It doesn't take long to find him sitting at his table surrounded by drawing paper and an iPad.

"Hey, man," I say, unsure how to start the conversation, fully feeling the tension that still lingers in the air between us.

"You ever going to stop just walkin' in? What if I had a lady friend over?"

"You haven't had a lady friend over since you bought this place, so I'm not worried about it. Can we talk?"

He drops his stylus and sits back in his seat to finally look at me.

"Depends. We good?" he asks.

"Depends. We got something not to be good about?"

"I told you that I didn't know who she was. In hindsight, I realize that it should have clicked right away. I also told you I didn't mean any harm."

"You did. But you forget that I also know you, Reid. The way you were looking at her . . ." I run my hands through my hair, trying to stay calm, reminding myself it's my best friend I'm talking to. "The way you talked to her. There's more to it. Isn't there?" I pull out a chair and take a seat at his table, leveling the playing field for the conversation.

"I don't know what you want me to say, Sawyer."

"The truth," I say confidently but bracing myself for the worst, not sure how many more tough conversations I'm prepared to have.

"The truth . . ." Silence stretches between us for a few moments and I know this probably won't be good, but I decide to wait him out anyway.

"Fuck. From the second I saw her, everything around me disappeared. I felt this instant pull to her. Was it physical at first? Yeah, I'm not going to lie to you, you've seen her. But seeing her breakdown? Holding her while she completely lost her shit? I felt this primal need to protect her, to take care of her. Like recognizes like, Sawyer, whether you understand that or not. She was clearly running from something or someone, I could see it in her eyes. So yeah, I felt something, a pull or whatever you want to call it. I had to weigh those feelings against my loyalty and love for you, man. You know what I chose, but that doesn't mean it was fucking easy on me to make things harder on her."

The last sentence was delivered louder and firmer than the rest and left no room for misunderstanding. It fucked him up to cause more pain for Ivy. A part of me loves him for that and wants to thank him, the other wants to gouge out his fucking eyes to make sure he can't ever look at her again. But this isn't just some random asshole I'm talking to, and I've got to figure this out.

Reid gets up from the table and walks to the kitchen, and I rub my palms against my eyes. I've never had to navigate something like this before. From sixth grade until the day she took off, Ivy was undoubtedly mine. She knew it and so did everyone else. I know she's been with others since, but I wasn't around to stop it or see it. This is different. I love Reid like a brother, and I need to make sure of a few things before I can move on.

"Is this something I need to worry about?"

"No."

"That's it? Just no?"

"Yep."

"I trust you. You know that, right?" I mean it. He's never given me a reason not to trust him. If Reid gives his word, he stands by it.

"Yep. Which is why you should know you don't have anything to worry about. She's off-limits. I wouldn't do that to you. Couldn't imagine doing that to you, brother." I release a deep sigh of relief. I knew that was the case, but hearing it makes me feel a whole lot better.

"Someone's out there for you. You're gonna find her. You got all of us, too, you're a part of this family. Whether you believe that or not, it's the truth."

He nods his head and I decide to leave it at that. I get up from the table and see myself out. Before leaving, I remind him of family dinner this Sunday.

I hop back on my bike and head out for a long ride. I've got a ton of shit to think about and process, not to mention a hundred missed texts from my siblings that I want to avoid.

Without Ivy on the back to worry about, I cut through town, speeding past the other cars and weaving recklessly through traffic. I reach the end of town where the road opens up and head straight for the lookout point at the edge of the ridge. I push my bike to the limit, the wind in my face, leaning hard into the winding mountain roads, causing my footpegs to spark against the asphalt. My thoughts don't leave her. Ten fucking years apart and my heart is still hers. I don't know what to do with all the emotions tearing me apart, but I know that I want her and nothing else matters. I race up the mountain, hoping time on the open road will give me a sign of a clear way forward. She needs options, and I need to make sure she knows that I'm one of them. My heart races with the possibilities of everything we could still be. I never stopped loving this woman and now that she's back, I feel like I can finally breathe again. I know that I need to be patient, that she needs my support more than anything else, and I'm willing to give her that. I've waited ten fucking years, I'll wait another ten if I have to. Our love has always been worth it, and I know deep down that it always will be. The memories of us come flooding back.

"How many babies do you want?"

"You're not putting a baby in me, Sawyer! We're eighteen!"

"Technically, I'm almost nineteen. We'll obviously wait until after college. C'mon, how many are we gonna make?"

"Fine, I'll play your game. Ten."

"Don't play with me, Iv, 'cause I'll happily put ten babies in you." *I grab her around the waist and drag her across the bed of my truck, the blankets we're laying on top of bunching under us in the process. Her legs spread open for me, and I settle my hips between them.*

"Mmm," she moans, nuzzling her face into my neck. I rub my hands up the outside of her thighs, pushing her little sundress up as I go, until my fingers meet the thin string of her panties.

"You make me crazy." I nibble on her shoulder, switching to little kisses as I work my way up her slender neck. I trace my finger along the thin fabric of her underwear, following it down until I meet her wet center. I swipe my finger across the damp spot and her hips gyrate against me.

"Can I have you, butterfly? Let's practice."

"Mmm. Practice? We've been doing this all year, I think we're getting the hang of it."

"Practice making those ten babies I'm going to put in you someday."

"Five. Just like your mom had. Five is perfect." I look up to meet her eyes and see nothing but honesty reflected in them.

"Five then."

I drag her panties down her thighs as far as I can and she kicks them off the rest of the way, leaving her completely bare to me. I pull out a condom from my pocket before pushing down my shorts. I sheath myself before lining up and pushing in gently, working into her tight center until I'm seated fully inside. She feels so damn good every single time. She moans and I love that she enjoys this. The first few times hurt her, and it killed me to know I was causing her pain.

"I can't wait until I don't have to wear one of these. I want to feel you around me."

"I want to feel you come inside me."

"Fuck, Ivy. You're making it hard to not say fuck it and take my chance without wearing one." I move my hips back and push into her again. Her legs wrap around my waist, holding me tightly. My thrusts stay quick and deep inside her.

"Someday," she says as she holds me close.

"Someday," I repeat before my lips crash down on hers.

I skid to a stop, my bike turning sideways and sparks flying again. Fighting to keep my bike upright, I scarcely miss wiping out, and pull over to the side to catch my breath. I take off my helmet and bend at the waist, bracing my hands on my knees. My legs are shaking and my stomach flops. Before I know it, I'm retching the contents of my stomach into the ditch. I wipe my mouth with the back of my hand before taking a deep breath of the clean mountain air and letting my emotions settle.

Fuck everything else.

I want my goddamn girl.

Time to get my shit together and make sure she doesn't ever question that.

ivy

Sawyer dropped me off at my house after breakfast but wouldn't leave without putting my number in his phone. He sent me a text so that I had his.

Unknown: You're so beautiful.

A blush blooms across my cheeks. This morning didn't go at all how I had pictured it in my head. I spent the last decade villainizing myself to the point that I genuinely believed the narrative I had created—that no one in this town would accept me back into it. Being met with kindness was a shock to my system. When I left Aspen Ridge, leaving Sawyer and everything I'd ever known and loved behind, I didn't get any closure. Everyone's lives kept going without me, as if I had been erased altogether. Every step I was forced to take on my own, a brick was laid, building my wall higher and higher.

I expected heartbreak and fear.

I didn't expect to lose myself entirely in the process.

Meeting Zoe saved me from years of complete loneliness. But overall, I learned to function, holding myself together but always living on the edge of uncertainty, walking through a life that I didn't want for myself.

Seeing Sawyer again has thrown me completely off my axis, rattling the foundation of the structure I deliberately placed to hold me together.

After so long on my own, to be seen, feel safe, secure, and protected? It's messing with me. The memory of Sawyer's filthy words and the feeling of his arms wrapped around me have been on repeat all day.

"Tell me, butterfly, if I touched your pussy right now, what would I find? Would you be dripping wet for me?"

He wasn't wrong. Being in such close proximity to him again lit my body on fire. It didn't matter the weight that hung between us like a heavy cloud before a storm. The tension and chemistry is stronger than anything else. He stokes a need in me that only he can sate.

Warmth pools between my legs, my core aching and pulsing in need at the thought of being with him again. If he had followed through on his threat to touch me, he knew the truth as much as I did. I was dripping for him, even while we fought and I poured my heart out. My hand creeps up under my shirt to touch my breasts. I pull at my nipples, twisting and pinching, knowing that they are a direct line straight to my aching center. I imagine it's Sawyer's mouth over my nipples, sucking and biting lightly, pushing me right to the brink of needy insanity. Closing my eyes and picturing him hovering above me, his hands all over my body, the rough feel of his beard on my soft, smooth skin, my clit throbs in need. I shimmy my leggings down past my knees and let my legs fall open, trembling slightly in anticipation. Lightly rubbing my fingers up the insides of my thighs, working myself up further, I'm lost to the desperate desire that it's Sawyer touching me instead of myself. I imagine his praise, something that I had no idea would feel so good to hear. I let his words from my panic attack wash over me, imagining the situation differently.

"You're doing so well."

"That's my girl."

I let my imagination spiral, adding some of my own that I would want to hear—"Such a good girl. Do you want to come, baby?" So, so badly.

I finally slip my fingers down my seam and dip them into the wetness at my center. I press in two fingers and pump them a few times before I slide them up to my sensitive, swollen clit and swirl them in firm, slow circles. Moans escape me as my hips and body start to chase the impending orgasm. My free hand continues to pinch and twist my nipples as I slip my fingers back down to press inside me. My orgasm builds and builds as I let myself go. I rub my clit with my palm as I fuck myself with my fingers, hips gyrating, Sawyer's name on my lips.

"Come for me." I hear him whisper as if he was really here with me. "Come for me, baby."

I combust. I'm washed away with wave after wave of pleasure that rocks through my body. My pussy pulses around my fingers as I come harder than I have in years. Once I'm too sensitive to be touched further, I remove my hand and catch my breath. Sex was good with Sawyer, but we were fumbling teenagers who had no idea what they were doing. The thought of him touching me now? Fucking hell. If it was even half as good as just the thought of him was, I wouldn't survive it.

I pull up my leggings and go to the bathroom to wash my hands as my phone starts to ring with Zoe's incoming video call.

I dry them quickly before returning to the couch and answering her. Her smiling face greets me, her short hair pulled in a half-up top knot that I swear only she can make look cute.

"Hi, ZoZo!"

"Holy shit, babe, you've got that 'I've been fucked' glow."

Nothing gets past her. I wiggle my fingers in front of the camera and give her a little smile.

"Ahh. A self-induced digit fuck. Whatever works."

I laugh at her.

"I miss you!"

"I miss you more. Now tell me all the things."

"I don't even know where to start. It's been a long two days. How has it only been TWO days!?"

"I've got the time, so spill it all."

I go into the details of the last forty-eight hours, my mental breakdown at the beach with Reid, finding out the hard way that Reid happens to be Sawyer's best friend, Sawyer showing up at my parents' house, the explosive conversations, breakfast, seeing some people from town. I verbally vomit all of it.

"Holy. Fucking. Shit."

"Yeaaaaaah."

"K, first thing. Are you okay?"

"I don't know, honestly. It's been emotionally draining and so much about it has been unexpected. Sawyer's reaction to me? Zo, he's never gotten over me. He's not married, not in a relationship, which is fine, but the way he stormed over here, the way he holds me and looks at me. It's not at all what I expected."

"Damn, babe. But are you honestly that surprised? It's not like you got over him either."

"What do you mean?"

"Iv, you didn't. You literally say his name in your sleep. And I know you have a lot of trauma from your parents, but I think he was a major reason you feared going back to that town. You were terrified of facing him. Plus, you've had like two hookups and one of those included Fuckface-Who-Will-Not-Be-Named."

I sit on that for a moment. She's not wrong. My parents have been gone for well over a year, going on two, and I had no real reason not to come up here and take care of the house. My own fears and insecurities came into play, and sure, some of those were related to how I would be welcomed back here, but a massive part was facing Sawyer. I had accepted the assumption that he hated me for ruining us, but knowing it for certain? I couldn't bear it.

The fact that I was met with the opposite?

It's a lot to process, but a part of my heart has healed from the compassion and love he's shown me. It's also confused me, forcing me to face things I've locked away, and has left me questioning everything.

***

The sun is setting by the time I hang up with Zoe. I go to the kitchen and pull out one of the wine bottles she packed for me as well as a bag of Chex Mix. Dinner of champions for someone who doesn't have the guts to return to town for an actual meal. I pour a glass of my favorite red and grab my bagged dinner before snuggling up on top of the sleeping bag on the couch. I can't bring myself to sleep in my old room. Or even go back upstairs again. The living room is bad enough. It never felt like a home here, and with both of my parents gone, it feels even more empty. Not that their presence filled it with anything other than disappointment and grief.

When I was in elementary school, my mom still had hope. She would make a show of preparing dinner for my dad every night. She turned on music and would dance around the kitchen with me while she cooked a meal. One of two things would happen: my dad would either come home, grab his plate, and eat in his office, ignoring us completely, or he wouldn't come home at all. My mom and I would eat together, just the two of us, and she would make it magical for me, a queen and her princess eating a lavish meal while the king handles his important work.

The music was the first thing to stop.

Shortly after, she stopped cooking altogether.

The house feels as though all the despair and heartbreak had bled into the very bones of it. It's gloomy, cold, and I find myself craving the comfort and warmth of Sawyer's space that I had last night.

. . .

"What are you looking at, butterfly?"

"Your parents. Look at them."

I point to his parents in the kitchen. They host Sunday dinner and I look forward to it every week. His dad is swinging his mom around the room to a Fleetwood Mac song, "Leather and Lace". One of my favorites. She throws her head back laughing at him. They are so in love and don't care who knows it. When they're together it's just them.

"Your dad looks at your mom like she hung the moon."

"And how do you think I look at you?"

I glance over to find him looking down at my face.

"I don't know. How?"

He grabs my wrist, pulls me down the hallway to his bedroom, and lets the door click shut behind us.

"You don't know? I must not be doing a very good job."

"Then maybe you should practice in the mirror more often."

He gives me a look that is all seriousness. A laugh bursts free from me and I clasp my hand over my mouth. My eyes widen as big as saucers. I hate my laugh. It's loud and people have always made fun of me for it. Especially my dad on the off chance I laughed in front of him.

He walks up close to me and pulls my hand away from my mouth.

"Don't do that."

"Do what?"

"Cover your laugh."

"It's terrible!"

"It's the best sound I've ever heard, and I love it."

He steps close enough that our toes are touching, his hand still clasped around my wrist between us. His thumb rubs aimlessly back and forth at my pressure point, igniting heat throughout my body. I meet his eyes and study his face. I've known this boy since we were eleven and twelve years old. The last six years has brought a lot of different looks from him, but I've seen this look on his face before. I just saw it reflected on his dad's face as he looked at his mom. He reaches up and drags the back of his knuckles down my cheek and across my jaw.

"How am I looking at you now?"

"I..."

"Like you're the most beautiful girl I've ever seen? Like the world would come to a complete standstill if you weren't in it? Like you're the only girl I'll ever love? Like you hung the moon?"

I close my eyes and lean into his touch, resting my forehead against his.

"I love you, Sawyer."

"Good. 'Cause I love you. Don't ever forget that."

At what point did I forget that? At what point did I start to question his love for me? I wipe away the tears as they fall. Sawyer only ever had eyes for me from the moment we met. He never wavered.

But most importantly, he always made me feel loved for simply just existing.

He never asked anything of me.

Never asked me to change.

He just loved me. For me. No questions. No expectations.

I know that truth down to the marrow of my bones as an image of Sawyer standing here yesterday flashes through my mind. The look on his face as he stared at me.

It was relief.

And love.

"Ivy, we need to talk. This is going to be really difficult for you to hear, but it's important that you have all the facts."

"Okay... what is it, Mom?"

"I overheard a conversation today between Sawyer and his father."

"Okay?"

"You didn't get into the University of Washington by yourself, honey."

"Yes I did. What are you trying to say, Mom?"

Her words aren't making any sense. I got my admission letter a week after Sawyer did. I read it myself. I accepted my admission to go there.

"You didn't, though. Sawyer was worried you two would be separated. He has to stay in Aspen Ridge because of the distillery. His dad made a phone call, it's his alma mater. I heard Sawyer thanking him and them discussing it. I'm sorry, Ivy. I know this is probably hard to hear. Men will do whatever it takes to keep the things they want. Remember that. This is a lesson."

My heart sinks.

My mom was wrong. She had to be. The last two days replay in my mind like a montage. He never got over me. The way he looks at me is still the same. The only thing that's new is the uncertainty that I put there. I did that. I hurt him and left him alone when all he ever did was love me and want to be with me.

I grab my phone off the coffee table and pull up his text.

Unknown: You're so beautiful.

I run my fingers over his words before adding him as a contact.

Me: Can we talk?

Three little dots appear and then disappear. My heart sinks. A fresh wave of tears threatens to burst free until there's a knock at my door. I jump up off the couch, sloshing my wine from the glass and onto my hand in the process. I set it on the table before jogging to the door, licking the wine off my skin, my heart in my throat. I whip open the door to find Sawyer pacing back and forth on the porch, running his fingers through his hair. He stops and looks me over, taking in my black leggings, tall wool socks, and loose tank top.

"Hi, butterfly."

"Hi."

Our eyes dance around each other's faces, trying to get a read on the other person.

"What are you doing here?"

"You said you couldn't sleep here. I didn't want you to be alone. I wanted you to have options."

"Sawyer . . ."

My eyes drift closed. My chest heaves. This man. I open my eyes to where Sawyer stands in front of me, bracing himself on the door frame. The look on his face is no longer of concern and affection, it's lust filled, unbridled desire, need, and desperation.

I know it matches my own.

We lunge for each other a moment later, coming together in the entryway, my arms wrapping around his neck as our mouths collide. My hands weave through his hair. His kiss is bruising and demanding and his rough facial hair against my smooth skin feels like heaven. I can't help the moan that escapes my lips, muffled by the press of his.

He wastes no time scooping me up into his arms. My legs wrap around his waist as one of his hands snakes up my side to cup my face and thread through my hair. He angles my face where he wants me while walking us into the house. The door slams behind us as Sawyer kicks it closed before he spins and pushes me against it. He pulls back and I grip his hair tighter, desperate not to lose contact. He doesn't leave me long enough to disappoint me. His eyes never leave mine as his tongue peeks out and traces the seam of my lips delicately.

"Let me in, baby," he pleads.

My eyes meet his and the double meaning of his words aren't lost on me.

My lips part for him and his tongue delves in. He kisses me as if it's the last thing he'll ever do. His hips press hard against mine, pinning me between his body and the door, my legs tightening around his waist to hold myself up. His hands roam everywhere, around my ass and thighs, to the curve of my hips, and up my sides and back down again. It's all-consuming. He's everywhere.

His mouth leaves mine to pepper kisses across my jaw and down my neck before sucking gently on the skin where it meets my shoulder. I moan and arch into him.

"Fuck. Ivy. That sound, baby. You feel so good in my arms."

I rock gently against his waist. He shifts and drops my hips lower, the hardness of his cock pressing right against my core. I rock harder against him and this time it's him who moans. The fire that started to build deep and low in my belly rises to a blazing inferno.

This.

This feeling that only Sawyer evokes in me. How could I ever walk away from this? From him. He's only ever loved me. How could I allow myself to believe the toxic bullshit my mother fed me? The epiphany slams into me and the realization of everything I gave up destroys what's left of my hesitation.

I frantically pull his face back to kiss him, tears streaming down my cheeks now. I grasp at his shoulders and pull him to me, not able to get close enough. Desperation. That's what I feel. Fuck, what have I done?

He kisses me hard, grasping my face in both of his hands before pulling back and looking at me.

"Do you know how long I've dreamt of kissing you again?"

A sob escapes me, and I drop my forehead to his.

"I'm sorry. I'm so sorry."

"Shhh. I know, baby."

He cradles me in his big arms and takes me to the couch. This time he sets me down next to him before leaning down and wiping my tears away. I pull my knees up to my chest and knead my hands together in front of my shins until I feel the bite of pain.

"Your tears fucking destroy me, Iv. Talk to me." He reaches for my hands, pulling them apart, and threads his fingers through mine.

"She said you were trapping me, Sawyer. It wasn't just thinking I could be pregnant. It wasn't just culinary school. She told me she heard you thank your dad for pulling strings to get me into U-Dub. That you had him pull strings to guarantee I would go there because you knew if I got in I would go, because that's where you were going. I'm so sorry, Sawyer. I believed her."

"Ivy . . . Fuck. You aren't going to ask me if it's true?" His eyes bounce back and forth between my own, looking for his answer.

I shake my head.

"I don't need to. I know you didn't. You wouldn't. But I believed her. She was my mom, Sawyer. She's the one who trapped me. She took away all my options. Not you. Never you. I'm so sorry," I choke out.

"C'mere, baby."

He pulls me into his lap, my head resting on his chest. He wraps his arms completely around me as I crumble into a million pieces and cry my heart out.

"I'm sorry."

My heart has been ripped completely open. Bare, empty, and raw.

I cry for the time I lost.

For the teenagers who mapped out their lives, only to be torn apart.

For the pain I caused Sawyer.

I cry for the young girl who trusted her mother.

But I also cry for my mother. For the life she never got to live the way she dreamed. For the lengths that she went to keep me from making the same decisions she did. She mothered me the only way she knew how. I ache for the woman who was taken from the world too soon, without ever having the opportunity to live.

"Hey, baby, you need to breathe for me before you hyperventilate."

Sawyer lifts me, pulling my back flush against his chest and my butt between his legs. He holds me tight against him and places one of his hands on the center of my chest, his palm flat against me, the other wrapped around my waist.

"Breathe in and out with me, baby. In, one, two, three, four, five. Hold it, baby girl. Breathe out. One, two, three, four, five."

I close my eyes and focus on my breathing, the feeling of Sawyer around me, his smell, his voice as he coaches me through the technique he saw me use earlier. I release all the tension in my body as I relax into him and let go.

"That's my girl. I'm so proud of you. Just breathe. You're so strong."

These are the last words I hear before sleep takes me.

Sawyer

I HOLD IVY ON HER PARENTS' SHITTY-ASS COUCH UNTIL my legs start to fall asleep before moving us to lie side by side. I carried her to the living room couch after she fell asleep on me in the entryway earlier. Tucking her into my body, my arms wrap around her to keep her close, and I settle her into my chest to cocoon her. I press my lips gently onto her forehead and take a deep inhale of her perfect, sweet scent when her phone starts vibrating on the coffee table in front of us. Ivy stirs slightly and I tighten my arms around her.

"Shh, baby. Sleep."

I reach forward and grasp her phone to silence it when I see the missed call from an Unknown number. I put her phone on silent as the text message previews start coming in.

Unknown: Ivy, Ivy, Ivy. I warned you

Unknown: Come home

Unknown: I won't say it again. You're mine.

Unknown: GET FUCKING HOME

.   .   .

My blood boils in my veins and I have to work hard to steady my heart and breathing so I don't wake up Ivy. Who the fuck is this motherfucker? This has to be the ex, Brooks. I wish I could unlock her phone to put an end to this right now and make sure he doesn't fuck with her anymore. Like hell will she be dealing with this psycho on her own. I'll be damned if he thinks he can threaten her and get away with it. There's no world where she'll be his again. I'll make sure of it. The texts stop, so I put her phone back on the coffee table and return my arm to wrap around her. My fingers rub aimlessly on her shoulder to calm myself. I hold her as close as physically possible with our clothes still on, and contemplate everything that's come to light.

The shit with her mother isn't surprising at all, and I've always assumed her mom played a part in her leaving. It seemed like even Ivy's dad didn't know where she had gone. Not that he would have noticed her absence anyway. I drastically underestimated the lengths her mother would go to see Ivy live the life she didn't get to.

I see the crossroads we're at, and I know that I have two choices. We can continue to hash out the past, or we can let it go and find our way forward. Knowing the truth is enough. Having her right fucking here? Wrapped in my arms while she sleeps peacefully? That's fucking everything. This is what I want to live for.

I desperately want to move forward. I want to let all the shit from the past go and find our way through it. I just hope she wants the same. It's time to move on.

I spend the remainder of the night restless, building on my plan to remind Ivy how happy she once was in Aspen Ridge, and with me. I may not know her like I used to, but her soul and heart are the same, and those two speak to me and recognize me as their counterpart. I know that this woman is the one woman on earth who was made for me. Just like she knows deep down she's right where she should be, she just needs a little reminder.

And I know exactly where we're starting.

***

I wake as Ivy starts to stir in my arms, stretching her lithe little body like a cat after a nap. Her eyes are slow to open, and I watch her face transform as she sees me.

"Hi, butterfly."

"Hi," she says as her lips turn up in a small smile. "I slept."

"Do you not normally?"

"No. Not a full night, anyway."

"Since you left." Not a question, and she doesn't deny or confirm. There's a part of me that is happy her body recognizes she's safe with me, that she can rest without worry. I'll happily hold her every night if it means she will sleep restfully.

Not able to help myself, I close the few inches between us and take her lips with mine. I watch as her eyes slowly close and her body goes lax in my arms. She doesn't hesitate to kiss me back, her mouth opening to deepen it. Her arms loop around my neck, pulling me closer. What was meant to be a simple good morning kiss heats quickly. I flip us so that she's on her back and I'm on top of her, her legs fall open for me and I settle between them. She responds by bucking her hips up into mine in search of friction.

Fuck. I wasn't expecting this. She wants me. Whether she's lost or confused, she can't deny what's between us, and this is my proof. Her brain needs time to catch up, but damn if her body doesn't know exactly who she's with. Pride and the reassurance I need fill my chest.

I kiss her thoroughly and she matches my intensity. I curl my arm under her knee and pull up, spreading her open further for me and letting my hips fall into her, my hard length pressing along her center. She grinds into me while pulling my shirt up. The moment her small hands glide across my abs, I moan into her mouth. She grips me tightly around my waist and pulls me down onto her, and I struggle to hold my weight up with one arm trapped between her and the couch and the other holding up her leg, but she seems to love the weight of me on her. Not wanting to crush her, I let go of her thigh and brace my forearm next to her head before rocking into her. We find a steady pace, dry humping and making out like fucking teenagers. She releases my mouth before arching her lower back and pressing her pelvis higher into me.

She's close. Her breathing accelerates and she grabs my arm tightly. Fuck, I know it's not going to take much more before I blow in my fucking pants. I keep fucking into her, grinding my throbbing cock over her core, back and forth, until she lets out the sexiest fucking moan. And then it's my name on her sweet lips as she comes undone under me.

"Sawyer!"

I come instantly.

"Fuck, Ivy, I'm coming," I moan against her lips.

Jerking one last time into her, my cock throbs painfully against my zipper as I unload cum into my briefs.

She pulls me into her as she settles down from her orgasm, breathing just as heavily as I am. I lean up enough to look at her face. She's flushed, her eyes lidded and heavy, and she's never looked more fucking beautiful than she does under me, the post-orgasm bliss relaxing her.

"Holy shit," she says.

"Yeah. Holy shit."

"Haven't done that since we were teenagers."

"Same."

"You're so beautiful, baby."

If possible, her cheeks flame brighter. She's so fucking cute.

"We need to get cleaned up. Especially me. Pack a bag, we're going to my place."

"What?"

I climb off of her and stand, adjusting my pants the best that I can. The drive home is going to fucking suck.

"Just what I said. You aren't staying here. So pack up all of your things and we're leaving in five minutes. We have plans today, anyway."

She sits back on the couch and looks at me, her mouth hanging open slightly, and I place my fingers under her chin to close it. She bats my hand away from her face and I chuckle.

"Five minutes, Ivy."

"What if I don't want to?" she protests.

"Do you want to stay here?" I ask, raising a brow.

"No," she doesn't hesitate to answer, and then covers her mouth like she didn't mean to be so transparent with me.

"Then pack. Your. Shit." I look down at my watch and then back at her. Four minutes, Iv. I'll be right back."

I go to relieve myself in the bathroom and clean up the best I can before washing my hands and returning to her. She's packed and standing by the front door in the clothes she woke up in, two duffel bags at her feet, and her purse in hand.

"We can't do that again."

"Yes we can," I tell her.

"I have a lot of shit to figure out, Sawyer. This morning doesn't change that. I can't think straight if we're doing . . . that."

Her words sting, but I'm stronger than to let them hurt me. I understand she needs time and I'm prepared to give her as much as she needs. Her body knows, her mind just needs a beat. It doesn't mean I'm giving her space though. I walk up to her and tilt her chin up with my fingers.

"Did it feel good to come with me?"

Her eyelids flutter closed and her breath hitches.

"Answer me. Did it feel good to come because of my cock rubbing against you, wrapped tightly in my arms, my mouth on yours while pleasure pulsed through your body? Did it feel good?"

"Yes. You know it did. Yes. It felt *good*," she says the last word patronizingly, like *good* couldn't possibly be used to describe what it felt like.

"Then don't say we can't do it again. Because we will. Trust me."

"I just. I need to focus, I need to figure out my life."

"I figured. You can do that from my place, but don't think for a second that we won't be repeating that. We're going to go shower." Her pretty eyes shoot up to mine and I can't help but laugh. "Separately. If that's what you want." I say with a wink.

"So smooth, Sawyer."

"Then we've got plans."

"What kinda plans?" She narrows her eyes at me skeptically.

"You'll see."

"Ugh. Fine. You win. Coffee?"

"At my place. Who do you take me for?"

I shoo her with my hands to get her going before grabbing her bags and following her out to my truck. I toss her bags in the back before opening her door and hauling her ass into it, dropping her into the seat with a little "oomph" that makes me laugh. I shut the door and round the front before climbing in.

"I really can't believe you still have this thing."

"I love it. Why would I sell it or trade it for something else?"

She shrugs her shoulders and looks out the window. I back out of her driveway and head down the long, private gravel road.

"Hey, baby. I gotta ask you something. Last night while you were sleeping your phone kept going off. Brooks is your ex, huh? Are his texts always that psychotic?"

"Yeah. I don't know what you saw, but it's fine. He won't chase me here and he'll move on soon enough. It's nothing."

"Those texts didn't seem like nothing, Ivy. He's deranged and he's harassing you, and I'm not okay with that."

"I'm ignoring him, and he'll get bored and find someone else to mess with. It's fine, Sawyer, really. I've got bigger things to worry about than Brooks."

She bites her bottom lip between her teeth and grasps her

hands, kneading and pulling at her fingers. My head cocks to the side as I watch her. She's anxious, panicky. So much has happened over the last ten years that has wound her up tight and left its mark on her. It's more than just a piece of shit ex-boyfriend. If it's the only thing I get to do for Ivy, I'll unravel all of the trauma, anxiety, and weight she bears, and make her feel like a goddess in the process.

I've got my work cut out for me, but I would do anything for this woman, and I'm going to prove it.

CHAPTER 20

ivy

WE PARK OUT FRONT OF SAWYER'S HOUSE AND I CLIMB out of his truck. He grabs my two bags effortlessly and I follow him into the house. It's a gorgeous home and it's clear he's worked hard on it. The front door opens to a small mudroom, where I kick my Converse off and set them to the side, then walk behind Sawyer down a short hallway that leads to an open-concept living space.

"I know you've been here before, but I didn't really give you much of a tour. My mind was elsewhere," he says.

"It's okay. Mine was too."

"Let me brew us some coffee, you mind if I shower first?"

"No, go ahead. I'm sure you want to get out of those pants. I can figure out the coffee." I give him a cheeky, knowing smile. He smiles back at me, his face lighting up, before dropping his lips to my forehead for a quick kiss.

"I'm happy you're here. I don't know if I've said that yet. I won't be long. Make yourself comfortable."

"K."

I watch Sawyer jog to the short hallway off of the main living space before disappearing. I make my way into the kitchen to make a cup of desperately needed coffee. I fell in love with his kitchen when I woke up looking for coffee the other morning. It's a sleek modern design, but somehow compliments the natural aesthetic of the rest of the house. The room makes a square "U" shape, with a large island in the center. The counters are a gorgeous white marble, and the contrast of the black cabinets pulls the room together beautifully. The top cabinets have glass doors, so it's not so dark that it feels like the room is closing in on you. I drop a K-Cup into the Keurig and walk over to the gas range while it brews. My heart aches to create in here. I miss cooking. Zoe's kitchen isn't much more than a kitchenette, and it's been weeks since I was let go from the restaurant. I run my hands across the stainless steel before grabbing the milk, sugar, and cinnamon to finish making my drink.

Coffee finally in hand, I head to the floor-to-ceiling windows that run the entire length of this side of the house, coming to an arch in the center. I look up at the exposed beams and practically drool. When I was out here the other night it was completely dark, other than the light given off by the fire, and the next morning I was so preoccupied I didn't really look around. I knew we were on the edge of town, but I had no idea the views he had. Past the tall Sitka spruce trees lay the gorgeous mountains with their white tips standing guard over our peaceful little town.

I turn to the living room and walk over to the brown leather couches that make an "L" in front of a large, stone fireplace. A flat screen tv rests above it. I sit down and curl my legs under myself, staring out the window while sipping on my hot coffee. For the first time in a very long time, I feel calm.

My thoughts drift to Sawyer moving on top of me this morning, making a heat bloom from my chest to my cheeks. That connection between us never faded, just laid dormant. It's like no time passed at all. Just being in his presence, I'm absorbed wholly, nothing else matters. He has the ability to knock down every wall I've built over the last decade and reduce me to my raw and bare form. He sees right through my carefully constructed façade.

I expected him to hate me. When he showed up that first

night, while stunned, I braced for wrath, a slew of angry questions, and a demand for answers. But none of that ever came.

It was as if the moment he saw me, everything he had been harboring was whisked away with the breeze. All that remained was concern and relief.

Everything since then has been nothing but supportive, holding me, both physically and metaphorically, with so much tender care.

I look around Sawyer's space, his woodsy sweet scent surrounding me, and can't believe I'm here. I know the truth now, deep down I always did, but I was terrified and wanted to make my mom proud. I didn't want to be the final straw that broke her completely by staying in Aspen Ridge because of Sawyer. It would have ruined her. I know I never should have left. The life I wanted was always right here with him.

But can I come back from that decision?

Can I just stay here after being gone for so long and leaving the way that I did?

Would this be what life was like with Sawyer? Comfort and safety, peace. Happiness that didn't ebb and flow, just calm and steady—so much like him.

Sawyer returns, shirtless, a pair of gray sweatpants hanging low on his hips, exposing his V. Why is it so ridiculously arousing to see men in gray sweatpants, no shirt, and bare feet? Panties are dropping all over the world every time a man dresses like this.

I slowly peruse his body from bottom to top before meeting his eyes. He's so fucking sexy.

"Like what you see, baby?"

I give him a seductive smile, unable to resist this power that he has over me.

"You know I do. You see yourself, right? Time has been good to you, Sawyer."

"You should talk. I thought you were beautiful back then, but fuck, Ivy, now?" He rubs his hand over the coarse stubble on his jaw and shakes his head. "There aren't words to describe how sexy you are."

My face flames as a blush rises.

"Thank you for saying that."

"I only speak the truth. Always have."

He leaves that lingering in the air between us as words from the past drift through my head.

"I know we're young, but I know we're meant to be together."

"I love you, Ivy, don't ever forget that."

"Easy, baby. Wish granted."

"Like you're the most beautiful girl I've ever seen. Like the world would come to a complete standstill if you weren't in it. Like you're the only girl I'll ever love."

"Do you really think you could do anything to make me hate you? Do you think I could share my life with anyone but you after what we had? You think any amount of time apart could change how I feel about you, butterfly?"

"Do you think any amount of time has changed what's between us?"

Tears prick my eyes but I hold them at bay. This man never stopped loving me. I buried it deep out of pure survival, but I never stopped loving him either. I get up from my seat and set my mug down on the coffee table before walking right up to him until our chests are pressed together.

"I missed you," I whisper, before reaching up on tiptoes and kissing him.

He may not know it, but ever so slowly, he's healing me.

CHAPTER 21

Sawyer

WHILE IVY SHOWERS, I CHECK MY PHONE FOR THE FIRST time since yesterday. A first for me. I'm never distracted, I don't have the time or the patience for distractions. But Ivy is everything. I'd let the world go up in flames around us to get this time with her. I've got a shit ton of missed texts to sift through, but one stands out above the rest.

Mom: When were you going to tell me that Ivy has shown back up, son?

Fuck. I pull up my asshole sibling thread to find out who the snitch is.

Me: Hey assholes! Which one of you told Mom?

Kins: Someone told her? What happened to sibling privilege asshats?

Liam: Wasn't me.

Carter: Nope. Dal?

Me: Being awfully quiet, Dickhead. Care to defend yourself?

My phone rings. Dallas. I roll my eyes before picking it up.

"Did you fucking tell Mom, Dallas?"

"Hi to you too. Works going just fucking skippy, thanks for asking, shithead."

"Answer the question."

"No. I didn't tell Mom anything. But you know who did? Cause the whole town's talking about it."

Fucking hell. Ms. Nettie. Goddammit.

"That old biddy. I should have known. Do I even want to know what they're saying?"

"Just that she's back and you two were getting cozy yesterday outside of Bean Haven. Hannah did talk to Liam, but he already knew, just not any details. Said she looked pretty good though."

"Watch it, Dallas. You want to see thirty, you won't talk about her like that."

"Calm down big boy. I meant health-wise, not her overall looks. Although . . ."

I growl into the phone and the fucker laughs at me.

"You doin' okay?" he asks.

"I think so, yeah. We worked through some shit last night and had a breakthrough. I refuse to abandon her, I don't give a shit what she did anymore. I moved her into my house this morning. She can figure her shit out from here, she doesn't need to be in that shithole that was her parents' house."

"Even if I'm not happy with how things went down, I gotta

hand it to you, that's exactly what I would do. You need anything?"

"Yeah, actually. She doesn't know yet, but I'm taking her to the gym in a bit. You think you can call Dom and see if he can block out an hour for us? Private. I want it just us, so she's comfortable."

"You're taking her boxing? Kinky."

"It's not like that. You remember what it was like for us? Fuck, we still get like that. All that pent-up energy with nowhere for it to go? And then to have an outlet to finally be able to channel it? That's what she needs." I huff and run my hands through my hair before continuing. "She started having severe panic attacks after she left Aspen Ridge. That's why I was comforting her outside of Bean Haven. It was like a switch went off and she couldn't breathe. She's got some nervous tics and she's wound tighter than a fucking spool. She asked me to take her for fun, but I think this'll be good for her."

"Damn, man. What happened to her while she was gone?"

"I'm still getting it all figured out."

"I'll call Dom. Anything else?"

"Yeah, I don't have a last name, but she's got an ex that is obsessed with her and won't let her go. He's blowing up her phone and the texts are maddening. I want to know who the fucker is and how to make him go away."

"Give me what you got and I'll see what I can do."

"Brooks. Mommy and Daddy own the restaurant Ivy worked at. I don't have that name either, but she was in Seattle. You still friends with that PI?"

"Wes? I'll reach out. If anyone can hunt someone down and do it silently, it's him.

"Make it a priority. Please."

"On it. We good? I call to check on you and get a laundry list of shit to get done on top of your daily workload."

"Asshole. One last thing, Blaire still work for us?"

"Unfortunately."

"Attaboy. Text me when Dom says we're good to go."

"You got it."

I hang up with Dallas and bring up my mom's text.

Me: Mom, I love ya and I was going to tell you. This is a phone convo though. I'll call you soon and explain everything. Yes, I'm fine.

Mom: I expect you both for dinner on Sunday.

Fuck. I toss my phone to the other side of the couch, deciding to ignore the rest. I walk into my bathroom just as Ivy is stepping out, one towel wrapped tightly around her body, another wrapped around her head, holding her hair up.

"Thank you for the shower. I needed it. I wasn't sure where to put my things, I don't mind living out of my bags, though, I was going to do that at the house anyway."

"I'm going to make space for you. I'd rather not be reminded that you may still leave. If you unpack, we can deal with everything else later."

She drops her head to look down at her bare feet and pulls that plump bottom lip between her teeth again.

Dammit. She's fucking killing me.

I walk up to her before putting my palm on her cheek. She releases her lip on her own and relaxes her head into my hand, eyes closing as she hums appreciatively.

Fuck yes. This is what I want from her. To find comfort in me. To let it all go and just be.

"That's my girl. Relax."

She steps forward on her own and rests her head on my chest. I love our height difference, she fits so easily against me. I wrap my arms around her and hold her tightly.

"I'm proud of you, baby."

"For what? I'm a fucking mess."

"No, you're not. You're so strong. Are you kidding me? Look at you, you're a goddamn queen, Ivy. You've been handling so much on your own for so long, but now I'm here. I've got something that I think is going to make you feel better. Trust me?"

She looks up at me and gives me the most gorgeous smile.

"Yeah. I trust you, Sawyer."

And if that isn't fucking music to my ears.

"Good. Now put some workout clothes on and let's go see your surprise."

I watch her jiggle her shoulders a little in excitement. She turns to walk away, and because I can't fucking help myself, I smack her towel-clad ass.

I pull into the parking lot of Dom's gym and look at Ivy in the passenger seat. She's wearing a pair of tight black running leggings and a bright pink sports bra. Her long black hair is in a high ponytail, and hell if I can't stop myself from imagining what it'd be like to wrap it around my fist while she's on her knees in front of me. I adjust myself with my left hand as I throw the truck into park.

"We're going boxing?" she says as she wiggles in her seat and claps her hand in front of her face. Right now, she looks so much like the young girl I fell in love with.

"We're going boxing. You gotta lot of energy you need to expel. Maybe this'll help."

"It helps you?" she asks, "usually I go on a run when I need to clear my head."

"Hell yeah, it does. The boys and I are still coming here weekly to knock each other around. Especially me and Dallas. I think it's what's made us so close. We can deal with the other person better if we get to beat the shit out of each other every so often." She laughs, but I can tell she understands.

"C'mon, let's get inside." She reaches down and pulls her hat out of her bag and goes to put it on. I reach over and pull it from her hands, tossing it behind me out the window into the bed of the truck.

"You can't work out in a hat. You don't need it."

"I do need it! Sawyer, I don't want everyone to notice me. I know it was fine with Ms. Nettie and Hannah, but can we just keep it quiet?"

"Trust me. Let's go." I jump out of the truck and round the front as she's climbing out and slamming the door. I reach for her hand and practically drag her into the gym.

Just like Dallas had texted me, Dom is waiting for us at the front desk and the place is empty. Dom's gym, formally named Knockout, has been around forever. Dom's dad was a former boxer who opened this place long before we were born. He was in an accident that left his left hand permanently disfigured, officially ending any chance he had of becoming a professional. Dom's been running it the last few years. He's five years older than Dallas and I, and we all grew up coming here and learning how to box.

"Hey, Sawyer. This your woman?"

"This is Ivy. Ivy, Dom. Not sure if you two remember ever running into each other or not. Thanks for clearing the place out for us. Want to get her stretched out and teach her a few things without all the eyes."

"You're good. You got an hour before classes start comin' in. That work?"

"More than works. Thanks, Dom. I owe you, man."

I put my hand on Ivy's lower back and guide her further into the gym. She's doing that nervous tic, wringing the life out of her hands in front of her. I lead us to a mat and face her.

"Let's stretch and then I want to teach you a few self-defense moves before I unleash you on a punching bag. I want to make sure you can defend yourself, and I also want to make sure you're punching correctly so you don't break your hands or wrists."

"K. I've got this." She shakes out her hands at her sides, rolls her neck, and begins working herself through stretches that look more like tortuous yoga poses. My dick threatens to bust free of my athletic shorts while watching her stretch her lean, tight body through the motions. She spreads her legs in front of me, bends at the waist, and leans to one side, her arms reaching and holding her ankle. Her perky, full ass is on display, her leggings clinging to her and leaving nothing to the imagination. I groan. Loudly.

"Fuuuuck, Ivy. Are you trying to kill me? I think you're good and stretched out. Get your ass in the ring before I haul you out of here like a caveman."

She looks at me upside down from between her legs.

"Problem?"

I drop my head back and groan at the sky.

She stays in that position and leans toward the other leg. Having enough of her temptress shit, I walk right up behind her and grab her hips firmly in my hands, yanking her ass right into my hard cock.

"You feel that, baby? Yeah, I'd say we got a problem. Now quit playing with fire and get in the ring."

She stands and turns in my arms with a smart-ass grin on her face. I lean down to kiss her and she shoves my chest. Hard. I'm not expecting it and it forces me to stumble back from her a few paces.

"Nuh-uh. We're here to work out. Come teach me something new."

She skips away from the mat and climbs under the ropes, into the boxing ring.

I look at her for a moment, trying to think of everything but what her body will feel like if I ever get to be inside her again. My dick has a mind of its own and doesn't want to settle down.

"You coming or should I go ask Dom for help?" she yells. That gets my ass moving. I climb into the ring and walk right up to her.

"Go ahead, Ivy. See what happens if you let him come over here and help you. But I don't believe you'd do it. You only want me in here with you. Looking at you." I roam my eyes over her body. "Touching you." My hands run along the length of her arm and goosebumps break out over her skin. She closes her eyes for a moment, and I take the open opportunity to catch her off guard. I push gently right above her breastbone, just hard enough to get her attention and force her to stumble on her feet.

"First lesson. Stance."

"You asshole." She glares at me.

"Time to get to work, baby."

ivy

I GET OUT OF THE SHOWER AND DRY OFF, THE adrenaline from working out with Sawyer earlier still coursing through me. I freaking loved it. I always thought it was kind of barbaric that Sawyer's dad had all the kids fighting in a ring together, even though they had lessons, but I never understood it as an outlet until today. It was everything I didn't know I needed. Sawyer knew exactly what would help me. I rub my cherry almond lotion over my legs, slip into a pair of panties, and pull a tank top over my head before realizing I left my night shorts in my bag. I shut off the light and tiptoe out of the bathroom. Sawyer is sitting on the edge of his bed, rubbing his hands up and down his thighs. When he notices me he freezes, his eyes perusing my body slowly as if committing me to memory.

"Baby, come here," he begs as he holds a hand out to me. I step close enough to grasp it when he pulls me to stand between his spread legs.

"Trust me?"

"Yes," I say nervously.

He turns me so that my back is to him, running his hands up the outside of my thighs, he curls his fingers into the band of my panties before dragging them down my legs. A shiver runs down my spine. Once they pool at my feet I kick them off, swaying slightly. Sawyer has seen me naked before, he's had sex with me more than anyone else ever has. But it's been so long, and my stomach knots with nerves and anticipation.

His hands return to my hips, guiding me down gently so that I'm forced to sit on his lap.

"Remember, baby, trust me," he whispers in my ear.

"What are you doing?" I ask.

"Helping you relax."

"I told you we can't do this anymore. It's distracting."

"And I told you that was bullshit and not happening."

His fingers lightly skim over my skin, down my thighs, until they reach my knees.

"Spread for me."

He pulls my knees apart before forcing me to lift my legs so that they're resting on top of his thighs. I'm spread open for him, and he groans before peppering my shoulder and neck with open-mouthed kisses. His tongue runs from the base of my neck to my ear, lapping at me like I'm his favorite snack.

"Wider, beautiful." He spreads his legs, forcing mine open as far as they can go. The cool air kisses my most sensitive area and goosebumps scatter across my skin in response. His hand comes up under my chin and pushes my head to face forward. It's then I see that we're positioned directly in front of his full-length mirror. My mouth drops open at the sight. Sawyer's massive body behind me, my legs draped over his thighs and spread open wide.

"Fuck, look at you, Ivy. So goddamn perfect. Don't take your eyes off of us. I want you to watch as you come undone for me."

"Holy shit, Sawyer." My heart rate skyrockets, pounding erratically behind my ribcage.

His fingers lightly caress up the inside of my thighs until they reach my apex. Keeping the soft, barely there touch, he runs two fingers up my seam.

"Aah." I squirm on his lap. One of his hands comes to my hip and grabs me firmly.

"Still or I stop. Trust me. Now watch."

I don't take my eyes off of us in the mirror. Sawyer's muscular body surrounds me, spreading me completely open and exposed for him. The hand that was on my hip rubs upward until he's pulling my tank top down and freeing my breasts. I watch as he continues to rub lightly back and forth up my center, barely touching me. He does the same to my nipples, circling them slowly and delicately. I drop my head back on his shoulder, but keep my eyes on the mirror. His gorgeous face is focused, and his eyes travel all over me.

"Sawyer. Please," I pant. I do my best not to move, out of fear of him stopping altogether. My chest is rising and falling rapidly, my skin covered in goosebumps, chills running up and down my spine. Everything feels so good. But I need more, desperately.

"Mmm. I'm not going to lie, I like hearing you beg, Ivy." He kisses my neck before biting lightly, sending a bolt of pleasure right through me and straight to my core.

"Yes, Sawyer. Please, I need more."

He freezes and meets my eyes in the mirror. His eyes are hooded and lust-filled. I can feel his breathing increase as his chest heaves against me and I chance moving slightly, pressing his dick into my back. He plunges two fingers inside me so hard and without warning that I rock back against him.

Oh, fuck. Yes. I moan loudly through the onslaught of his fingers in me.

I can't take my eyes off of us. He palms my breast firmly in his big hand before pinching and twisting my nipples. He curls his fingers deep inside of me, rubbing the spot that has me seeing stars, his palm sliding back and forth on my clit as he does.

The orgasm is almost instant. I explode. There's no slow build-up, it's a massive, explosive grenade that only Sawyer could detonate. The pleasure plows into me with such force that I scream his name as my back arches and my legs shake. I reach behind me with one hand, grabbing Sawyer behind his neck and pulling him closer to me. He nuzzles into my neck and never stops fucking me with his fingers, forcing me to ride out the most intense orgasm of my life. I grip the sheets below us and rock into his hand.

"God! Sawyer!"

"Just me here, baby. God has nothing to do with what just happened to you."

My orgasm starts to slip away, and I relax fully into him. He pulls his fingers from my body before closing our legs slowly.

"Fuck, that was so beautiful. I would watch you come every day if you'd let me."

He's not wrong. Watching him take me like that, in such an exposed, vulnerable way was so hot. It heightened the feeling of everything. Life changing. That's what that was.

I have barely caught my breath when Sawyer stands with me in his arms and lays me down on the bed, dropping a kiss to my forehead before leaving to go to the bathroom. Fucking hell that was incredible. That's two orgasms Sawyer's given me now, when no other man—not that I've allowed many to try—could get me there. I'm able to completely relax with him and let him take the reins and I forgot how incredibly freeing that is.

"Let me clean you up, baby, and then we're going to bed."

I close my eyes and relax into the mattress while he wipes down my overly sensitive area. He returns and I watch as he pulls his shirt over his head, not taking his eyes off of me. His muscles are sculpted expertly, each ab its own beautifully ripped layer leading down to his sexy V. He tosses his shirt at me and it lands in my lap. I look up at him in question.

"Put it on or I'll do it for you."

I laugh at him as I strip my tank top off and replace it with his shirt.

"Better?" I ask him.

He hooks his thumbs into his joggers before pushing them down his toned legs, standing there and allowing me to take my visual fill of him. He smirks at me like he just fucking knows. I lick my lips when I let my eyes drag down to his black boxer briefs, his hard cock facing upward, straining against the fabric. He's so hot. My mouth waters and I so badly want to reach out and touch him.

"I see that look on your face, Iv. Not tonight."

I roll my eyes and he lifts the blankets and lays down before dragging me under with him. Instead of pulling my back flush to his, he pulls my front and holds my hands between our chests, our legs tangled together.

"We're going to figure this all out. Just trust me, baby."

"I believe you."

And I do. For the first time in a decade, hope fills me.

brooks

She let him touch her. Rage floods my system like I've never felt before. How fucking dare she let him touch her. She just signed his death warrant.

I walk through the woods behind the dead man's house and reach the main road before climbing back into my car. Fucking filth covering my shoes and the bottom of my pants. The sight of her spread out in his arms while he touched what's mine is forever burned into my brain. I'll fucking kill him, and she'll be punished. I have a lifetime ahead of me to erase his touch from her body and make sure she doesn't remember anyone but me.

I slam my hand into the steering wheel over and over.

"FUCKING WHORE!" She'll pay. She'll pay.

I drive to the other side of town and take the turn that leads to Ivy's house. I know there is another house on this street, so I find the clearing in the woods I used this morning, turn off my lights, and drive my car deep into the trees before trudging back through the wooded shithole until I reach her house. The back door was left unlocked, safety clearly not a priority for these hicks, and I easily slip into her childhood home undetected. I meander through the dusty house, musky air assaulting my nose, until I find Ivy's bedroom. I walk over to her perfectly made bed and pick up the pillow, disappointed that it doesn't smell anything like her. Still, it's her room and my thoughts are overloaded with her. I unbuckle my pants, letting them fall to my ankles before stroking my cock to thoughts of slipping into her tight cunt. I'm ruthless, gripping my dick hard, reaching down with my other hand to cup my balls. I lean forward and shoot my load all over her pillow.

I know I could have found someone to fuck tonight in the next town over, it's not difficult to find a willing participant, but I'm going to be a husband soon, and Ivy's pussy will be the only thing I fuck. Well, and that and her mouth. Something she'd never do for me before. That'll all change soon.

Soon.

CHAPTER 24

Sawyer

THE NEXT MORNING COMES FAST AND HARD AND I'M not ready to leave Ivy. But I need to go to work and return to some type of normalcy. So does she.

I look at her sleeping body sprawled out in my bed, and it still doesn't seem real. She sleeps like the fucking dead, and since I know she hasn't slept well since she's been gone, I'm sure it's because she's relaxed enough to let her body actually rest. I'm dressed in my work clothes—a pair of navy slacks and a white button-up shirt. I roll up my sleeves, put on my watch, and walk back over to her side of the bed. I kneel next to her and hate that I'm about to disturb her sleep, but can't bring myself to leave her to wake up alone. I brush her silky black hair from her face before leaning down and peppering her forehead and cheeks with kisses.

"Mmm." She starts to stir, turning over from her stomach to her back before cracking her eyes open. "What time is it?"

"Early, baby. I have to go to work and make sure Dallas hasn't fired everyone and burned the place down."

"Okay . . ." She starts to sit up, but I place my hand on the center of her chest to hold her down to the bed.

"Nope. Sleep. And then I want you to do whatever *you* want to do today."

"I need to figure out what I'm going to do with my parents' house and schedule a bunch of things," she says, her voice groggy.

"You can do all of that from here. Let me know the plan and I'll do whatever I can to help,"

"Thank you. You really don't mind me staying here? I can go get stuff done at my parents' house."

My head rears back like she smacked me. Does she really not understand?

"Ivy, I don't know how to make this any clearer, baby. I want you here for as long as you are willing to be. If it were up to me, you'd never leave. I just ask that for today, you be here when I get home. Please."

I love the slow smile that creeps over her face.

"I can do that."

"Good. I'm going to take the motorcycle, so the truck is here and you don't feel trapped. We can go back and pick up your jeep tonight or tomorrow. I should be home around six, that work?"

"Thank you, Sawyer."

She reaches out and places her hand on my cheek before rubbing her thumb back and forth across the scruff of my beard. I hold her eyes hostage for a few moments before giving her forehead one last lingering kiss and standing, smoothing out my shirt.

"See you tonight, Iv."

"Tonight."

I walk to the bedroom door before giving her one last look. She's mid-cat stretch, and I groan out loud. It takes all my strength to walk away from her. But at least I'm leaving her in one of my T-shirts and in my bed.

She'll be here when I get home. I feel it.

"Dallas, what the fuck are you doing in my office?"

He glances around, a puzzled look on his face.

"Who the fuck are you? This is my office now."

"I don't think so, dickhead, get out of my chair."

I walk around my desk and Dallas scoots away from it in my office chair like a fifth grader.

"Dallas, what are you, ten? Get up and give me my chair. We've got shit to talk about."

"This is my chair now, shithead. Who bought it anyway? This one is way better than the one in my office."

"I did. Now get the fuck out of it and let me sit down."

He pushes his feet to propel him further away. You've got to be fucking kidding me. The sight is laughable. My twin, a grown-ass man, who is slightly taller and has about thirty pounds of weight on me, is sliding around in an office chair like we're in elementary school.

"Dallas. Give me my fucking chair. We aren't kids anymore and I've got shit to do."

"Come and get it, fucker. This is mine now."

He scoots further and further away, white-knuckling the armrests. The moment he reaches for the door to open it wider, I launch myself at him, wrapping my arm around his neck in a chokehold, and dropping my weight forward into the ground, forcing him to bend with me. We fall to the hardwood floor, my expensive Herman Miller chair tipping over on top of us. Dallas punches wildly, connecting with my ribs. I tighten my hold around his neck and jerk us back straight, sending the chair scattering away, I throw a blow into his stomach that causes him to make a horrendous noise.

"If you puke on me, dickhead, I swear I'll make you clean my office with your toothbrush!" I say through gritted teeth.

He reaches his free arm around to grab my shoulder and I lift and drop my elbow down onto his forearm.

"Fuck! That fucking hurt!"

Using all of his weight, he turns us and I lose my hold around his neck. We shove each other, wrestling on the ground, trying to get the other to submit. I get him on his back, one of my knees on his chest, my hand pressing the side of his face into the ground. He continues to push me, throwing wild punches, and flips again, rolling us.

"What the fuck is going on in here?"

Dallas and I both freeze, he has my arm cinched behind my back, my fingers nearly touching the back of my head, and I'm throwing punches with my free hand into his ribs and stomach. We stare at Liam and Carter, neither of us wanting to be the one who lets go first.

"He started it," Dallas says.

"Holy shit. Dad left these two in charge?" Carter says to Liam.

"Technically he left just me in charge," I reply as Dallas yanks up further on my arm. It fucking hurts, but I'd rather he dislocate my shoulder than give him the satisfaction of besting me.

"We've got shit to talk about. Get the fuck up."

Liam's face leaves no room for misunderstanding. Dallas and I release each other, and I move to pick up my chair when he does the same.

I push him out of my way before moving it back to his rightful home behind my desk.

"I'll give you the link, you moron. You can buy your own. Now sit down or fuck off."

I look down at my now-wrinkled shirt and pants and do my best to comb my fingers through my hair. I take a seat and my brothers do the same.

"Alright. What have I missed?"

"Nothing. What have we missed?" Liam says, straight to the point. I should have known that they'd corner and force information out of me.

I shoot daggers at Dallas.

"Seriously? Is that why you stole my chair? Killin' time?"

He shrugs his shoulders. What an asshole.

"We're not leaving until you give us something."

"Alright, let's get this over with. What do you want to know?"

They look at each other before turning back to me.

"Everything. What is she doing back?"

"How did you find her?"

"What the fuck has been going on?"

"Is she back for good?"

"Where has she been?"

Their questions come in rapid fire, and I put up my hand to stop them.

"I'm not going to get into Ivy's business with you. It's her story to tell and I'm still getting to the bottom of it, but she left because her mom convinced her that I was controlling the outcome of where she'd go to college so that she'd stay with me. She told her that Dad paid off the admission board to get Ivy in and that I was all for it. She made it clear to Ivy that she needed to leave me and Aspen Ridge to guarantee she didn't end up like her. Her mom really fucked with her head. There was some other stuff going on, but that's between me and Iv."

"Holy shit, man," Liam says. "I'm so fucking sorry."

"Yeah. She's not doing so hot. I want to do whatever I can to help her feel better."

"You don't know why she's back? What's her plan?" Liam asks.

Carter sits back in his chair and rests his ankle on his knee, listening.

"So, some shit went down with an ex-boyfriend, and she found herself in a situation where she's back here. Details aren't important. She's staying at my house, she's safe, and we're working through shit. That's it right now."

"What's the endgame here Sawyer? You considering getting back together with her?" Carter asks, finally breaking his silence.

"It's not even a question. You may not understand it because you guys were fourteen and sixteen when she left, but she is my endgame. She always has been. If she's willing to stay and still wants me, which I think she does, then that's what's happening. Nothing, and I mean nothing will stand in my way this time, as long as she'll have me."

"That's bullshit."

"Excuse me?" I narrow my eyes at my brother.

"That's bullshit. You talk like it's all on her to decide what your fate is. She left you once and believe it or not big brother, I do fucking remember. I remember you not leaving your bed. I remember Mom crying because she was so worried about you and didn't know what to do. Why the fuck is it all in her court? She's the one who left you!"

I look at my youngest brother. He's the most emotionally unavailable, stoic, easygoing one out of all of us. He loves women, but has never been in a relationship. I didn't realize the effect my depressive episode after Ivy left had on him.

"Carter, I get it. I do. But I *love* her. I've never stopped, couldn't if I tried. There is no me without her. I'm not saying you have to be her best friend, but you will accept her eventually. She is scared to death that no one in this town will accept her back into the fold, and I'll be damned if it's my own blood that makes her feel unwelcome. You don't know what she's been through, so don't you dare fucking pass judgment on her." My voice slowly rises and I notice Dallas brace himself in his seat, ready to get between us if needed. Probably smart, because I'm about two seconds from smacking the shit out of Carter.

"We got you, shithead. Right boys?" Dallas says, looking at our two brothers, trying to deflate the situation.

"We do," Liam agrees.

"Carter?" Dallas says firmly.

Carter looks at me for a beat before nodding his head.

"Good. Now get out of my office and back to work."

Liam and Carter rise and leave, but Dallas remains sitting with his phone in his hand.

"You got anything about our issue?" I ask as soon as the door shuts.

"Wes found his info. Wants to know if he should dig deeper or tail him. I wasn't sure how deep you wanted to go. I know what I'd do if it were me."

I rub my hands through my hair while I think it over. I don't want to betray Ivy's trust, but I need to know if this fucker means to cause more issues for her.

"What would you do?" I ask.

"It's not a question. There's no depth I wouldn't go for my woman. When I settle down, there's nothing I wouldn't do to ensure her safety. When she's mine, she's fucking mine."

He's not wrong. If there is even a small chance that I could prevent Ivy's pain or fear, I need to take it.

"Make it happen. And send me the info you have."

Dallas nods before leaving my office.

I spend the rest of the morning sifting through emails before attending a meeting with our CFO and Carter to go over numbers, growth, projections, and plans. While I was gone, Dallas surprisingly stayed out of Blaire's way and allowed her to move forward with the installation of a bar downstairs. The company she chose creates custom pieces and the mock-ups look great. She's got great ideas and will do good things here.

I walk back into my office and shut the door behind me before pulling out a protein shake from my mini fridge when it hits me.

Fuck. I wonder if there's food in the house for Ivy to eat lunch.

I sit down in my chair before pulling my phone from my pocket and opening up my texts with Liam.

Me: Hey man, Can you find out if Hannah has that teenager working deliveries right now?

Liam: Give me a min

. . .

I toss back my shake while waiting for a reply. I hope she's having a good day. I hope she's relaxed while alone in my space. I wanted to stay with her. The last few days it's been so easy to give her all of my focus.

Liam: Yeah what do you need?

Awesome. Hope she likes breakfast for lunch.

Me: A dozen apple cinnamon muffins, coffee with milk, sugar, and a sprinkle of cinnamon and a cake pop.

Liam: A cake pop? Really? She's not three.

Me: Everyone likes cake pops, fucker. Who doesn't like cake pops?

Liam: Whatever. Han's taking care of it.

Me: Thanks

Lunch handled, I redirect my focus on work.

About thirty minutes later my phone chimes with incoming text messages. Ivy's gorgeous face stares back at me as she holds a muffin to her mouth mid-bite. Her face is bare of makeup and her hair is piled on the top of her head in some type of twisty, messy bun.

I rub my fingers over her pretty face.

. . .

Ivy: Was a dozen necessary? Thank you. I
missed these.

Me: More than you missed me?

Fuck. I know I'm playing with fire here. But damn if I don't want to hear it.

Ivy: Maybe? They're delicious and they make
me so happy.

Me: I made you pretty happy last night

Touching her like I did last night was mind-blowing. So much so I almost blew in my pants again, not needing her to touch me at all. Having her relax completely and allowing me to worship her body was such a gift. Damn if I don't crave her.

Ivy: You mean after boxing when you fed me
pizza and beer and we sat outside with the
fire? That did make me happy.

Oh she thinks she's cute.

Me: Nope. When I had you spread open in my lap and I worked your pussy over until you came all over my fingers. I know that made you happy.

Ivy: Oh. That. That was good too. Very. Very. Good.

Me: I had your cum all over my fingers, baby. I know it was good.

Me: I miss you.

Three little dots appear and then disappear several times, leaving me nervous and on the edge of my seat. I bounce my leg while I wait her out. I knew saying that I missed her was pushing it, but I can't filter myself. She knows where my head is at.

Ivy: Then hurry home.

Home. Holy shit she called it home. I know she didn't mean it the way she said it, but fuck if I don't wish she thought of my house as her home. Of me as her home.

I bust my ass to get the rest of my work done for the day and I'm hopping back on my bike at five-thirty to race home to my girl. I park it out front before walking across the gravel driveway and taking the stairs of my porch two at a time. The smell of garlic, onions, and tomatoes immediately consumes me and my mouth waters. I remove my jacket, hanging it on the mudroom hall tree, and kick off my boots. I walk through the narrow entryway and stop in my tracks at the sight before me.

Ivy is standing in my kitchen, hair still piled on the top of her head, dressed in a tight tank top and a pair of denim jeans with bare feet. She's got music on and her hips sway side to side as she stirs something at the stove. It smells delicious, almost as good as she does.

I walk as silently as possible before I sneak up behind her, sliding my hand across her side and around to her stomach before pulling her lightly into me. She doesn't jump and instead leans into me, unable to resist. I kiss her temple lightly.

"Hi, butterfly." I nuzzle into her hair, breathing in her cherry scent.

"Hi." She wiggles a bit in my arms.

"I could get used to this."

"Mmm. Yeah? I hope you like it. I remember you used to love Italian. I haven't cooked in weeks and I've missed it so much. This is therapeutic for me."

"Baby, you can cook for us as often and as much as you want. Tell me what you need and I'll get it."

I lean down and kiss her neck twice before releasing her and turning to lean against the counter.

"What are you making? It smells incredible."

"Lasagna with bechamel sauce and a garden salad."

"I can't wait. Do I have time to shower and wash the day off of me?" I ask her.

"Absolutely. Go."

I smack her ass and she whips around to face me.

"Sawyer!" she yells.

I grasp her face between my hands before taking her mouth in a deep kiss. Our tongues meet in the middle in a caress. The kiss is deep and passionate, I can't get enough. I drop my hand down to her hip and trail my fingers along the bit of exposed skin between her tank top and jeans. She's so soft and I love how her body melts into mine.

She's perfect. So fucking perfect for me.

I slow the kiss and pull her bottom lip into my mouth as I pull away, releasing it with a little pop.

She looks up at me, her eyes dreamy and lust-filled, and my chest swells with pride at how quickly I can turn her on, how good I know I can make her feel. I rub my thumb over her swollen lip before turning and heading straight to my bathroom for a quick cold shower. Withholding sex until I know I'm it for her is harder than I thought it'd be.

It'll be worth it in the end.

I hope.

CHAPTER 25

ivy

I SIT DOWN ON SAWYER'S COUCH WHILE I WAIT FOR THE lasagna to finish baking and pull out my phone to check in with Zoe. Ever since Brooks showed up at her house, I've been checking in with her daily, not that she'd have it any other way. So far he hasn't reappeared, and although he's still trying to contact me, I'm doing my best to brush it off. There's no way he felt strongly enough to chase me all the way to Aspen Ridge.

Me: How's Seattle and the finance world?

She answers immediately.

Zo: Not the same without you. Ugh. Annoying AF honestly. People continue to surprise me with their stupidity.

Me: LOL Still nothing from Brooks right?

Zo: Nope. Haven't seen him. He still texting you?

Me: Yeah. Was not expecting all this. It'll fade.

Zo: You still planning on coming back here after all this?

Me: I don't know anymore. I'm so confused.

Me: It's too much for text but it's like I've been in this haze and being back here, especially being with him, the fog cleared. Does that even make sense?

Zo: It does babe. You gotta do what's best for you. Am I gonna miss the hell out of you if you stay? Duh. But it's not like we won't visit. If he's home to you, you gotta make that decision. I support you no matter what you do. But sell that fucking house so you can be done with your parents baggage. Yeah?

Me: I love you, hussy, you know that?

Zo: Yeah yeah. Call me when you get space to talk and not text. Ily

I swipe away the notifications from Brooks and power down my phone, really not wanting to work Sawyer up if he sees them.

The timer on the stove goes off so I walk back into my dream kitchen and pull out the lasagna to let it cool while I toss the salad together and drizzle it with my homemade house dressing.

"It really smells amazing, Iv. Thank you for cooking," he says sweetly as he kisses my cheek from behind. "Anything I can do to help you?"

"Thank you for letting me use your kitchen, I'm nervous for you to try it, but excited at the same time. Grab the plates?"

"Whatever is mine is yours, baby. Make yourself at home." He smacks my ass as he reaches for two plates and pulls out silverware. I plate the food and we sit together at the table to eat. It's easy and comfortable.

"Ivy, holy shit. I mean, I assumed you could cook, but this. Wow."

I watch as Sawyer takes another large mouth full of lasagna. I love watching people eat. There's something so fulfilling and wholly satisfying about preparing a meal and watching others enjoy it.

"Thank you. I enjoyed making it."

"How was going to the store? I wasn't sure if you would go out or not."

"Well, I'll keep to myself just how long it took me to find the courage to get my ass out the door, but it wasn't that bad. Granted, I wore a hat, kept my head down, and used the self-checkout option. I hustled, in and out."

"So no public stoning then?"

"Sorry to report. I did not get stoned."

"No shame-walk through the town square?"

I laugh at this one.

"They did not Cersei my ass, no."

"Well," he says with a mouth full of food, "there's always tomorrow."

"I suppose there is. Speaking of . . ."

He looks up from his plate and meets my eyes. I love how he always gives me his full, undivided attention. He's always looked at me like I was the only thing in the room. It's a heady feeling, and I'm not going to lie, I missed it.

"I got a lot of plans ironed out today. Someone is meeting me at my parents' house tomorrow to do a full appraisal of everything in it. Once I have that information, we'll have the estate sale. I also contacted the realtor and put the house up for sale. We agreed on a quick sale price so I can hopefully get it sold. Not sure how many people are looking to buy a fixer-upper in Aspen Ridge, Washington, but we'll see."

I watch as Sawyer swallows his last bite. His jaw working and Adam's apple bobbing. He rests his fork down on his plate before meeting my eyes again.

"That's great progress. You were busy today. I think the house has great bones and you won't have trouble selling it. So many people are looking for fixer-uppers."

I hoped he would say that. I really need the place to sell.

I clear the plates and set them in the sink before pulling a couple of ramekins from the refrigerator and dusting the tops of the custard with a thin layer of sugar. I pull out my new kitchen torch to burn the tops until they're a deep amber color and nice and bubbly.

"I hope you saved room for dessert." I pick up the ramekins and two spoons and return to the table, placing one in front of Sawyer.

"You made these?"

I laugh at him. "I'm a trained chef, Sawyer, yes I made crème brûlée. It's my favorite so I hope you like it." I watch as he uses his spoon to dig in, breaking the crisp topping and pulling out some of the custard with it. I keep my hands in my lap and study him, watching for his reaction. He pulls the spoon from his mouth slowly, a smile creeping over his face.

"You like it?"

"Ivy. This is incredible. You're really something, baby. I'm proud of you. It's delicious."

Pride fills my chest and I take a deep breath before digging into my own.

I could get used to this. Cooking meals for us, sharing space. This is what I imagined my life would be like. This is what happiness feels like.

I wake up with Sawyer's warm body wrapped around me, his leg pushed between both of mine, and his arm curled around my waist. The sun is peeking through the windows, casting the room in an orange glow. Peace settles into my bones as I snuggle myself closer into his warm embrace.

"Someday I won't need to sneak into your bedroom like a criminal," Sawyer says as he slides into my bed behind me, pulling me close.

I grab his arm that's now wrapped tightly around my body and hold him close to me. I take a deep breath of his scent, and peace and calm fill every one of my senses. My heart finding its natural rhythm in sync with his.

"Someday we're going to have our own place and we'll wake up just like this. I can't wait to have you to myself."

"You promise? Because I can't live without this feeling, Sawyer."

"I promise, butterfly. I'll take care of you."

"I love you, Sawyer."

"I'll love you forever, Ivy."

I roll to my side, tossing my leg over his hip and resting my head on his thick bicep as I run my fingers aimlessly through the small patch of hair on his chest.

I wake him up slowly, arching my back and grinding on his already hard dick. He feels so good, his cock rubbing back and forth right where I need him, only thin pieces of fabric separating us. His hand comes around then, running up my thigh until it's flat on my ass. He hikes me up a little higher and pulls me closer to him, the new position allowing him to hit my clit perfectly. I moan into his neck, moving my hips back and forth, chasing my orgasm that's just out of reach.

"Sawyer, I need more."

"I got you, baby. Shh."

He moves his hand between us, pushing down the front of

my panties until his fingers slide easily through my slick folds. He pushes a finger deep inside me and pumps twice before pulling out and up to my clit.

"Fuck. You're drenched. I love how wet you get for me. I can't wait to be inside you again. Feel you around me. So tight. So warm. You feel like home, baby."

"Aah!" I moan. His sweet but filthy words speak right to my heart and pussy simultaneously.

He circles my swollen nub, his fingers moving easily with how wet I am, until my legs begin to shake, my orgasm building.

"You're close, baby. Come for me. Let me feel you."

My orgasm barrels through me, sending pleasure throughout my entire body. My legs shake, my toes curl, and my nails dig into Sawyer's back, leaving crescent-shaped marks on his skin.

Sawyer continues to rut, his hips moving in frantic motions, rubbing against my body until he jerks against my core, saying my name on a deep moan as he fills his briefs once again with his spend. The sound of him coming makes me even wetter. And even after just finishing, I want more of him.

I want all of him.

"Careful, Ivy. I could get used to waking up like this."

He's not wrong. Especially because I can't imagine not having this now that I've had it again.

Sawyer drops me off at my parents' house with barely a minute to spare before the appraiser gets here. Not wanting to go in, I wait outside for him, taking a seat in one of the Adirondack chairs left on the front porch when Reid walks across the large lawns and gravel driveway.

"Did you get permission to be here?" I ask him. His gigantic form takes up almost the entirety of the opening to the porch.

"There's that sass."

I roll my eyes at him. This is the first time I've seen him since that evening at Sawyer's house. I wasn't sure how it would go, and the awkwardness flowing between us right now leaves something to be desired.

"I just want you to know that I'm sorry. I didn't mean to cause you any pain, but Sawyer is my best friend, the brother I never had. I should have told you, but I didn't want to spook you."

I get it, and if the tables were turned and it was Zoe, I would have done the exact same thing.

"Honestly, you did me a favor."

His eyes shoot up from the ground to meet mine.

"I did?"

"Yeah, I mean, don't get too excited, it sucked. But it forced me to work through a lot of personal shit."

"And you and Sawyer?"

"You haven't talked?"

"Not much. He's been a little, uh, preoccupied."

With me. I really haven't had the time to pause and think how me coming back has uprooted Sawyer's life. I'm glad he's back at work and at least divvying up his focus. The last few days we've been in an emotional bubble, hashing everything out and getting reacquainted with each other, in more ways than one.

"Ahh. We had a lot to talk about. He's the same, you know? It's like no time was spent apart and all it took was seeing each other again to erase anything that happened over the last ten years. I wasn't expecting that."

"Because he waited for you."

"What do you mean?"

"I only met him in college, you had been gone over a year at that point, so I didn't know him before. But he's never had a relationship, Ivy."

I feel like I've been smacked across the face. It's obvious his feelings for me never changed, but to never have had a relationship?

"He had to have slept around, though."

"I'm not going there, but we're all human, so don't be too naive."

Fair answer. "Still, what was his plan? To live a life of solitude because he couldn't let me go?"

"Look, when your parents passed away, things got rough for him. He expected you to at least come back for their funeral, and when you didn't show up for the service, he slept in his car with a view of their plots at the cemetery so he wouldn't miss you if you came back."

I drop my head to look at the floor, emotion filling my body, and tears burning behind my eyes. I couldn't bring myself to return to my parents' funeral. I couldn't bear seeing them laid to rest by myself, in a place that I had long abandoned, at least in the physical sense. My mother begged me never to return, and I knew she wouldn't want me to come back for that. If I hadn't fled Seattle because of Brooks' incessant stalking and my life falling apart, I don't know if I ever would have found the courage to come back at all.

"When you didn't, he got piss drunk, and then really fucking angry. My dad was staying at the hotel in town. Sawyer walked there and lost his shit, demanding that he tell him where you were. Luckily my dad called me instead of the police. Dallas and I had to force him back home and calm him down. But the crash after? Ivy, he was broken. I don't know if a man has ever loved a woman the way he loves you. I'm not telling you this to make you feel bad, sweetheart. I'm telling you so that you hopefully understand and stop questioning it."

A light blue Honda Accord pulls up and parks in front of us, signaling the end of our conversation. I meet with the man I'm hiring to handle the estate sale and I allow him privacy as he goes through and marks everything in the house while Reid's words play on repeat in my head. How could Sawyer have meant everything he ever said to me all those years ago? He truly never stopped loving me. My mom's words, once a loud scream in my head, have faded to nothing more than faint whispers that no longer matter.

I love him.

I've always loved him.

I couldn't ever hurt him like that again.

Tonight I plan to show him that.

———

I return to Sawyer's house around five-thirty and brew myself a cup of tea before curling up on his couch to wait for him to get home. Anxiety has been plaguing me all afternoon. I want to be with Sawyer, but I'm still terrified of how I'll be accepted back into town. We haven't even spoken about his parents yet and I've convinced myself that they will have no interest in supporting Sawyer being with me after everything I put him through. When I left Aspen Ridge I didn't just lose Sawyer, but his entire family, my friends, and the town that I was raised in. His mom, though, holds such a special place in my heart. I hated comparing our moms, but the difference was night and day. While my mom's depression kept her from completing basic functions, Sawyer's mom thrived. While my parents showed me exactly what I didn't want, Sawyer's showed me everything I did. I loved them all, but her especially. When Sawyer brought me home for the first time, she was the most accepting, most loving woman. I'd really love to be able to keep those memories of her without gambling with the fact that they very well could be tainted once she sees me again.

Sawyer arrives home and struts down the hallway, his button-up shirt rolled up at the sleeves, exposing his veiny forearms, with a tall box in hand. He reaches me and sets it down on the coffee table.

"What's this?" I ask as he drops a kiss to my forehead.

"A gift. Open it."

My face scrunches up in curiosity, doing my best to hide my excitement. I don't remember the last time someone gave me a gift, unless I count the vibrator Zoe gave me on my birthday last year.

I slowly open the white box and fold the tissue paper out revealing a pair of bright red Hunter rain boots. I smile so big my cheeks hurt. I look up at Sawyer as he smiles down at me.

"Time for you to tap back into your roots, city girl."

"They're beautiful, Sawyer. Thank you."

"Get ready, we got plans tonight."

"We do? Where are we going?"

"Bonfire at Grace Beach."

My heart sinks to my stomach and I reach for my hands, twisting my fingers between them.

Sawyer sits down next to me, prying my hands apart and holding them in his.

"Baby, you said you trust me. Now breathe."

I take a deep inhale and hold it, never taking my eyes off of his.

"Good girl. Now, you're going to grab one of my hoodies, because that's what I want to see you in. Pull on your new boots, and we're going to go to your favorite place in the world. Yes, the town will be there. But you will be safe, and if it becomes too much, we leave. No questions asked. It's going to be fine."

"Are you prepared for it to not be fine, though, Sawyer? Honestly?"

I watch as he cocks his head to the side and looks at me incredulously.

"Cut the shit, Ivy. We're moving forward, so let's move forward. I said it was going to be fine, you say you trust me, so do it."

My head jerks back at his tone. Sawyer is never harsh with me. I stare at him with my mouth open for a moment before a deep laugh bubbles up and out of me. Now it's his turn to stare with his mouth hanging open, his eyes widening in surprise over my outburst.

"Care to share what's so fucking funny, Iv?"

I laugh harder.

"Cut the shit, Ivy," I say in my best impression of him before laughing harder. I pull my hands from him and wrap them around my stomach as my head falls back in a laugh. It takes all of two seconds for Sawyer to join me in laughing, which makes me laugh harder. He grabs my wrist before hauling me forward into his lap where his hands begin to torturously tickle around my stomach. I push at his hands before tumbling to the floor, bringing him with me. We land on the hardwood with a thud, his hand cushioning my head from bouncing off the ground.

Our laughs settle as he lays on top of me and pushes my hair from my face.

"Fuck, I missed you so goddamn much."

"You sure about that?"

"Shut up, Ivy," he says right before he kisses me. It's short and sweet and absolutely perfect.

I finish getting ready, trying to smooth out my tangled hair and attempt to make myself a little less frazzled before heading out the door with Sawyer. I guess this is my chance to see if staying in Aspen Ridge is an option, even if I'm starting to accept that I don't know how I'd ever walk away from him again.

Sawyer jumps out of the truck before rounding the hood to get my door and hauling me out of it.

Once I'm on my feet, he crowds my space, caging me in between him and the open door. He lifts his hand to rest a palm on my cheek before combing his fingers through my hair.

"I've got you, baby."

I close my eyes and breathe, my chest rising and falling, rubbing my nipples against his hard chest. He fists his hand in my hair and angles my head to the side before claiming my lips in a deep, bruising kiss. I can't help the moan that escapes as he kisses me ruthlessly. His free hand grips my hips tightly, fingers moving under my sweatshirt and dancing around the exposed skin.

Fuck, this fire between us. It always burns so fast. He breaks the kiss before I'm ready, and I know why. The lust-filled look in his eyes, his hard length pressing against my abdomen, I know that if we don't stop now the chances are high that he'll be fucking me right here against the side of his truck for the whole town to see.

He leans his forehead against mine, our breaths mingling as we work to compose ourselves.

"Fuck, Ivy. I want you so bad."

"I know. Me too."

He breaks away from me before grabbing my hand and pulling me toward the beach. His touch keeps me grounded and I welcome it.

The sun has nearly set as we walk up to the beach. At the end of every summer, usually in early to mid-September, the town has a massive bonfire right here, signaling the start of fall. Everyone used to come out for it, there's music, food tents, drinks, and everyone has a good time. A massive fire burns in the center of the beach, and people are everywhere, standing or sitting on logs or lawn chairs that they brought from home. I used to love coming to this event. It's where Sawyer and I lost our virginity to each other in the back of that very truck, parked off in the distance, away from everyone else.

"Let's find my siblings, yeah? We'll start small."

"That is not starting small, Sawyer. They're Chernobyl and I'm the nuclear reactor."

He grabs my face, forcing me to meet his eyes. "Were you always this difficult? I don't remember you having such a mouth on you."

I smile up at him.

"Baby, you said you trusted me, now fucking trust me. Let's go find my family."

"Fine. But remember that you brought me here, I'm not responsible if they all flip out on me. Well, I am, but you get what I'm saying," I ramble.

"Ivy. It'll be fine. Do you need me to say it ten more times? I can do it now and get it out of the way," he says as he practically drags me to the spot where some of his siblings are standing.

We approach the group and their conversation immediately halts. Talk about fucking awkward. Fuck my life.

"Hey, fuckers," Sawyer says, breaking the silence.

"Hey, shithead. Ivy. It's good to see you, you look good." Dallas pulls me into an unexpected hug. I hug him back, one-handed, Sawyer refusing to let go of his hold on me as he makes a deep rumbling growl. Suddenly, I'm yanked out of Dallas' embrace and tucked tightly under Sawyer's arm.

"Thanks," I say sheepishly, a little shocked. "It's good to see you, Dallas."

You'd never guess that he and Sawyer are twins. They couldn't be more different from one another. Dallas has aged much like Sawyer has. He's wearing a henley with the buttons undone, exposing his neck and a thin gold chain. His right arm is covered in a half sleeve of tattoos. His facial hair is trimmed close, slightly shorter than how Sawyer keeps his.

I look to Liam, who has probably changed the most. He's the largest out of all of them, and that's saying something since Sawyer and Dallas are both six feet tall. He's bigger in both height and width, and really grew into a gorgeous man. They all clearly work out, each of them so physically fit that it's painful to be around so much masculine beauty at the same time.

What were the Hayes drinking when they procreated?

"Hi, Liam."

"Hey you. You doing okay?"

Taken aback by his question, I look up at Sawyer before meeting Liam's face again.

"I'm getting there. Thanks for asking. How are you? I saw Hannah the other day. Her little girl is so cute."

"She's somethin' huh? Everyone's pretty obsessed with her."

"I can see why. Her sweet smile is infectious. I can't wait to be a Mama someday." The words escaped me before I had a chance to filter myself. Sawyer nuzzles into my hair before making a deep, rumbling sound that only I can hear.

Fuck. Did that turn him on?

I lift my shoulder to push his head away a bit, reminding him that we're in public. He stands to his full height, but not before giving my neck a little bite.

I stay nestled into Sawyer's side as I catch up with two of his brothers. The conversation is easy and some of the tension I was holding is released. Sawyer rubs my arm, providing me with comfort that he knows I need. I breathe in the crisp, salty air and it's so difficult to not feel at home.

brooks

I WATCH HER FROM A DISTANCE, THAT PIECE OF SHIT'S arm wrapped tightly around her shoulder. Anger continues to course through me at the sight of her being touched by anyone but me. I didn't put in all that work just to lose her. Especially not to him and this little backwoods town. The entire town came together, making it easy for me to hang back and out of sight. I've been staying at a shitty hotel a few towns over, biding my time. I'll get her alone soon enough and then I'll make sure she can never leave me again.

Soon enough.

CHAPTER 27

Sawyer

Ivy relaxes more and more as Dallas and Liam converse with her, putting her at ease. Dallas meets my eyes and nods at something behind me, and I crane my neck to catch Carter, Kinsey, and Reid walking up to us. I squeeze Ivy's shoulder and pull her closer to me as they join our group.

"Oh my god! Kinsey?" Ivy squeals, shocking the shit right out of me. "You're all grown up. Oh my god. Look at you! You're so beautiful!" I let Ivy go as she meets my sister halfway and they hold each other in a hug. I release a deep sigh of relief. Kinsey was my wild card. She was little when I first brought Ivy home, only five. Ivy was the big sister Kins never had. When Ivy left she had just turned eleven, a year younger than I was when I first met Ivy. My mom handled explaining to Kinsey that Ivy had moved away, and it was hard for her to get through. She'd visit me in my room every day and it was comforting my baby sister through my heartbreak that eventually pulled me out from rock bottom. Because of that, though, I'm fiercely protective of her. Us four boys don't baby her, but I'd kill someone if she ever got hurt, and she knows how protective I feel. It's probably why she's never dated.

"Hi! Me? Look at YOU!" Kinsey says as she holds Ivy out in

front of her. "Damn girl, you are just as beautiful as I remember. You look happy. That my brother's doing?"

Ivy looks back up at me and I can't help the smile I give her. She takes my breath away.

"Yeah," she says, holding my eyes. "Yeah, he's got a whole lot to do with it."

Carter stays on his best behavior, quiet, but that's better than me having to kick the piss out of him in front of the town. The conversation flows, everyone catching up, and in this moment, not much could make me happier than being surrounded by my family with Ivy next to me.

My sister and Ivy are lost in a conversation with Reid about how Kinsey wants a tattoo. Luckily, Reid refuses to tattoo Kins, which may or may not be due to me threatening to break his hands if he ever did. But, hey, that's my baby sister.

Dallas comes up next to me with beers in his hand and passes one to me and Ivy.

"Thanks, man. Where are Mom and Dad?" I ask him. I've been avoiding my mom since her text demanding that Ivy and I come to dinner on Sunday.

"Dad's having a rough day. She didn't want to come down here and leave him. But she said to tell you that there's no excuse that will get you out of dinner and that she expects you both. So big ole family dinner on Sunday," he says as he smacks me on the back, sloshing my beer over the rim.

"You're such a dickhead," I say as I shake out my hand in his face. But he isn't paying attention. I look at his line of sight and find Blaire chatting it up with Cole Barnes. Cole's around our age and a top-notch douche canoe. Expert level asshat.

I smack Dallas in the stomach to get his attention.

"You gotta problem? Blaire can do what she wants and it's good she's out making friends."

"No problem. Just further reason to not like her. They're perfect for each other."

I roll my eyes at him before turning my attention back to Ivy.

She looks up at me before pulling me down so she can whisper in my ear, even on her tiptoes she can't reach on her own. I lean down, breathing in that sweet cherry almond scent that I could get lost in.

"I love it here. Thank you for bringing me." She turns my face and kisses me sweetly on the lips. And fuck if it doesn't feel good to have her initiate kissing me in public. She has all the power over me. Good or bad, my heart has always been in her hands. I will gladly get on my knees and worship this woman if she'll let me, but fuck if I don't want her to feel the same for me. I need her to.

"C'mon, let's go walk around."

I lead her by the hand, and it's like I can feel each hesitant step she takes through our connection, she's winding up tighter and tighter again. Pulling her next to me and wrapping my arm around her shoulders, I gently kiss her temple.

"You're okay, butterfly." She relaxes into me as we walk around the crowded beach.

"Is that Ivy, Sawyer?" I look behind us to see a dumbfounded Luna. "You didn't mention Ivy was back at lunch!"

Ivy tenses next to me and I rub her arm reassuringly. She can't seriously think I was on a date with Luna, but damn if I don't appreciate the slight jealousy it brought out in her.

"She actually just arrived and we've been hiding out a bit. Lots to catch up on. This is her first time being out with everyone. Sorry, Luna."

"It's okay! It's good to see you, Ivy. Welcome back. I'm not sure if you remember me—"

"I do! Luna Mills. You were in the class right under ours. It's good to see you. How are you?"

"Oh, life is busy! I work at Barrel House and boy is it just crazy right now! But life is good!"

"Hendrix come back, Luna?"

"Ugh. No. Actually, he decided to stay with his family. So the kitchen staff is keeping up with the basic menu, but man has it been tough! We're the only real restaurant in town, you know, so people aren't thrilled that they're missin' more than half of the dinner menu."

I look up at the stars then, thanking every fucking power that be for paving the way for my girl to come back to me.

"Ivy?"

"Sawyer . . . don't." She grabs a fistful of my shirt and tries to pull my attention back to her but it's too late, my mind is already made up. I told her I'd give her choices, but fuck if I'm going to make this easy on her anymore.

"You're in luck, Luna. Ivy is a trained and experienced chef. She graduated from the Culinary Institute and has worked her way up in the kitchen. She's in between jobs right now, but her last one was as a sous chef at a fancy restaurant in Seattle."

"Are you really? Oh, Ivy. I don't want to speak for the owners, but I'm the manager and will be calling them first thing in the morning! You'd be saving us if you'd consider coming to work as our chef, at least for a bit."

I look down at Ivy, prepared for her wrath, but instead find her mouth gaping open at me. I push under her chin to close it.

"What do you say, Chef? Want to get back in the kitchen?"

Watching the smile grow across her face is priceless. She turns to face Luna.

"Absolutely, Luna. You can get my contact info from Sawyer. Just reach out if you want me to come in."

We say goodbye to a very relieved Luna, and I steer Ivy back to my truck.

"Sawyer, what you just did back there . . ."

I open the passenger side door and push her up against the seat, shielding us from anyone passing by.

"Baby, it'd be good for you. Just go with it. Nothing has to be permanent, but you said it yourself, you miss being in the kitchen. Do this while you figure the rest out."

"I don't need to figure anything out, Sawyer."

Her words freeze me to the spot, my eyes on hers, my heart

stops beating and all the air whooshes from my lungs. Fuck. Is she still leaving? Did I push her too far? Did I misread everything?

"Aspen Ridge is my home. *You* are my home."

I blink at her a few times before all of my restraint breaks, I grab her face between my palms and slam my mouth down on hers. Her hands grab my forearms, looking for purchase as I devour her mouth. I fuck my tongue in and out, tangling with hers, taking as much of her as I can get. My hands roam down to her sides, grabbing her around the waist and lifting her into the seat of the truck before breaking the kiss. I look at her now, lips swollen and pink, face flushed with arousal, and her breathing ragged.

Fuck. I need to get her home.

Now.

"I may have been okay taking your virginity in the back of this truck at seventeen, but that's not how this is going to go the second time around."

I push her legs in before slamming the truck door closed and jogging around to get into the driver's seat. I take one look at her again before cursing under my breath and starting up the engine.

"Seatbelt, baby," I say as I peel out of my parking spot.

I get us home in record time, breaking about a hundred traffic laws in the process. I jump out of my truck before rounding the hood to get Ivy's door and haul her out.

Once she's on her feet, I crowd her space, caging her in between me and the open door again. I run my palm over her cheek before combing my fingers through her hair where I keep a grip on the back of her head.

"Fuck. You are so goddamn beautiful."

A blush blooms on her cheeks and I can't help the smile it brings me. I lift her, wrapping her legs around my waist as I shut the truck door and walk us up the stairs and into the house. Her fingers thread into my hair as she pulls my neck back to take my lips with hers. She kisses me like she means it, like she can't get enough of me, and fuck if my heart isn't pounding out of my chest.

I finally feel whole again.

It's cliché as fuck, but this woman completes me. She's the other half to my whole and I'll be damned if she fucking leaves me again. I'm going to make it hard as fuck this time so there's not a lingering question in that pretty little head of hers how I feel.

I kick the door shut behind us before spinning her and pushing her back up against it, dropping her feet to the ground. Her little fingers run through the coarse stubble of my beard and she moans into my mouth. I grab her wrists and hold them above her head.

Releasing her lips to look at her, my heartbeat in my ears, her gorgeous face leaves me breathless.

"Fuck, Ivy."

I rest my forehead against hers, taking a moment to slow down so I don't blow my load before I even get inside her. Our eyes connect as we hold each other close.

Fuck, I hope this is it. I'm giving her my all.

Please don't break me, Ivy.

CHAPTER 28

ivy

With his forehead pressed to mine and lips hovering so close that our breath mingles, he releases my wrists and roams his hands over the waist of my sweatshirt, up my arms, shoulders, and neck until he's cupping my face in his hands. His hooded eyes bore into me, holding so much intense passion and desire.

"Fuck. I've been waiting for this. For you. You wreck me, Ivy. I was ruined for anyone else from the moment you came into my life. It's always been you. Only you."

His words speak straight to my heart, healing it completely.

I drag my hand slowly down his firm chest, soaking up the feeling of him under my palm. My hand continues south until I find his hard erection under his jeans and rub gently. His breathy moans give me life, and the courage to explore him further.

"Always knew you'd find your way back to me, baby. I never stopped believing it. Tell me you feel it too. Tell me it's still there for you," he whispers as he trails soft kisses along my jaw. Reaching under my thighs, he hoists me up to lock my legs around his waist, pressing his mouth against mine in the process.

"I feel it. It's still there. Don't stop."

Running my hands through his gorgeous, tousled hair, I reciprocate his kiss. Our mouths coming together in a desperate race to connect, our tongues tangling, moans slipping past both of our lips. Only Sawyer has kissed me like this. I could kiss this man forever and it still wouldn't be long enough.

He carries me effortlessly through the house before reaching his bedroom, kicking open the door, he slowly lets my body slide down his. Careful to ensure I'm steady on my feet, he separates our kiss and takes a few steps back.

"Fuck, I missed you so much." His voice is desperate, his normal control slipping and leaving behind a primal hunger. His eyes devour my body, carnal lust etched into his features.

I grab his face between my hands, forcing him to look down and meet my eyes.

"I missed you too. I need you, Sawyer. Take me. Make me yours again."

"Baby, you've always been mine. Not a day in your life have you not been only mine."

He puts his hands around my wrists and pulls them free of his face before prowling around me and sitting on his bed.

"Strip for me."

Turning to face him, I start to remove my sweatshirt. Slowly pulling it over my head while Sawyer's eyes eat me up. I let it fall from my hand and tumble to the floor at my feet. Then I unclasp the clip of my bra that's nestled in between my breasts and let it float down to meet my sweatshirt in a heap. His eyes peruse my body from top to bottom and back again. His body rigid, eyes glassy, fists clenching and unclenching at his sides. His control is slipping further and further. He's had so much restraint, he's taken care of me, touched me, but never let us get any further than using his fingers or dry humping like teenagers.

"Fuck, you're perfect," he says, his voice deep and demanding.

I rub my hands up my stomach until I reach my breasts. Cupping them until my nipples become stiff. I gently tweak the peaks just until I feel the slight sting of pain. "Mmm." The moan escapes from my lips. That's all it takes. Sawyer releases a deep growl and pulls me onto his bed, quickly climbing on top of me.

"I need to taste you. Now."

Roughly pulling my leggings and panties down my legs and tossing them to the side, leaving me completely bare to him, he settles between my legs, pulling them over each of his shoulders. His hands cup under my ass, lifting me into the perfect position for him to devour my pussy. With his sexy blue eyes on me, he drags his nose through my center, breathing in deeply as he goes.

"Fuck, baby. Yes." He licks me slowly with the pad of his tongue from entrance to clit, moaning as he goes. The hum sends the most delicious vibrations throughout me, causing my legs to tremble around him. My eyes immediately roll to the back of my head, and I grasp the sheets in an effort to keep me grounded. The pleasure pulsing through me has me fearing I'll drift away with it.

"Eyes on me, Ivy. I want you to watch as I finally feast on your perfect pussy."

Sawyer continues to lick my sensitive nub, swirling his tongue and driving me to the brink of insanity, keeping me forever hovering on the edge, but not letting me fall off of it. I keep my eyes locked on him as he moves one of his hands between my legs and presses two fingers deep inside me, curling them toward my stomach to hit that magic sweet spot he knows will make me go crazy. I let loose a scream as my body fights to adjust to the abrupt intrusion. It's such a delicious mix of pain and pleasure.

"Mmm," he hums again. "You're so wet for me, baby."

"Sawyer," I plead on a moan. "Please, I need you inside me."

"Patience, butterfly." He swipes the tip of his tongue back and forth on my throbbing clit.

"Thinking about tasting you . . ." More swipes, slightly firmer this time.

"The feeling of you coming on my tongue with my fingers buried deep inside you"—his fingers press deeper, then pull almost all the way out and twist on the way back in—"has consumed my thoughts for as long as I can remember. I'm going to eat you until you can't take anymore. Not ever tasting you was one of my biggest regrets. Let's see how many orgasms I can pull from this sweet, tight body of yours."

His words go directly to my core, heating me from the inside and spreading like wildfire throughout my body. Our hearts may beat as one, but everything about being with Sawyer right now is different. I run my fingers through his thick hair, loving the feel of his mouth between my legs. I never want this to end.

He continues his ministrations, keeping his tongue in perfect sync with his fingers as they slide and twist in and out of me. His other hand digs roughly into my ass cheek, pulling my body closer to his face.

"Come for me, baby. I want to feel your legs shake and hear you scream my name."

Then he gently bites down on my clit and sucks it. Hard.

That's all it takes.

"Sawyer!" I scream.

The orgasm erupts in me so hard and so fast that I see stars and scream his name over and over again. My thighs squeeze around his head and my body convulses under him. The orgasm goes on and on and he doesn't stop until I'm a languid puddle under him.

"So. Fucking. Good," he lulls, peppering my pussy and inner thighs with kisses.

I release my hold on his hair and drop my head back to the bed, doing my best to return to earth after that life-shattering orgasm.

"Just so you know, I was wrecked for anyone else, too. And no one has ever done that to me before."

CHAPTER 29

Sawyer

Her confession fills me with satisfaction. Laying
between Ivy's legs, the taste of her on my tongue, listening to her
catch her breath before me, I can't believe I'm not dreaming, and
fuck if I don't love the fact that I'm the only man to do this for
her. I meant what I told her, not going down on her when I had
her was a huge regret. I knew if she ever came back to me I would
take my time with her. She tastes sweet like honey and I can't get
enough. When she starts to sit up and reach for me, I gently press
her back flat on my bed.

"I told you, baby. I've waited a long time for this. You can have
my cock when I've had my fill of you coming undone on my
tongue."

I slowly rub my hands up her thighs, curving over her perfect
hips and down again, gently placing soft kisses across her freshly
shaven pussy, keeping eye contact with her the entire time. She
rewards me with a moan. I'll never take that sound for granted.
Fuck, I'll never take anything that has to do with Ivy for granted
again. I rub the rough stubble of my beard back and forth on the
inside of her thighs, loving the scatter of goosebumps it creates on
her skin.

"You ready for another one?"

"Sawyer, I want you inside me. Please, I'm begging."

"As much as I love to hear you beg for my cock, I want at least one more orgasm from you first. Give me what I want, Ivy."

I let my light pecks turn into deep French kisses, touching everywhere but where she wants me the most. She wiggles in my hands as I roughly grip both sides of her hips. Her legs are still tossed over my shoulders, her heels digging into my back, and I truly have no intention of ever leaving this spot. Moving my hand from her hip, I drag my finger slowly through her slick folds and dip into her center up to the first knuckle. I circle her entrance, loving how wet she is for me.

"Aah! Sawyer!" she moans. I look at her, my lips turned up in a satisfied grin. I love that I can reduce her to a puddle of wanton desire and need.

"That's it, baby. You're fucking dripping for me. I love seeing you like this. At my mercy. Letting me take care of you. You like handing everything over to me? Letting me make you feel this good?" Her only response is a deep moan.

Driving my finger in deeply, I pump in and out in firm, slow strokes while I continue to shower her in kisses before adding a second finger, curving up when I press in. She's soaking wet, warm, and her pussy is so fucking tight. I can't wait to feel her around me again. God, I've missed this. Missed every single thing about her.

Her legs begin to tremble on my shoulders, her breathing coming in quick pants. She's close already.

"C'mon, let go for me. I've got you. Trust me."

I descend on her throbbing, swollen clit like my life depends on it, swirling my tongue right where she wants me. Just when I feel those first flutters around my fingers, I suck on her clit, granting me the most amazing scream from her lips.

That's my girl.

I continue to work her over as her orgasm pulses through her and I don't stop until she's ridden every ounce of pleasure from it. As her thighs open further and fall from my shoulders, I sit up and marvel at her languid body, blissed out and still coming down. Getting up to remove the rest of my clothes, I watch as her face rakes over me, stopping as she sees my dick. Her tongue peeks out and swipes across her lips, making my cock throb in response.

I lay down on top of her, settling between her legs and bracing myself on my forearms, cradling her head between my hands. I brush her wild black hair out of her face and breathe her in deeply, laying a firm kiss on her forehead before meeting her eyes.

"I'll always give you choices, Ivy. I'll never trap you or ask anything of you that I know you don't already want. But when I take you again, there won't be anything between us, baby. I'm okay with the consequences. I'm more than okay with it. I've lost enough time with you, fuck, I'll never get it back. But we're moving forward. If we're doing this we're not going back. I'm clean, and fuck if I don't want to gamble the outcome with you. If you're not ready and that means we wait, then we wait. But I need to hear that you understand and agree before we take this step."

If I ever thought my heart couldn't beat out of my chest before now, I was inherently wrong. I watch her face as her eyes fill with tears as I wait for her response.

"What are you saying, Sawyer?"

"That when I fuck you, I'm taking you bare. I know you're on birth control and even if you weren't, if we make a baby, then so be it. I can't wait for the day I get to watch your belly swell with our kid. But I need to hear you say that you're on board. I won't force anything on you in this life or the next, but I've lost ten long fucking years with you and I'm not wasting any more. I'll beg you to stop taking your pill another day." I can't hide the emotion lacing my words.

The tears finally spill out of the corners of her eyes as she leans up to kiss me, slowly and passionately.

"Take me bare then, Sawyer. Don't make me wait another minute."

I sigh in relief and look back down at her beautiful face. God, those words. I feel them in my core, settling deep within my bones. After a decade away from her, left an empty, heartless man in waiting, I finally feel whole again. My heart beats rapidly in my chest, coming to life again after all these years. Nothing could make me happier than finally being one with her again.

"I love you, butterfly," I say as I line up my cock with her slick center and thrust inside her. She arches into me, allowing me to fill her completely.

"Aah. Yes, Sawyer!"

Fuck. She feels so good. Tight and warm, her pussy gripping me like it never wants me to leave.

I stay seated to the hilt, still holding her head between both of my hands, and stare down at her. Her beautiful green eyes are glassy and hooded, looking back at me with so much love.

"Who have you always belonged to?"

"Sawyer . . ."

"I need to hear you say it."

"You . . ."

A few more tears escape her eyes and I lean down to kiss them away. I start to move my hips, pulling out of her before pushing back in deeply. My god she feels perfect. Her soft hands run over my shoulders and up and down my back before finally settling low on my hips and pulling me close to her, like she can't quite get me close enough.

"Baby. You feel so fucking good."

I reach down and pull her leg up over my arm to deepen my penetration as she meets each of my thrusts.

"Yes. Yes!" she screams.

I pick up my speed, Ivy still meeting me thrust for thrust. Our muffled moans fill the room as we consume each other, kissing like we need each other to breathe.

"Ivy, I need you to come. I'm so close. You feel too good, baby. Please," I nearly beg her.

I reach my free hand down between our bodies to pinch her clit and thank fuck, it sets her off.

Her pussy clenches tight around my cock, milking me. I give her two more deep thrusts, capture her mouth in mine, and let my orgasm erupt, jerking inside her while her pussy tightens around me, her body spasming under me. I empty my seed deep inside her for the first time without a condom. We come down from our orgasms and slowly break our kiss. I hold her face in my hands, looking down at her swollen lips, her flushed cheeks, heavy eyes, and brow that is beaded with sweat. Her hair is a mess of unruly waves and fuck if she isn't the most gorgeous woman I've ever seen. I know at this moment, without a shadow of a doubt, that I am the luckiest man alive. Call it fate, destiny, or just luck, I'm thankful for whatever brought my girl back to me.

My Ivy.

CHAPTER 30

ivy

I WAKE UP SOMETIME LATER, THE SUN BARELY STARTING to peek over the mountains, not quite casting a glow into the bedroom. Sawyer leisurely licks between my folds like he has all the time in the world. My hips thrust up, wanting more. This is the second time since last night that he's woken me up to take me again. The first time he took me on our sides, entering me from behind with his thick, hard cock. He started by making love to me slowly, kissing my shoulder and whispering naughty things in my ear before his control snapped and he flipped me onto my knees, pounding into my pussy ruthlessly and with abandon. This time, though, I woke to his face between my legs, licking and kissing my center.

"Please, Sawyer."

"Feeling needy, baby?"

"Please!" I arch into him again, trying to get him closer to where I need him the most.

He flattens his tongue, licking me from entrance to clit, slowly, methodically. He eats me hungrily like I'm his favorite meal.

"Please. Please, Sawyer!"

"So impatient."

In a move that seemed practiced and must come from years of wrestling, Sawyer flips onto his back and pulls me on top of him, thighs on either side of his head.

"Take your pleasure then, baby. Use me."

I don't hesitate to comply. With Sawyer's hands on my waist, I sit down and press my pussy right to his perfect, waiting mouth. His tongue delves right into my core, fucking in and out of me while I rock my hips back and forth.

"Oh fuck, yes!" My moans echo off the walls around us.

His grip on me tightens, forcing me to sit down further. The rough stubble on his face elicits the most delicious pain mixed with the pleasure he's giving me. I rock back and forth, chasing my impending orgasm. It builds quickly, a fire in the pit of my stomach that spreads out across my body. I arch forward and brace myself over his head with my palms on the mattress as he devours my pussy through my orgasm, pulling every bit out of me. My body convulses, the violent waves pulsing through me.

Ecstasy.

That's what this euphoric feeling was. Pure, unfiltered ecstasy.

I feel the warmth leak out of me and Sawyer moans, flattening his tongue again and taking one last slow lick up my center, gathering my moisture and pulling it into his mouth.

He flips me onto my side and lays next to me, the evidence of my orgasm on his glistening face.

"Fuck, you're delicious."

He kisses me then, the taste of me on his tongue. I roll him to his back before sliding down his body, kissing every hard ridge of his toned stomach. Grabbing his thick, hard cock with my hand, wanting nothing more than to taste him right now, I lick him from base to tip before swirling my tongue around his engorged, mushroom head. A bead of precum leaks from his slit and I lick it away with my tongue, moaning at the heady taste of him.

"Suck it, baby. Please."

His hips jerk forward and I don't waste any more time before taking him all the way to the back of my throat. I keep him there for a moment, trying to take him deeper, before sucking all the way back up and repeating the motion. His hand moves to the back of my head, just resting there, allowing me to do all the work. I suck him hard, taking him as deep as I can go and gagging around his thick length. Tears spill from my eyes, but his moans are all I need to keep going. Wetness pools between my legs, and even though I just came minutes ago, my core aches to be filled with him again. I moan around him and he thrusts his hips up, forcing him impossibly deep. I pull back and grip his length tighter with my hand, working my mouth and fist in tandem, up and down.

"That's it, baby. You're doing so well. Fuck, that feels so good."

His hips move of their own accord, thrusting and pushing his cock down my throat further. I hum around him in appreciation. I love being able to make him lose control like this.

"Fuck, yeah. Don't stop. So fucking good, Ivy."

I reach my other hand around to grab his balls, rolling them gently in my hand and stroking the soft skin behind them.

"Ohhhh Fuuuuuuuuuuuck. Ivy, I'm coming!"

He explodes, his hips quake as he stills completely, his cock pulsing in my mouth as ropes of cum shoot down my throat. I suck him hard, milking every bit from him, and pulling off of him with a pop, loving the taste.

I sit up on my knees next to him, his cock softening against his abdomen. I wipe my fingers across my lips and smile widely.

"Need me to wipe that smug look off of your face, baby?"

He grabs me around the waist, hauling me next to him, our naked bodies sated for now. He tucks me in tightly to him, wrapping his arms completely around me, my head resting on his muscular bicep.

"It's different from what I remembered."

"Well, we're not teenagers anymore," I say with a little laugh. He swats at my ass before returning to hold me close, his fingers rubbing lightly up and down my back, goosebumps trailing in the wake.

"That's not what I mean. It's always been intense, more than sex with you. But now? I still feel like I'm on borrowed time, Iv. Like I need to savor every second and it's still not enough."

I look up at him, my fingers tracing the features of his face, committing them to memory. His blue eyes have slowly come back to life but the fear of losing me is still there. I gently lay a kiss to his swollen lips, closing my eyes and breathing him in.

"I'm not leaving," I say with as much conviction as I can muster. My mother's voice no longer a lingering presence in my head.

"I never should have run, Sawyer. I knew it the moment I left, but I was so confused. It still hurts to think about my mom."

"Does it hurt to lay here with me knowing it's not what she wanted for you?"

"No," I answer without hesitation. "The moment you showed up at my parents' house and scooped me up into your arms, I was home. I've been floating around the last ten years, unhappy and unsure, lost. Seeing you? Being in Aspen Ridge? It grounded me. My mom thought she knew what would make me happy because of her fear, and I know she loved me so much, Sawyer, but the dreams she had for herself aren't my own."

"What are yours?" His fingers are still sliding up and down my back, bringing me so much comfort from just his touch.

"This. Going to the Culinary Institute was the right choice, but I know now you would have supported me and we would have figured it out. But this?" I wave my hand between the small space between us. "This is my dream. A life with you, Aspen Ridge, Grace Beach, the overcast skies and mountain air, a lot of babies, cooking."

"I want to give you all of that, Ivy. I always have. I love you. I've never stopped. Not for a moment."

"I love you too."

He rolls me onto my back and my legs spread wide for him.

"How about we work on that baby part? And then after we go to Grace Beach and try again there."

He makes good on his promise. He takes me once more in the bed, again in his arms, shortly after with my back against the tile of his shower, and twice more later in the day bent over a cold, dead piece of driftwood with nothing but the waves crashing and birds chirping around us.

"You ready for this? It's gonna be a madhouse, you remember, right?"

"Oh, I remember. The five of you? Plus whatever friends you all would bring. Your poor mother. She's a saint."

"She is. How are you feeling?" His eyes dance over my face, looking for any clue of panic. His concern isn't misplaced. While his siblings have been nothing but welcoming, I have yet to see his mom. I'm filled with nerves but not panic. My memories of his mother have been carefully preserved. I wouldn't allow myself to envision the hatred she could hold for me for how badly I destroyed her child. She was a second mother to me. Sometimes my only mother when mine was too depressed to get out of bed. I've missed her warmth, her smile, and her love. This is the last hurdle for me to get over. After everything I've been through, I know it won't break me if she's cold, it's justified. Part of me welcomes it. Sawyer accepted me back as if I hadn't ripped his heart out in the most brutal way. I haven't paid any penance and I anticipate it; it's deserved.

I put on a pair of dark denim jeans and pair them with a white pocket tee and my favorite pair of brown booties. I braid my long hair off to the side so that the wind doesn't completely destroy it on the back of Sawyer's bike, and add minimal makeup. I'm looking in the mirror, giving myself a silent pep talk when Sawyer walks into the bathroom behind me.

"Hi, butterfly."

"Hi."

I lean forward and put on a few coats of mascara before meeting his eyes in the mirror.

"You look gorgeous."

I roam over his appearance in the mirror. He's wearing a button-up shirt with the sleeves cuffed up to his elbows, and a pair of jeans that hug him perfectly. His hair is styled on the top, and he's cleaned up his beard to a perfect scruff that begs for my touch.

"Not too bad yourself, handsome. I'm ready if you are."

"Let's go, baby. You've got this."

We pull up to Sawyer's parents' house and I wait in the passenger seat of his truck for him to open my door, something I've learned he likes to do. I think it's just an excuse to touch me more but I'm not complaining. Once I'm righted on my feet in front of Sawyer, I reach for his free hand instead of wringing mine together like a nervous wreck. He settles me, calms all of my fear and anxieties, and brings me a peace I had long forgotten existed.

He lifts my hand to his lips and kisses the top of it. His parents' house is exactly how I remembered it. Instead of sitting further into the woods like Sawyer's, or surrounded by trees like my parents' house, Craig and Amy Hayes' home sits all by itself in the middle of a wide-open space, wild lupines growing as far as you can see. The backyard hosts a custom-built table that sits well over a dozen. Their deeply rooted Sunday dinner tradition centers around that table until the winter months force them inside. We make our way to the steps of the porch when Amy swings open her front door and steps out. She's aged, sure, but she is still absolutely stunning. A life spent surrounded by her loved ones, being adored by a man who puts her at the center of his world, and living out her life exactly how she wants to. She's the picture of happiness.

"Ivy Paige."

"Ms. Amy," I say with a hesitant smile. Sawyer squeezes my hand in reassurance, a silent reminder to trust him and to breathe.

I take the last step up the porch where she meets me and wraps her arms tightly around my shoulders.

"Welcome home, honey."

I sob into her. My chest heaving.

"Absolutely no crying. This is a happy thing! You're home. I'm so happy to see you. Look at you!" She holds me away from her and looks me over in such a motherly way.

I let a small laugh loose and she swipes her thumbs under my eyes.

"I'm okay. I just missed you."

"Oh honey, I missed you too. We've always loved you like one of our own and I'm so happy to see you again. Right now there's a houseful of people waiting to be fed, so let's get in there before they start to riot."

"That sounds great, yes please."

Sawyer recaptures my hand and together we walk into his childhood home with his entire family and friends waiting.

"Look who it is! Glad you two could leave the bedroom long enough to join us," Dallas announces as we walk into the kitchen. Sawyer smacks him on the back of his head which causes Dallas to laugh. I know my cheeks have flamed a bright crimson.

"Dallas, don't even start. Do you two have to be so feral? Ivy, I tried my hardest, but these two are thicker than rocks. I apologize for their behavior."

I laugh out loud, and it makes my chest feel so much lighter.

"Oh, I remember."

"Mom, Ivy made this. Want me to leave it in here or bring it out back?" Sawyer holds out the pan containing the apple frangipane tart I made.

"It smells delicious, Ivy, thank you. You can leave it in here. Go. Go say hi to everyone."

"C'mon, let's go see everyone out back," Sawyer says as he pulls me to follow him.

We walk through their home, and I stop at every photo on the wall, memories of our childhood hung everywhere. Sawyer and his siblings growing up, their faces throughout different stages that I remember so clearly. I stop at one that takes my breath away. Sitting on the mantel above their fireplace is a photo of Sawyer and I. We're sitting on some driftwood at Grace Beach after Sawyer brought me out to surf for the first time. I remember being terrified.

"Do you trust me?"

"Sawyer, you know I do. But this isn't me. This is you! And you're out of your mind. That water is freezing! Even with a wet suit."

"I would never let anything happen to you, Iv. Pull up the suit and get your ass over here," he says with a smirk, knowing full well I'll listen.

He watches me as I shimmy my body into the wetsuit and push my arms through. He walks up to me, eyes never leaving my chest, and bats my hands away from the zipper. He pulls it up until right over my breasts before hauling it in his direction. I stumble forward, colliding with him before looking up and smiling ear to ear.

"You look so good, you know that right?" I laugh at him with an eye roll before pushing him in the chest to shove him away. I finish zipping up my suit and watch as Sawyer grabs his surfboard and heads back to me, determination written all over his face. He clasps my hand tightly in his before dragging me begrudgingly into the water.

"Shit! Shit! Shit! Sawyer!!" I screech. It's mid-June but the water this far north is still cold, it's not the Arctic but damn near close as far as I'm concerned. Sawyer turns to face me, putting his back to the waves crashing not far from us.

"Iv, it's not that bad, you'll get used to it. Trust me?"
"Okay, okay. I've got this."
"You do. I've got you if you don't. You're going to love it."

Sawyer's hand on my back breaks me of the memory.

"You remember that day?" he asks.

"Of course I do. I was terrified, you pushed me out of my comfort zone, and I ended up loving it. I did not love freezing in the water though."

"I warmed you up after, didn't I?" He winks before pulling me outside where the rest of his family is congregating.

This man is going to be the death of me.

CHAPTER 31

Sawyer

"HEY GUYS! WE MADE IT, IVY IN TOW, JUST LIKE MOM demanded," I deadpan to the group containing my family and some friends sitting around the large table outside. "Hey, Dad. How you feeling today?" I say as we approach my father, who's sitting relaxed in one of the patio chairs.

"Oh, I'm fine. Cut it out. Get your ass out of the way so I can see our girl." The stroke left him with a bit of a slur, but it doesn't seem to bother him when communicating and he rarely gets frustrated with himself, at least not in front of us. He's been the best role model for how to take punches and bounce back from life knocking you on your ass. The five of us kids are lucky to have him. I press my hand to Ivy's lower back to scoot her forward, stepping out of her way.

"Hey, Mr. Craig. It's so good to see you again."

"Ivy, it's good to see you back home."

"It's really good to finally be home."

"C'mere, let me hug you." Ivy leans down and my dad wraps her in a huge bear hug. I know how much Ivy loved and looked up to my parents, so I can imagine how needed this is for her right now.

"You want something to drink?" I whisper to her.

"Yes, please."

"Go have a seat, you've seen everyone already. I'll go grab us something." I lean down, kiss her, and push her forward lightly with my palm on her lower back. She looks up at me like a deer in headlights, her eyes big, round, and nervous. "You're fine, don't be a big baby."

I leave her with my siblings, plus Hannah and Charlie—Reid nowhere to be found per usual—and turn to go back inside the house. Dallas catches me in the hallway on his way outside to join everyone.

"You heard back from Wes yet?" I ask him.

"Not yet, but I'll follow up with him later. She still being bothered by that asshole?"

"Not sure. She's relaxed a lot, but she keeps her phone off. I haven't brought it up or asked if he's still harassing her."

"Maybe make that a priority instead of poking her with your stick."

I shove him in the chest with both of my hands, forcing him to fall back into the wall, knocking down a picture frame. Luckily it doesn't break.

"Boys! Why? Why? Knock it off!" our mom yells from the kitchen.

"Look what you did now, dickhead, made Mom all mad." I walk backwards toward the kitchen, pointing at him. "Follow up with Wes. And it's a log, not a stick."

"Sure, shithead, sure."

I turn and walk back into the kitchen, finding my mom. I open the fridge and pull out two Elysian Bifrost beers that I know Ivy will love. Not sure which of my brothers got ahold of a pack this early in the season, but I'm stealing two regardless.

"You need any help, Mom?" My mom stops chopping cucumbers for her salad and looks at me.

"I need to know that you're okay and be reassured you know what you're doing. I know you're an adult but you're still my baby." She quickly bats away a rogue tear. I set the beer bottles down on the island and wrap my mom in a big hug. She leans into me and rests her head on my chest.

"I promise I know what I'm doing. I'm okay," I reassure her as best I can. "Better than okay, Mom. I feel whole again, like I'm me again."

"You two were always like that. Even from a young age. When you were apart it was like all the light died out from both of your eyes. I always hoped you'd two find a way back to each other. I'll let Ivy tell me the story when she's ready, but I support you. You've always got us behind you."

I kiss the top of her head before releasing her. "I know. I love you."

"I love you too, son. Now get back outside before your wild brothers eat her alive."

I pick the beers up and head back outside to find Ivy sitting on one of the outdoor couches with Charlie sitting in her lap and Hannah and Kinsey on either side. Charlie is facing Ivy with her little hands clasped over Ivy's cheeks, squeezing them together. Ivy makes a funny noise and Charlie breaks out in a fit of giggles that is infectious to everyone else around. I lean against the door frame and watch her for a moment, and fuck if I'm not imagining what it would be like to see her with our daughter.

"Quit looking at her like you want to put a baby in her, shithead."

"Fuck off, Liam. I do want to put a baby in her."

"You sure about that? I was there when Han had Charlotte, they cry. A lot. Put Hannah through the ringer."

"It's worth it, though. Look at Charlie. Hannah would never change the fact that she's here, and I know you wouldn't either, you love that little girl."

Liam looks over at the girls sitting together on the couch.

"Yeah, I do," he confirms. "Don't be moving things along too fast."

"There's no such thing as too fast with Ivy. She's it."

"Whatever you say, big brother."

"How's things with Levi?" I ask, to change the topic from me and Ivy.

"He hasn't shown up in a month. Keeps making plans to come down and spend the weekend with them, Hannah shuffles around all her plans and then he's got some excuse as to why he had to cancel. It sucks because I know if Charlie wasn't in the picture, Hannah wouldn't put up with this bullshit. She's stuck. I want to kill the bastard for what he's doing to them."

"She's lucky to have you in her corner. Just keep doin' what you're doing."

"Yeah. What about you? How's things with Ivy? She looks more settled today."

"We're good. Figuring it all out, moving forward. Pretty sure she's taking Hendrix's job at Barrel House, guess he decided to stay with his family, which worked out for us."

"That's great, man. I hope it works out."

I pat my brother on the back before walking up to the girls.

"Hey pretty girl, I'll set your drink right here for when you're done playing with the toddler." I wink at her. Her face lights up when she looks at me and I love the feeling of knowing that it's just for me.

I sit back and enjoy my beer while everyone mingles and catches up. Ivy fills them in on working in a restaurant and raves about her friend Zoe and the things that she has gotten Ivy to do over the years. Zoe sounds more like a menace to society, but I'm glad Ivy has someone who loves her so thoroughly.

"Dinner, you hooligans!" my mom says as she waltzes onto the back porch, trays of food balanced in each of her hands.

She sets them down on the table and Carter and Liam follow her into the house to get the rest. I sit next to Ivy at the table and rest my hand on her thigh under it. I bob my head against hers to get her attention.

"You doing okay?"

"Better than okay. I missed this. Thank you for bringing me, not that you had much of a choice." She laughs and I settle in next to her, letting go of the worry that plagues me.

We pass bowls of salad, chicken piccata, and homemade breadsticks around the table and everyone chats. It's peaceful and normal and feels so right to have Ivy at Sunday dinner with us again.

"Reid didn't want to come?" Kinsey asks from across the table.

"I told him he was expected, but once again, here we are and no Reid." I motion my hands around the table.

"Maybe someday he'll feel like one of us and come. We'll keep offering until he does," my mom states.

"How's work?" My dad breaks the silence. Ever the quiet one, even before the stroke, always watching and listening.

"Great, Dad. Dallas hired an event coordinator and we're in the middle of construction, putting in a bar to be able to serve flights, host events, and do tours. It'll be a new way to bring in revenue. He picked a great new team member, you should be proud of him." I wink at Dallas who's glaring at me.

"If by great new team member you mean the Wicked Witch of the West, then yes, we have a new employee."

"That's a lot to take in. What's she like?" my mom asks. I open my mouth to answer but Dallas beats me to it.

"Whelp, she's a bit of a princess, fiery red hair, curves for days, bit of a mouth on her that likes to talk back, and an attitude that just won't quit."

Everyone at the table freezes and looks at Dallas, confusion and a bit of shock written across all of our faces.

"Interesting," Kinsey says, breaking the silence.

"What?" Dallas asks.

"Well, I was expecting you to tell me more about her qualifications and what she will be doing at the distillery, but the information you just gave told me a bit more."

Dallas just rolls his eyes.

"She likes to get under my skin. That's all."

"I'm sure that's exactly what you mean, dickhead," Carter quips.

Ivy laughs next to me, hiding her mouth under her napkin. I grab her wrist and pull it away from her face.

"Don't do that."

"Do what?" she asks, confused.

"Cover your laugh."

She rolls her eyes into the back of her head with an exaggerated huff.

I replace my hand to the top of her thigh and squeeze. She looks up at me and kisses my cheek before smiling and returning to her meal. I move my hand up higher, rubbing her inner thigh, wondering if she'll stop me. Fuck, I wish she wearing one of those little sundresses she used to live in when we were teenagers. I want to feel her skin against mine. I climb further up until I reach the apex between her legs and she slowly spreads for me. Fuck she's going to kill me. I swipe the back of my hand across the seam of her denim jeans and watch her cheeks pinken. I laugh before removing my hand and placing it down closer to her knee, done fucking with her at the table with all of my family surrounding us.

Dinner went smoothly and everyone raved about Ivy's apple tart. It's late when we finally head back to my house. Ivy and I walk into my home like we've done it a million times before, silence stretches between us, and the mood is hard to read. She's quiet, her focus clearly on the thoughts in her head. I follow as she walks through the house and into the master bedroom. She doesn't say anything as she goes into the bathroom to wash her face and brush her teeth. Sitting down on the bed to wait for her, dinner replays in my head, scared that I wrongfully assumed that it went well. She seemed so happy while we were there. I can't help the worry and uncertainty that I feel. I lean forward between my spread legs, resting my forearms on them and rub my hands together. When she leaves the bathroom she's completely naked, her long black hair cascades down her sides and back in loose waves from the braid it's been in all day. She's fucking gorgeous. Her breasts are perky and just enough to be a palmful in my hands. Her rosy nipples are already hard, jutting out and begging for my mouth. My eyes travel down to her toned navel, her bare, pretty pussy, down her long legs until I reach her red-painted toes. I meet her eyes, unable to form a complete sentence. Her beauty takes my breath away. She walks up to me and stands between my legs, my hands automatically finding their home on the back of her smooth thighs. She grabs a fistful of my hair and pulls my head backward to look up at her fully.

"I love you." My heart stutters at her proclamation.

"I love you," I say in return. Moving my hand up her thigh until I reach her warm center, I swipe two of my fingers through her pussy, finding her wet for me. Curving my hand so that I can easily sink a finger inside her, loving her moans at the intrusion, I pump a few times before removing it slowly and bringing it to my mouth, my eyes still on her as I suck my finger, licking it clean.

"Fuck, you taste so good." I jerk her forward, pressing my nose to her center and taking a deep inhale of her perfect scent. "Fuck, Ivy. You're perfect for me."

I grab her around the waist, pulling her on top of me as I lean back, dragging her with me.

"You know what I want, baby. Sit."

She straddles my head without complaint, and I wrap my arms around her thighs to hold her in place, her sweet pussy right over my mouth where I want her.

I swipe my tongue up the length of her center, coating it in her sweet essence. She moans and I keep up my assault on her, driving my tongue deep inside her and pulling her closer to me. I move her thighs back and forth, encouraging her to rock on me, to use me and get exactly what she needs. I flatten my tongue and let her move across it, lashing across her clit. She's warm and so slick and I love every minute of going down on her, surrounded by her smell, her taste, listening to her moan and cry out. I drive my tongue back inside when I feel her pussy fluttering around me. I move my tongue back up to her clit and suck. She spasms, screaming out her pleasure as she comes on my tongue. I let her ride it out as I move my hands to my hips and shove down my pants to my thighs.

She gets the hint and moves down, lifting herself as I hold my cock up for her. She sinks down in one thrust, her wetness not giving us any resistance.

"Oh god, Sawyer. You feel so good, baby."

I thrust my hips up into her as she rides me, rocking back and forth. She presses her hands down on my chest and lifts her hips up, letting herself fall down hard, impaling herself on my rigid cock over and over again. I rub up and down her sides, grabbing a handful of her breasts, massaging them and groping her.

"That's it, baby. Ride that cock. You're doing so well."

"Fuck, Sawyer. I'm going to come again."

"I'm right there with you, baby. Milk me, make me come with you."

I lean up and suck one of her pert nipples into my mouth, swirling my tongue around the tight little bud before dragging my teeth across it.

"I'm coming! Fuck, fuck, fuck." Her pussy tightens around my cock like a vise, pulsing and quivering and I can't hold back a second longer. I grab her waist and lock her down, pressing my dick into her until our bodies are flush and I can't go any deeper. I come hard, filling her with my cum while I jerk inside of her.

She collapses on top of me, both of us sweaty. I wrap my arms around her waist and hold her close to me, her head resting on my chest.

"Dammit, I love you, Ivy. So fucking much it hurts," I confess.

We lay there together, spent. All my hopes and dreams resting on top of me with this woman who I'll never get enough of.

ivy

Sunday night while we were at Sawyer's parents' house for dinner, he got a text from Luna asking for my number and if I'd be available to come in on Tuesday to meet with the owners. For the first time since coming back into town, I had zero hesitations. The thought of being back in a real working kitchen again, creating meals for people to enjoy, fills me with so much excitement that I think I would have taken this job had it been anywhere. Barrel House wasn't around when I lived here before and was opened a few years after I left by a couple I'm not too familiar with. Which is great for me, they most likely won't be harboring any resentment toward me for breaking Sawyer's heart.

Barrel House is located, quite literally, in the cellar of an old brick building. The entrance is on the side, down a set of stone steps that lead to a heavy steel door. It has a dark, speakeasy vibe with exposed brick walls, gorgeous lighting, and emerald-green tufted booths. The bar and tabletops are dark cedar wood with a matching green epoxy river through the center. Everything is gorgeous and I immediately fall in love.

The owners meet me at the hostess station, looking every bit the part of someone who would own such a gorgeous, hip space.

"Hi, I'm Ivy Turner. It's nice to meet you."

"Ivy, nice to meet you. My name is Dawson, this is my wife, Sybil. Thank you for coming in."

"I'm happy to be here."

"So this is really just a formality, Luna and Sawyer both put in a great word for you, and honestly, there aren't many chefs, if any, in Aspen Ridge, and no one is willing to relocate here for the job at the moment."

I chuckle at that. Small-town problems.

"Thank you. I can completely understand that. Is there anything you'd like to know? I'm formally trained at the Culinary Institute on the California campus and I've been working in a kitchen for the last four years, the last year as a sous chef. Sorry. I'm getting ahead of myself. Please continue."

I give them a small smile. I'm suddenly nervous and I don't know why. I know they said this interview was a formality, but there seems to be something else lingering in the air between us.

"You're fine, we appreciate all the information. Sawyer sang your praises. We're both happy to finally find someone qualified enough to handle the kitchen. We'd like to keep the menu as our former chef had created it, but if this works out and you'd like to stay on, then we can discuss you making changes to it."

My heart does some weird flips in my chest. I've always wanted to be able to create my own menu and run my own kitchen. That's the dream.

"Thank you for being open and transparent about those details and that sounds like a wonderful plan."

Dawson releases a deep exhale and looks at his wife, who hasn't said anything up until now. I look at her and smile, but don't get one in return as she looks away too quickly. I get an uneasy feeling about her, but I can't put my finger on it.

"That sounds great. Can you start tomorrow? Luna will get you all set up. Come in around nine-thirty? You'll have time to get situated and start lunch service."

"Thank you. I'll be here."

We shake hands and Dawson excuses himself while I gather my purse and jean jacket to head back to Sawyer's house.

"So, you're her."

I look over at Sybil, who finally broke her vow of silence.

"Her? I'm not sure I understand who you mean."

"Sawyer's one who got away."

My heart sinks. Do she and Sawyer have history? She's clearly married now and surely Sawyer would have given me a heads up before letting me meet with someone he's been with.

"Do I know you?" I ask.

"No. Sawyer knows my younger sister though. Emily. She thought she could change him, get him to fall for her and be more than a hookup. But you were always in the middle of him and anyone who came after you. I see why now," she says as she looks me up and down, as if my body is the sole reason Sawyer never moved on from me. I swallow the evil retort threatening to burst from my lips and decide to kill her with kindness so that I don't lose another job. Especially one I haven't even started yet.

"Yes. Well, the heart wants what the heart wants. I hope Emily's okay and was able to move on and find her happiness. Have a good day, Sybil."

I walk quickly out of the restaurant and into my jeep before finally breathing deeply. Her unprofessionalism should bother me, but I can sympathize with her being protective over her sister. I'll give her this one pass. Especially because I really want to work there. I know Sawyer has been with other people and I should be thankful she wasn't right in front of me. Still, the jealousy burns like wildfire. I start up my jeep without thinking further on it and drive to the distillery.

Sawyer

"HEY BOSS MAN, YOU GOT A VISITOR COMING IN HOT. And I mean HOT. She yours?"

I look up from my desk to the windows that line my office and see Ivy walking my way. She's wearing her long hair down her back in loose waves, her cheeks are flushed and she's kneading the life out of her hands as she walks.

"Yep. Mine. Cancel any meetings I have and forward my phone, please, Marcus," I reply to our intern without taking my eyes off of my woman.

I watch her walk, her hips swaying side to side until she meets my eyes through the window. Her steps falter for a single beat before she picks up her pace and waltzes into my office like she owns the place. I lean back in my chair and lace my fingers together behind my head.

She shuts the door behind her.

"Ivy, this is quite the surprise but I'm not complaining. How was the meeting?"

She stands in front of the closed door, my desk and twenty feet of space between us. She looks around my office, taking in the sparse space that I haven't bothered to decorate.

"Do the windows have shades?"

I arch a brow and look at her questionably.

"They do," I confirm.

"Close them?"

I take a breath and move slowly to the remote on my desk and press the button to fog over the windows, not letting her know how much she just worked me up, how hard my cock already is for her. The windows glaze over as she sashays toward me, still nervously wringing the shit out of her hands. I spin my chair in her direction and lean back slightly.

"I just had an interesting conversation with Sybil."

My heart stops. There's no way Sybil would bring up her sister. I decide to play it cool.

"Did you? Did they decide to hire you? They'd be stupid not to."

"They did. Super exciting. But still, not as interesting as finding out that Sybil is the sister of a former hookup of yours."

Fuck.

"You see . . ." She pauses and kicks the inside of my left foot, pushing it outward before doing the same with my right, essentially spreading my legs further open. A chill runs down my spine. I steady my breathing and wait for her to continue.

"Apparently, dear Emily was hung up on you." Ivy steps between my legs before leaning down and grabbing a fistful of my hair and pulling my head back to meet her eyes. Fuck, she's so jealous. My cock hardens to the likes of a steel rod in my pants. I've never seen her like this before.

"I didn't like hearing about someone who's touched you." She rubs her lips featherlight over mine, just a whisper of a touch before dropping to her knees.

"In fact, I really, really didn't like it." She rubs her hands up both of my thighs before running them over the length of my hard-on.

"Feeling jealous, Iv?"

"You know I am. I know we each have a past, but mine is all out of sight. Yours is right in front of me."

"Baby, you don't have anything to worry about. You're the only woman for me."

She unbuckles my belt before unbuttoning my pants and slides down the zipper.

"Then tell me, Sawyer. Please." She pulls my cock free, holding it firmly in her grasp. She bends her head down, eyes on mine, and licks me slowly from base to tip. "I know it makes me look insecure. But . . . I need to hear you say it." She looks up at me from between my legs and she looks so damn sexy sitting there with my cock in her hand, eyes heavy-lidded. She gives my hard dick a squeeze. "Who do you belong to, Sawyer?" Fucking hell, she's throwing my words back in my face and I'm all for it.

"You, baby," I say, my voice raspy and drunk on the way she's making me feel.

She swirls her tongue over the head of my cock, licking up the bead of precum leaking from the tip.

"Who have you always belonged to?"

"Fuck, Ivy. You. You know it. Like it's even a damn question."

"I wanted to hear it," she says as she swallows my cock whole. She bottoms out, my cock down her throat, and I can't help the moan that comes out of me. I do my best to keep my hips still so I don't hurt her. She swallows twice before pulling back up to the tip and doing it all over again. The sensations are unreal, tingling and shooting out through my entire body.

"Fuck, baby."

I let her suck me down a few more times before grabbing her under her arms and dropping her down on my desk.

I flip up her sundress and expose her bare pussy to me. I groan too loudly for being in my office.

"Jesus, Iv. Such a good girl coming into my office ready for me. You had better have had panties on at your interview though." I rub the flat of my palm down her bare stomach and across her pretty pink pussy before circling my fingers around her entrance. "You going to be quiet for me, baby?"

"Yes."

I thrust two fingers into her opening before curling them up toward her navel. She lays completely back on my desk and covers her mouth with her hands. Her muffled moans sound so good. I take a moment to look at her, half-naked, sprawled across my desk.

My Ivy.

I lean down and swipe her core from opening to clit before lining my dick up with her entrance.

"This has to be quick. Try not to scream."

I pound into her in one swift motion, bottoming out on the first thrust. Her warmth surrounds me, her pussy spasming, her wetness dripping out and leaking onto my balls. I pause only for a moment to give her a second to adjust to the intrusion before releasing myself on her. She takes it all and stays quiet. I stay buried, keeping my thrusts quick and so deep I feel her cervix keeping me from going any further. I put two of my fingers in my mouth, covering them in my saliva before placing them on her clit, pressing down just like she likes it and moving in quick little circles. Her hips buck into my hand and my dick pushes slightly deeper.

"Come for me. Take me over the edge with you, baby."

I pinch her clit and her orgasm barrels through her. She squeezes her eyes shut and presses her hands down hard over her mouth, her perfect pussy tightens and spasms over my cock, clamping down and forcing my orgasm from me. I thrust in deep, grabbing her hips and pulling her further onto me as I come, unloading inside her before collapsing on top of her.

"Fuck, I hate to say it, but I like you jealous."

She laughs, her body rumbling underneath me.

I stand up to pull out of her, silently hoping like hell I don't pull out all of my cum in the process, only to see a streak of blood covering my dick and a bit on Ivy.

"Shit, baby did I hurt you?" My hands go to the side of her thighs, forcing her heels on the edge of my desk.

"Fuck, Sawyer, this isn't the gynecologist, stop it." She sits up on her elbows and puts her legs back down, but I don't move from between them. I rub my hands up her sides, not looking away.

"Did I hurt you? Was I too rough?"

"I probably started my period. I'm sorry. I'll go get you some wet paper towels."

She goes to get up but I press her back down on my desk.

"Like hell you will. And don't apologize for something like this again. Don't. Move." I point at her as I start to walk away to my ensuite bathroom. I wet some paper towels, making a mental note to get some feminine wipes and products to have on hand in my office for her.

"I can do it, Sawyer." She reaches her hand out to take the paper towel from me. My gaze softens as I look at her and sigh. She's going to let me in completely someday.

"I know you *can*. But I *want* to." She relents and I wipe her as gently as possible before picking her up and righting her dress. I push her into my chair and walk to my bathroom again to clean myself up.

I get myself tucked away and join her back in my office. She's right where I left her, looking flushed and so beautiful. I walk up to her and kiss her forehead before shutting my laptop and pulling her to stand.

"Let's get going." She gives me a questioning look before making a show of looking at her watch.

"I just fucked you on my desk, and whether you started your period or I fucked you so hard you bled, I'm taking you home, we're going to watch whatever you want, eat whatever you want, take a bath, and then I'm going to hold you until you fall asleep. Don't bother arguing. Go get your ass in the truck."

She shakes her head and sighs before listening to me without argument. It must be an early Christmas miracle.

We get outside the distillery and Ivy heads to her jeep. I should have known better. She may not have verbally protested but she was still going to be difficult.

I walk up behind her before bending and picking her up bridal style and carrying her to my truck, making sure she doesn't flash her bare ass to anyone around.

"I said truck. Not jeep."

"Ugh. Whatever. Take me home."

I stop walking and look down at her.

"That's the second time you've called my place home. The first time it was questionable what you meant, but right now there's no confusing the context."

"I said what I said, Sawyer. Let's go."

I close my eyes for a brief moment and let happiness run through me.

I just hope she means it.

CHAPTER 34

ivy

Snuggled in bed, surrounded by everything I could ever crave, I can't help but feel loved and taken care of. On the way home from the distillery, Sawyer stopped at the grocery store and purchased every snack, treat, and candy he knew I liked or would like, pads, tampons, feminine wipes, ibuprofen, you name it, he made sure I had it. He settled me on the bed with pillows and blankets like a precious gem and then dumped the bags of groceries in front of me. He put the ice cream in the freezer and returned with bottles of water and climbed into bed, tucking me into his side, his arm wrapped around me, rubbing circles on my shoulder.

"Why don't you eat the rye chips?" he asks after a while, interrupting Jim from imitating Dwight on the screen in front of us. I pause the tv, 'cause this is one of my favorite pranks.

"'Cause they're gross. And Zoe loves them. It's kinda our thing. Sometimes I'll eat the whole bag and leave nothing but the rye chips. She obviously isn't happy that I didn't save her any of the other good stuff, but we get a good laugh."

"That's pretty awesome. Tell me more about her."

"Ugh. She's incredible. I miss her so much even if we talk every day. We met in California. I got a job as a barback while in college and she was waitressing. I kept screwing everything up at first and she took pity on me. We've been inseparable ever since. After college, I knew I wanted to be back in Washington and she was down for living in a new place. She's originally from Maine, a little town a few hours north of Boston."

"Ahh. That explains the Bruins hat."

I unplug my phone from the end table and power it on to show him some photos. I hold my breath, nervously anticipating text messages from Brooks to start coming in, but they never do. I sigh in relief. Maybe he finally got the hint and moved on. I knew it would just take a bit before he got bored of the chase and found someone else to play with, the poor thing.

I open my photo album and start to scroll through pictures, showing Sawyer the last few years of my life. He smiles while he looks at all of them with rapt attention.

"I'm glad you found each other, that you've had someone in your corner all these years."

I reach up and run my fingers along his gorgeous face, his stubble tickling my palm.

"Me too. I wish she were here. She came from a small town, though, and has vowed to never live in one again. She'd hate it here."

"Small-town living isn't for everyone. Just like city living. I know I wouldn't thrive in one. Do you, do you think you'll miss it?"

"No," I say without hesitation. "It's not for me. Honestly, it's claustrophobic. I felt like I was dying of suffocation. And being back in Aspen Ridge? I can breathe again. It's the only way I can explain it and it probably sounds so silly, but I feel like I've been holding my breath for ten years and the moment I was back in this town, suddenly my lungs started working again."

"That doesn't sound stupid. It's how you feel. I understand more than you know."

I study his face before asking him to elaborate.

"How so?"

"It's how I feel about you."

"You really love me, huh?" I ask.

"Always have."

We turn back to the tv and I press play. Jim's voice fills the room as he pretends to be Dwight in one of the most iconic pranks on television. We spend the rest of the afternoon and evening binging on *The Office* and eating junk food. My bleeding stopped after he cleaned me up in his office, so I'm assuming he fucked my poor vagina into oblivion. I fall asleep with Sawyer wrapped around me, my head resting on his bicep, and his other arm wrapped around my stomach. His strong hand rubs lightly across my lower abdomen and I don't dare ask what he's thinking about. I know we haven't been using protection and are both okay with any outcome that may come from it, but a part of me can't help but wonder if we're rushing. Can this be rushed after all the time we lost?

Walking into the kitchen of Barrel House for the first time to work felt incredible. Luna met me here this morning and helped me fill out paperwork and get acquainted with the kitchen, the menu, and the rest of the staff. The menu is small and complex and rotates seasonally, sourcing local ingredients like fresh fish from the docks, and vegetables and fruits from Yakima Valley. I'm impressed and extremely excited to get to work. I spend the rest of the morning preparing some of the meals and instituting family dinner before we serve lunch. It will give me the best opportunity to get to know all of the staff on a personal and professional level. Together, we all sat at a large table and enjoyed our practice meals so that I was ready for service later. Tomorrow we will use whatever leftover ingredients we have to create something to share.

Ready to start, Luna announces the beginning of lunch service. I shake out my hands at my sides and begin.

Lunch service starts to fly by, the restaurant meeting max

capacity within the first hour of opening, and we still had a line out front. I guess having the majority of the menu unavailable for the last month has brought in a ton of hungry mouths to feed. It's a mad dash of chowders, salads, crab cakes, fish and chips, sandwiches, and oysters. As we start to clean up before prep for dinner service begins, Luna comes to the back.

"Great first service! Lots of happy families. You've got a visitor, though," she sing-songs.

I pull off my apron as I walk to the dining room and immediately spot Sawyer sitting with Reid at a little table that looks entirely too small for Reid's large body.

Sawyer stands and places his palm on my hip before leaning in and kissing me quickly on the lips.

"Hi, butterfly."

"Hi, you." I smile up at him.

"Ivy." Reid nods in my direction.

"Drogo." I nod back.

"How do you feel?" Sawyer asks.

"Like I'm on cloud nine and nothing could drag me down. I missed being in the kitchen and working. It feels so good to be back at it. And look at this place!" I say as I motion my hands around the span of the room. "I can't believe a place like this exists in Aspen Ridge."

I look back at both men who are smiling like loons at me.

"What?" I ask them, puzzled.

"I don't know why the hell he's smiling so big but you're so damn cute when you get excited," Sawyer says. "Quit smiling at her like that or I'll knock your teeth out so there's no chance of her leaving me for you."

I smack Sawyer in the stomach. "Cut it out. I'm not leaving you for anyone."

His face goes serious. "I'm holdin' you to it, baby."

Dinner service goes by with few hiccups, and I walk into Sawyer's house around nine with achy feet and a sore lower back. I forgot how exhausting back-to-back services can be and will be happy once I get used to it again. I haven't been running every day since I got back in town, and I need to push myself so I don't lose it.

Sawyer meets me in the living room wearing nothing but a pair of gray joggers. My eyes roam his body from his bare feet up his legs that are hidden behind the fabric of his sweats, they hang low on his hips, and I lick my lips picturing running my tongue along that sexy V.

"Are you boys pulled aside and told all the secrets that will have women all over the world falling at your feet? It's ridiculous how sexy you look right now."

He laughs as he walks up to me and threads his hand through my hair, tilting my head back.

"I loved seeing you work today. You seemed so happy. That's all I want for you."

"It was amazing. The atmosphere there is incredible, the energy, the staff. Sawyer, I really, really loved it."

"I'm glad, baby. Now, c'mon, your bath awaits."

He drags me to the bathroom and slowly undresses me from my clothes that reek of olive oil, garlic, and seafood, before picking me up and setting me into the huge clawfoot tub. He sits on the floor next to me, his arm draped over the edge, fingers running through my hair. I settle down into the water and let myself relax, something I hope to get used to being able to do again.

brooks

I RETURNED TO SEATTLE AFTER WATCHING IVY LEAVE with Sawyer the night of the beach party. Sawyer Hayes. Eldest son of Craig and Amy Hayes, the family that owns and operates Aspen Ridge Distillery. Also, Ivy's ex-boyfriend. Unfortunately, they have a family member in every single department of their business, so infiltrating it with my family name wasn't a smart move in case Ivy got wind of it. Fucking with their business is out, so I went with plan B. This plan happened to fall right in my lap. Ivy didn't run back home to live. No. She ran back home to sell her parents' house. Luckily for me, my family has multiple LLCs to use to purchase the house without Ivy ever knowing it was me. Until I'm ready for her to know, anyway.

My lawyer put in the offer this morning. We made it one she can't say no to.

I couldn't have planned this better myself.

Not much longer now, Ivy.

CHAPTER 36

Sawyer

Ivy's birthday is coming up quickly and I know
exactly what I want to do to celebrate her. Last night I watched
her enter her passcode to unlock her phone, and I know that's a
huge invasion of privacy, but she'll forgive me. I wait for her to get
in the shower, and I power on her phone, enter the passcode, and
open up Zoe's contact info before plugging it into my phone. I
click out of it quickly and turn her phone back off, putting it
exactly where she left it. No harm, no foul. Didn't even feel the
urge to snoop.

I open my texts to send Zoe a message, hoping that I'm giving
her plenty of notice to plan.

Me: Hey Zoe, this is Sawyer. Ivy doesn't know
that I'm reaching out to you but I was hoping
we could connect to get you over here for her
birthday. I'm planning a little surprise party for
her for Saturday and I really want you to be
here. Not much would make her happier. Let
me know.

A reply comes in immediately.

Zoe: I wouldn't miss it. Send me the details
and I'll be there.

Thank fuck.

Me: Saturday starting at 8. Ivy will be home by
9. But show up whenever you can and we'll
make it work. You can stay here with Ivy and
I'll crash at a friend's so you two can have
time together. Thanks Zoe.

Next, I pull up my sibling group chat to finish the plans.

Me: Having a surprise party for Ivy at my
place this Saturday at 8. Don't miss it fuckers.

Liam: You sure that's a good idea? She seems
a little skittish still.

Carter: Yep. Like a baby fawn.

Dallas: Will you two shut the fuck up? We'll be
there shithead. Need anything?

Me: She'll be fine. She wants to be here and
she wants family. She just needs to continue
to feel accepted and she'll feel more solid.

Kinsey: I think it's a great idea. She'll love it.

> Me: Liam can you get with Hannah and see if she can make a few dozen apple cinnamon muffins?

> Liam: Yeah but who the hell wants muffins on their birthday?

> Me: Ivy does. They're her favorite. Can you get them for me?

> Liam: Yeah I'll talk to Hannah

> Me: Feel free to bring guests

> Dallas: You really going to let Carter do that?

> Me: Carter don't fuck up, yeah?

I send a text to my parents and Reid to extend an invite before pocketing my phone and joining Ivy in the shower.

Today the bar is being installed in the downstairs area of our main building. Blaire is instructing the crew where to place everything and so far it looks great. I find all three of my brothers on the porch watching, Dallas shooting daggers in Blaire's direction.

"Careful, she might erupt into flames if you keep looking at her like that," I say as I walk up to them.

"We can only hope," he deadpans.

"Seriously, what is it with you and this whole project? I don't get it. Do you guys?"

Carter and Liam both shrug and shake their heads.

"I don't know. I just don't want to invite everyone into our space. Dad and Grandpa didn't host events here. We're a goddamn distillery. It's not a vineyard for fuck's sake. You guys seriously want this place crawling with visitors? Carter? This is good for us?"

"We ran the projections, Dal, it's good. It's going to bring people into the town, create jobs, spread business, it's a good thing. Plus, if we go ahead and host weddings like Blaire wants to, think of all the single bridesmaids that'll be lingering around."

"Fuck off, Carter," Dallas says as he storms up the stairs into his office.

I point at Carter. "Stay away from the bridesmaids, loverboy."

I leave my brothers and get settled into my office when my phone goes off.

Ivy: Are you free?

I click the call button and she answers on the first ring.

"Baby, I got an offer!" she screams into the phone. My stomach does a weird twisting thing like I'm sitting on a rollercoaster. What could she be talking about?

"An offer for what?"

"The house, Sawyer! Get with it! I got an offer for my parents' house!"

Holy shit, that was fast. I knew it would sell but that was exceptionally quick for this area.

"That's amazing, Iv. Is it what you were asking?"

"No. That's the best part. They want a quick sale and offered me twenty grand over my asking price. Over. Twenty thousand, Sawyer. I'm on my way to sign the paperwork now. Some business is purchasing it to do a flip. I'm sure they're going to quadruple their money on it, but I don't even care. I'm going to be free of it all. This is the boost I needed. Now I just need to schedule to get the house emptied and by this time next week, it'll all be in the past. I can finally move forward!"

My heart sinks as I listen to her. I'm happy for her, ecstatic, how can I not be when she's this excited? But is this what she was waiting for? Was she hanging on to me for comfort and is still planning on leaving me and going back to Seattle?

"I'm so happy for you, baby. We'll celebrate tonight. I'm here if you need anything, okay?"

"Thank you, Sawyer. For everything."

We hang up and I'm left feeling sick to my stomach. I hope everything we've shared over the last few weeks has been enough to remind her what we have between us. I sit at my desk, staring blankly at the computer screen in front of me. My mind should be focusing on reviewing the financials our CFO sent me, the upcoming meetings, and my endless to-do list. But every time I try to get work done, there's one thought that keeps creeping in—her. The woman I love more than any of this. The same one who left me once before. I can't control the fear that slithers in, warning me that she'll leave me again after selling the house. I want to call her, to hear her voice and confess all of my insecurities, but I don't want to burden her, I don't want to make her feel more guilty than she already does. I take a deep breath and try once again to refocus on the task at hand, but my mind keeps wandering back to her. Always her.

Will she stay this time?

CHAPTER 37

ivy

Walking out of Barrel House at the end of dinner service, I'm surprised to see Sawyer outside waiting for me. This morning, he woke me up to say happy birthday with his head between my legs. He made me come twice before he was willing to come up for air. When we left each other for work, we made plans to meet at his house after. I give him a questioning smile before reaching up on my toes and kissing his lips. He's wearing a pair of denim jeans, black boots, a white tee that fits him ridiculously too well, and his leather jacket unzipped. He's painfully handsome and sexy.

"Hi, butterfly."

"Hi." I narrow my eyes at him.

"You up for a little ride?"

"Always. What about my jeep?"

"We'll get her tomorrow, don't worry." He grabs my hand and leads me to the motorcycle, which I've come to love being on the back of.

"Happy Birthday, baby," he says as he sets a helmet on my head that fits perfectly.

"Is this mine?" I ask.

"Yes ma'am. And this." He picks up a gorgeous leather jacket from the seat of his bike and holds it up for me. I turn and slide my arms into it before facing him again. He zips it up for me. I know the smile on my face is massive.

"How do I look?" I spin in a slow circle for him.

"Like you belong on the back of my bike. You're beautiful, Ivy." He hooks his fingers in the top of my jacket and gently pulls me forward. He licks across the seam of my lips before I open for him, accepting his tongue and sucking on it. A groan escapes him before I let go.

"Naughty girl. Let's go. You ready?"

"Yes. Thank you, Sawyer. I love them."

He gets on his motorcycle and holds it steady.

"Hop on, baby."

I get on behind him and scoot in close, flush against him, wrapping my arms around his waist as he starts it up and it rumbles under us.

We pull out of Main Street and he heads straight for my favorite place. Grace Beach.

It's dark out, no one on the road but us. He takes the winding route and I lean with him as he takes each hard turn. We hit the straightaway that leads directly to the beach, and I chance letting go of his waist, keeping myself flush against his back, and rubbing my hands over the top of his thighs. A moan vibrates through his chest. My heart rate starts to pick up, my breathing increasing along with it. I rub toward his inner thighs, pressing down over his hardening length. He moans again as the heel of my palm strokes against his dick. I love the feel of him under me, and touching him while going this fast on his motorcycle is exhilarating. We reach the end of the road where it dumps into the minimal parking lot of the beach and Sawyer drops his speed. All my quick-lived confidence leaves me, and I quickly grip his waist again.

As we finish our ride, he lets me off first to ensure my safety. I can't help but admire the way the man steps aside his bike and rips his helmet off as if in slow motion. As he sets the helmets back on the bike, I stand patiently, waiting for him. He turns and hauls me close before I can even look up.

"You think you're funny? Torturing me like that while I'm trying to keep us safe?" He nuzzles into me, taking a deep inhale. I laugh until his tongue moves up the length of my neck, sending chills down my spine. I arch to the side to give him more access because it feels so good.

"I couldn't help myself. Plus, I trust you," I confess.

"Mmm. I love hearing you say that. Walk with me down to the shore?"

"Like you have to ask." I skip ahead of him, stepping over roots, rocks, and driftwood, loving the crunch of the rocky shore under my shoes. I walk right to the edge where the water laps at the tiny bit of sand that's here. Holding my arms out to the sides and letting my head fall backward to face the sky, I inhale the salty, fresh air as peace burrows deep into the marrow of my bones.

Sawyer walks up behind me and slides his hands over my sides until they meet in front of my body, one hand splayed out across my belly the other bending up and resting over the center of my chest.

"Do you know how beautiful you are when you let go like this?"

I let my head rest against his chest and relax into his big, warm body, keeping my eyes closed, just breathing in the clean air.

"You always were so at ease here. How does it make you feel? Explain it to me."

I think about his question for a moment before answering.

"It feels like you. Peace. Comfort. Ease. Nothing is expected of me or needed of me. I just get to exist and let go."

"Baby . . ."

I turn in his arms.

"I mean it, Sawyer. I love you so much. I hate that I ever left you. I hate the time we lost. But all I want is to move forward with you. I don't want to waste any more time. I want to live for myself. For us."

"Fuck, Ivy. I love you. You don't know how good it feels to hear you say that. I spent so long just walking through life because I had to, but I was never living either. You took the best part of me with you when you left, and I finally feel whole again. I don't ever want to be away from you."

He reaches into his jacket pocket and takes out a small black velvet box, my heart pounds against my ribcage.

"Don't freak out. It's not what you think it is. That'll come soon, trust me, but not now."

He hands me the box and I open it to find a gorgeous gold medallion with a lion mid-roar on it. Its edges are rough, like it was an old coin at one point. It's attached to a long, thin, gold chain.

"Sawyer, it's gorgeous."

"It's meant to be worn as a reminder to be brave in moments of self-doubt."

My eyes immediately pool with tears.

"How are you so perfect?" I ask, and he laughs.

"Turn around, let me put it on you."

I turn and lift my hair as Sawyer clasps the necklace on me and I tuck it inside my jacket and under my shirt, the cool metal falling between my breasts and triggering goosebumps that scatter across my flesh.

"Thank you. I love it."

I pull him down by his neck to force his mouth on mine. The kiss is deep, slow, and everything I've ever wanted. He breaks away too soon before speaking.

"Alright, before we get carried away, let's get back home so I can keep you up all night in our bed."

I take one more longing look out at the water, the only light coming from the moon and stars above us, before being led by the hand back to Sawyer's bike.

———

We pull the bike into Sawyer's garage and take off our helmets to place them on a shelf. The anticipation of what's to come has me already wet, my pussy throbbing in need, as Sawyer dwarfs my hand in his again and pulls me toward the house. We walk into the mud room and kick off our shoes before I push him against the door, my hand going straight to grab his package over his jeans. The groan that leaves his mouth as his head falls back and hits the door fuels my confidence. I lean forward and kiss along his jaw, his rough stubble rubbing against my sensitive skin just as he reaches down and grabs my wrist, pulling me away from touching him.

"Baby . . . you're killing me. Let's get inside."

A little stunned, I take a step back from him.

"Oh no you don't. Don't go there. I'm not turning you down, so get that look off your face. Follow me." He pulls the wrist that he hasn't let go of and I follow him, confused.

We leave the narrow hallway and Sawyer flips on the light to the living room.

"SURPRISE!" rings out as I instinctively cover my ears and turn into Sawyer's body. His arms bound around me as he laughs and it takes me a full minute to process what's going on.

"Surprise, baby. Happy birthday."

He releases his hold and I look at the room full of people standing in front of me. I can't believe all of these people are here for me. Tears cling to my eyelashes. Everyone starts to part in the center and the tears spill over in rapid succession. Because walking straight toward me is Zoe. Her beautiful blonde hair bobbing with every step and a smile spreading from ear to ear. I cover my face with my palms before running the rest of the way across the room and tackling her to the ground. We land with a loud thud onto the rug.

"I missed your face, you hussy!"

"I missed you wicked bad too!" she screams.

"How? Did you do this?" I ask her.

We sit up and pull each other to stand.

"Nope. This was all your man. Who is fine as fuck by the way, are his brothers single?"

"Do not go there, Zo. No. And Sawyer did all this?"

"Yep. Stole my number from you when you weren't paying attention and set it all up."

"And the best part," Sawyer says as he joins us, "I'm crashing at Reid's so you two get the house to yourself to catch up and spend uninterrupted time together."

My heart soars. How did I get so lucky to get a second chance at life with this man?

The party winds down and Sawyer kicks everyone out. I still can't believe he did all of this for me. I've never had a surprise party before, and having everyone come out for it made me feel accepted back here in a way that I never could have imagined. Zoe walks down the hallway to the guest bedroom to give us a moment of privacy, which I'm thankful for. I walk right into his open arms.

"Thank you for all of this. Especially for getting Zoe here. This has been the best birthday I've had in a really long time. Longer than I care to admit, actually."

"You deserve the best, Iv. That's all I want for you." He holds my face in both of his palms and tilts my head back to angle me just how he wants me. His lips swipe back and forth over mine in a gentle caress before he kisses me firmly. It's sweet and tender, but not lacking an ounce of the passion that that is always simmering between us. He pulls back and pecks me twice on the lips before planting one on the center of my forehead.

"Have the best time tonight. Zoe's awesome. I love you, baby."

"Thank you. I love you."

Sawyer grabs his backpack and heads out the front door to go to Reid's house for the night. His thoughtfulness knows no bounds and I'm still stunned by the extent he went to make me feel special today. I haven't spent a night away from him since arriving in Aspen Ridge and hate to see him go, but I couldn't be more excited to spend the night with my best friend.

I join Zoe on the guest room bed and she dumps two plastic bags out in front of us. All of our favorite snacky junk food sits in front of us. I snatch up the bag of Chex Mix and rip it open.

"You look so much happier, babe."

"Do I?"

"Yeah. I kinda hate to say it. It's actually super rude of you." I laugh at her.

"How so?"

"Cause, now you're going to stay here in this little town and I'm going back to the city."

"I know. I hate that part, too. But, Zo, it's like two and a half hours. It's not the end of the world. We'll see each other. You think I'm down for just letting you walk out of my life forever? Nope. Fuck nope. You know too much; you're stuck with me." Now it's her turn to laugh.

"Good. Cause you're stuck with me too. Now, tell me all the juicy things. He fucking you senseless yet?"

"Uhm, yes. Every chance he can get."

"Better than when you were teens?" She shoulder bumps me because she knows the answer by the look on my face.

"On a different planet. The connection has always been wild between us, Zo. Electric. That's still there, but times a thousand. It's intense. And so addicting."

"God, where can I find some of that? I'll take male or female, either works for me. Just find me that connection, please. I want that can't live without you shit." She makes prayer hands and closes her eyes, sending up her pleas to whatever gods that be.

"You'll find it when you least expect it, Zo. It'll be incredible once you do. And who knows, knowing you, you'll probably find both and end up in some wickedly hot throuple situation."

"Gods. One can only hope, right? One of each sounds like heaven." She smacks my leg. "C'mon! Manifest it with me!"

"Fine, you weirdo." I close my eyes and grab her hands. "Zoe is going to find both a man and a woman, who are both equally obsessed with her, deliver her with all the mind-blowing orgasms, are faithful, and super uber sexy. Happy, lunatic?"

"Very."

"Alright, help get these nasty rye chips out of my way, and I'll put on *The Office*," I say as we get comfortable in the bed together. We spend the rest of the night eating junk food and binging on our favorite TV show. As much as Sawyer and Aspen Ridge have healed me, having this time with Zoe means everything.

CHAPTER 38

Sawyer

We step into Dom's gym, the lights dim, and the familiar scent of sweat and leather fill my nose. My brothers are already here per usual, wrapping their hands and stretching before we spar. The sound of gloves hitting bags echoes through the open room, and I watch as Reid unleashes on a heavy bag near us. Everyone's a little hesitant to get in the ring with him since he's such a beast. If only they knew what a big softie he really is.

"You goin' to watch, or I can get you set up on a bag?" I ask Ivy.

"Oh, I'm definitely watching this." I laugh at her before stepping into the ring with Dallas. My heart rate quickens with anticipation. I bounce on the soles of my feet and stretch my neck side to side. Our gloves touch in the center and it's go time.

"You ready, dickhead?"

"Always shithead. Let's see if I can mess up that pretty face of yours in front of your woman."

"You can try. But you'd actually have to hit me first." We begin dancing around each other, each looking for an opening. My muscles tense as I dodge a punch to the cheek, ducking under his right hook. I land two jabs in quick succession to his face before he makes contact with my ribs. With each landed punch, either hitting or taking, I feel the tension melting off of me. The adrenaline coursing through my veins, knowing Ivy is watching, is addictive and I push myself harder and harder. Sweat drips down my face as I land a solid hit to Dallas' jaw.

"Keep your fuckin' hands up, dickhead. That's gonna be a nice shiner in the morning," I taunt him.

Dallas shakes his head back and forth and stretches his neck. I take a chance to look over at Ivy, who's watching me intently, ringside, just wanting to sneak a glimpse of her pretty face.

"Sawyer!" she screams at the same time I see a flurry of punches coming at me, the sound of his gloves smacking against my flesh. I brace for the hits, lifting my gloves to protect myself. Fuck. He's pissed. I can't let myself lose, though, not in front of her. Call it whatever you want, but that masculine part of me doesn't want my ass handed to me by my dickhead brother in front of my girl. After what feels like an eternity of blocking his hits, Dallas takes a step back, panting heavily. I lean forward, chest heaving, before looking at my brother straight on. I give him a smile and a wink before bouncing back up on my feet and slamming my gloved fist down on his jaw.

"Shit!" I hear him say. I pummel him, my fists raining down like a hailstorm. He holds his own, and we fight, giving it everything we've got until we both fall to our knees, covered in sweat and out of breath.

"One of our best yet. Maybe you should bring Ivy here more often."

"You might be right. We good?"

"You know we are." I leave the ring and find Ivy standing between Reid and Liam, her hands twisting ruthlessly in front of her. I walk right into her space, capture her head between my gloves, and devour her mouth with mine, not giving a single shit how covered in sweat I am or that my lip is busted open. She drags her hands down my sweaty chest and moans softly into my mouth.

A slap hits the back of my head causing our teeth to knock together.

"We're standing right fucking here. Could you guys not?" Liam says, looking at us incredulously. I laugh before holding out my hands for him to help get my gloves and tape off.

"You want to work out or head back?" I ask Ivy.

"I ran this morning. I want to head back. Now." I meet her eyes then and see lust written all over them. Fuck, this turned her on. Yanking off the gloves and dropping them into my bag, I grab her hand and drag her out of the gym and into the rainy Washington weather. I open her door and toss my bag into the back before scooping up her tight little body and plopping her on the seat. I climb in and peel out of Dom's parking lot. I'm not two seconds down the road before she unbuckles her seatbelt and moves over to the center of the bench seat, her mouth going right for my neck. She plants open-mouthed kisses, lapping at me, not caring at all what a sweaty mess I am.

"I need you. Watching you, god that was so hot."

"Fuck, baby. Pull your leggings down and spread your legs for me." She complies without hesitation. I've gotten used to her smart mouth protesting everything I tell her to do, she must be really fucking horny to comply so willingly. She pushes her leggings down past her knees and spreads open as wide as she can. I look down at her bare pussy and can tell from here how wet she is. I put my eyes back on the road, focusing to keep us safe as the rain pummels down, while I move my right hand down to her sweet little pussy. Her skin is soft and so smooth, and I'm dying a slow death not being able to eat her out like she deserves. I'll never get enough of making her come on my tongue.

"Mmm. Yes. Please," she moans. I slide two of my fingers easily through her soaking wet core before curving them inside her as far as I can at this angle. I pump into her twice before dragging her wetness up her slit, parting her softly and rubbing her clit in little circles.

"Oh god. Sawyer, don't stop."

"Never, baby." Her hips move up and down as she chases her pleasure. I continue to rub her swollen nub until I feel her start to quiver. Focusing on the road is fucking torture as her legs start to shake, telling me she's right on the edge. I apply more pressure and look down at her, the sight alone is almost enough to make me blow in my shorts.

"You look so hot right now, baby. You going to come all over my fingers? Soak them for me, I want to taste you." She comes like the good girl she is, my name echoing off the walls of the old truck as she falls into oblivion. As she relaxes against the seat, I slide my fingers through her, gathering up as much of her essence as I can. Keeping my eyes on the road, I suck both of my fingers into my mouth and moan as her taste explodes on my tongue. I feel her eyes on me as I lick them clean of her cum. "Mmm. So good, baby."

"Fuck, Sawyer. I need you inside me right now. Don't make me wait." She kicks off her sneakers before freeing herself from her leggings.

"Shit, Iv. Give me a second." My heart beats rapidly as I take a quick turn off the road and pull into a clearing next to the woods, thankful for my old girl and her off-roading skills as mud sprays up from the tires. I barely have time to put her in park before Ivy is yanking at my gym shorts to get them down. "Fuck, baby. Let me do it." I pull them down to my thighs, my hard cock springing free as she straddles me, her little body trapped between me and the steering wheel. Grabbing her hips, I help guide her as she sinks down on me, my cock sliding easily through her wet center, filling her completely.

"God. You feel so good inside me. How did we ever live without each other?"

"We weren't livin', baby, now we are. So fucking ride me. Let me feel how badly you missed me."

She rocks her hips back and forth, keeping me deep the entire time. I lose myself completely, her wet pussy squeezing the life out of my cock while the rain pelts down on the truck, shielding us from the world.

"Holy shit. God, you're so deep."

"You can take it, baby. You were made for me. Don't stop until you make us come."

I rub my hands up her thighs and rest them back on her hips, helping her rock on me, the bottom of my cock rubbing exactly where she needs the friction. "That's it, Iv, just like that, baby. You're doing so well."

She feels so good; tight, warm, and fucking perfect. I feel her pussy contract and tighten around me, my cock stiffening further as the release builds. Leaning forward, I lick along the length of her neck, sucking the soft skin where it meets her shoulder. Her hands tighten around me as she starts to shudder, her orgasm blazing through. She throws her head back, leaning against the steering wheel, and moaning while I drag my palm down the center of her chest. Her cheeks are flushed, rosy blotches scatter across her neck, and the sight of her sets me off. I let go, my cock jerking as I fill her with my load.

Leaning forward, she rests her forehead against mine as I wrap my arms around her lower back, holding her close to me as we catch our breath. I'll never get enough of her.

"Well, we broke the Ford back in," I say, breaking our silence.

"I'm the last girl you've fucked in here?" She sits up to look at me in question.

"You're the only girl I've fucked in here, baby. But please don't mention another woman again, especially not while my cock is still buried inside your pussy. Now let's go home."

"Yeah, take me home."

And fuck if hearing her say that doesn't make me the happiest man alive.

ivy

I WALK THROUGH MY CHILDHOOD HOME FOR THE LAST time. Today I pass the keys off to the new owners who are meeting me here with the realtor. Since the offer I accepted on the house was so much more than I needed, I decided it was easier to donate everything inside. The place was emptied a few days ago and I felt nothing at all as I watched as everything was removed. Sawyer offered to help me go through my room, but the only things I wanted to keep were the photos on my pushpin board. Saying goodbye to this place today is the last big hurdle I need to get over to move completely on, to let it all go.

I stand in the empty living room, looking over the barren space when a hand slaps around my mouth and I'm hauled into a pair of strong arms.

"Hello, my darling. Miss me?"

My heart stops beating and sinks into the pit of my stomach.

Brooks.

Fuck. This can't be happening.

I try to jerk out of his hold when I feel the cold press of a gun to my temple. All the blood drains from my face.

"Tsk. Tsk. Nope. I don't think so. You won't be getting away from me this time, Ivy. You've been a very bad girl. You've got some apologizing to do, darling. Let's get home, shall we? Scream and I shoot you. Try to run and I shoot you. And then I'll come back and kill that pathetic piece of shit you let touch you. Got it? Nod if you understand."

My stomach turns and bile rises up my throat. I do my best to hold it down and try to keep a level head. Knowing I don't have any other options, with a gun pointed at my skull, I nod in understanding. He slowly releases his hold from around my mouth only to grab a fistful of my hair in a bruising grip. I wince at the sting on my scalp. I need to think. How am I going to get out of this? My entire body shakes with fear and shock. Sawyer. Oh god, Sawyer. He's going to think I ran again. I do my best to turn and face Brooks. He looks nothing like the man I spent nearly a year of my life with. His expertly styled hair is a mess of blond that peeks out from under a baseball cap, his eyes are dark and empty, devoid of any emotion. His normal attire of dress pants, button-up shirt, and jacket is replaced with denim jeans and a baggy black sweatshirt.

"Brooks. Please. Please. I can't go with you. Please don't do this."

The slap comes unexpectedly and with no time to brace for it. The force of the blow is so hard it sends me stumbling to the left before I fall to the ground with a cry. The sting is immediate as the burn spreads across my face. I wipe the blood from my split lip, tears pooling behind my eyes involuntarily. Shock keeps me frozen to the ground, my hand splayed across my tender cheek.

I can't leave with him.

Fight, Ivy. You have to fight.

For you and Sawyer.

For your future.

No one is going to take your life from you again.

CHAPTER 40

Sawyer

SOMETHING IS WRONG. IVY'S PHONE IS OFF AND GOING straight to voicemail. I should have asked her to keep it on. She left to do the final walk-through at her parents' house and hand over the keys an hour ago, and hasn't returned. I offered to go with her, but she said she needed to do it alone. My chest starts to ache and my fist lifts to press against the spot above my heart. I need to get to her. I feel it.

I grab my phone to dial Reid when an incoming call comes in from Dallas. I click to answer as I'm slipping into my leather jacket and slamming my door behind me.

"Talk to me."

"Wes just got back to me, man. Where's Ivy?"

"I'm on my way to her right now, something's off. She's at her parents' house but her phone is off. Something doesn't feel right."

"Fuck. I'm calling Reid! Brooks is here! He's in AR!"

"What!?" I roar.

But the call isn't connected anymore. I start up my bike and I'm fucking gone, pushing it to its absolute limit. Fear like I've never felt before takes over. Fuck. Fuck. Fuck!

I'll never forgive myself if something happens to her.

reid

I FINISH BREAKING DOWN MY STATION FOR THE NIGHT when my phone rings. It never fucking rings. It's always a text message. I don't have enough people in my life to get phone calls.

Tingles trickle down my spine, anxiety taking root.

"Dallas, what's up? Everything okay?"

"Where the fuck are you? Ivy's in trouble."

Nausea takes over the anxiety, rolling over me in waves, my stomach souring.

"Fuck, I'm at Rogue. Where is she? What's going on?"

"Shit, I still think you're the closest. Get to her, Reid! She's at her parents' house. Her psycho ex is in town and he's been stalking Ivy. Get there! NOW! Sawyer and I are on our way."

I'm already out the door, my leg swinging over my bike and I'm revving it up before taking off down Main Street. Memories of a past I'll never let myself forget flash behind my eyes like a sick montage, a reminder of what a failure I am. That I failed her, and I'll fail Ivy too.

Fuck, if anyone touches her. No. I can't let myself go there. I can't let this be Ivy's end, too. I focus on the road and getting to her as quickly as possible, hoping like hell I'm fast enough.

ivy

Brooks walks up to me, grabbing a fistful of my hair and yanking me up to stand. I reach out to grab his wrist in a failed attempt to loosen his hold.

"Should I just fuck you now? Erase every memory you have of someone else touching you? Does that cunt miss me?" His breath is hot on my neck as he whispers in my ear, rubbing his cheek across my own. He's going to rape me, this evil bastard is going to try to rape me. That one terrifying thought consumes me as I feel his powerful grip on my hair tighten. My stomach churns with acid, and my heart feels like it's about to bust out of my chest.

I can't move.

I can't speak.

All I can do is stare into his cold, dead eyes.

"Yeah, that sounds good. I'll fuck you into submission." I see the gun move in the direction between my legs and I break free of the fear holding me hostage.

"Don't fucking touch me! You'll never touch me again, Brooks. Fuck you! Let me go!" I scream. I know it's stupid to piss off your attacker, especially one with a gun, but I refuse to allow this to happen. I have to fight my way out of this somehow. He pulls my hair hard, forcing me to arch my back.

"How could you let someone else touch you? HOW? After everything I've done to make you mine! You're MINE!" he screams, spittle spraying across my face. He smacks his head twice with the hand that's holding the gun. He's completely deranged. I never would have imagined him behaving this way.

"Because I love him! Let me go, Brooks. You can walk away from this. Just let me go and you can leave."

I watch as his face transforms, melting from rage to eerily calm. His voice softens when he speaks again.

"Darling. You really should stop trying to make me mad. I can't be responsible for what happens if you push me too far. Now. Where were we? Ah. Yes."

He drags me by my hair, my body tripping after him. I grip his wrist and arm tightly, but he's relentless in his hold on me, until we reach the kitchen bar where he bends me over it. This can't be happening. Every part of my body shakes as fear spirals through me, my mind wars with fighting him off and taking the chance that he'll kill me, or giving in and letting him take a piece of me and hope like hell someone comes looking for me. I need to survive.

I start to dissociate as my body goes lax against the cold counter. I think of my mom. Being locked in this house with a man who didn't love her and only wanted to control her. Who died being tied to a man who didn't make her happy and too depressed to do it herself. "Fight, Ivy. Don't let any man steal your life from you. Make your own path." Her voice rings in my head. I think of Sawyer. "You're so strong. Are you kidding me? Look at you, you're a goddamn queen, Ivy. You've been handling so much on your own for so long . . . Just breathe. You're so strong."

I take a deep breath and hold it.

"I'll leave with you. We can go back now. I'll go. Let's go. Take me home, Brooks." I say as resolutely as possible, trying like hell to hide the tremors in my voice and doing my very best to listen to those voices inside my head. I need to survive by any means possible.

I just need to buy some time.

CHAPTER 43

Sawyer

I FLY THROUGH TOWN, HITTING A TOP SPEED OF 100 before I see Reid's bike up ahead. He's fast, but my bike's faster, or I'm just so far gone trying to get to Ivy that I'm reckless. I speed up next to him as we race onto their lane, spinning rocks and gravel as we fly up the long drive to the cul-de-sac. Whipping our bikes into the driveway, I'm off of it and running up her steps before I register anything else, Reid on my heels. Fear like I've never felt strangles me. I vaguely hear Dallas pull in fast behind us in his souped-up Audi, but my head's under water. I race through the house, screaming her name, not finding her anywhere.

"Fuck, where is she, Reid? Where the fuck is she?"

"Breathe man, we'll find her," I think Dallas says from behind me.

We run through the house looking for any sign of her but she's not here.

"Dallas, I can't do this again. Where is she?"

Dallas grabs me by the shirt and shoves me hard against the wall.

"Get your fucking shit together. She didn't leave you! She was taken! Her fucking jeep is still sitting out front. She needs you!"

His words hit their mark. She was taken. Fuck, this isn't like last time. Her piece of shit ex-boyfriend has her.

Rage.

Fear.

"Over here!" Reid yells and Dallas and I jog over to where he's standing at the back door that leads to the woods behind her house. He's holding the thin gold chain with the small lion medallion. The gift I gave her for her birthday. She must have dropped it knowing I'd come looking for her.

"Fuck. The woods. Dallas, call the police, call our brothers." I'm already out the door, Reid at my side.

ivy

I know I need to buy myself time, and that no matter what I agreed to, I can't get in the car with him. Who knows where he'll take me and if I'll have another opportunity to break free. The sky is angry and the rain starts to come down on us, quickly drenching my clothes, my shoes sliding in the mud at every step as we trudge through the woods behind my parents' house. I stumble behind him as he keeps a brutal grip on my upper arm. A few steps ahead, I spot a patch of roots sticking out of the earth and I know this is my chance. Brooks steps over them and I scuff the toe of my Converse under it. Brooks yanks hard on my arm the moment he feels resistance and I go down hard. I scream out as loud as I can as I crash down to the forest floor, hoping like hell someone out here in middle-of-nowhere Aspen Ridge hears me. How long before Sawyer realizes something is wrong? Would Reid see my jeep parked out front all night and come to check on things?

I can't leave him.

This isn't how my story ends.

reid

Fear is holding me hostage as I race through the woods with my best friend, no idea what we're going to find. If Ivy is hurt, I'll never forgive myself for not getting here fast enough. I can't fail her. There's no other option. We hear a scream not far ahead and I grab Sawyer's shirt to pull him to a stop. I motion with my pointer finger in front of my lips for him to be quiet. We both look around and listen. It's definitely Ivy. It has to be. I motion with my head for Sawyer to follow as we walk as quietly as possible over the wet forest ground, the rain aiding us in our pursuit, muffling the sounds of our boots. We head in the direction of her yell, and it isn't a few minutes before we hear her voice. I sigh in relief, but we still don't know what we're up against.

"Get the fuck up, Ivy, and don't make another goddamn sound," we hear a male voice hiss at her, and anger takes over all other emotions. I'll fucking kill him. He'll never have the opportunity to hurt another woman ever again.

ivy

"Please stop, Brooks. You're hurting me!" I plead as we reach a blacked-out car parked in a small clearing in the woods.

"I wouldn't have to hurt you if you'd just behave. You shouldn't have left me. I told you what would happen, didn't I? I gave you far too much freedom, but that's okay, I learned my lesson. I'll chain you to my fucking bed if it means you never have the chance to leave me again. I fucking warned you!"

"Oh, god," I can't help but say. What life was I on the path of living had I not left him? We reach the car and he tucks the gun into his pants before pulling open the passenger-side door for me to get in. I know this is it, my last chance, I can't get into this car.

I make one more attempt at begging him to leave without me. "Brooks. Please let me go. Please don't make me do this. I don't love you. You need to fucking let me go!" He moves quickly, grabbing my throat with his hands and squeezing. My eyes widen as I claw at his wrists with my nails. I throw my knee up as hard as I can and catch him in the top of the thigh.

"You think I'm stupid enough to not be prepared for that again?" His hold on my throat tightens and my sight starts to darken as I gasp for air. I don't want to leave this world yet. I haven't started to live. I just got Sawyer back. I want a life with him. I want babies. I want to be a successful chef. There's still so much to do.

How can this be the end?

CHAPTER 47

Sawyer

W E   F I N D   I V Y   W I T H   B R O O K S   S T A N D I N G   I N   F R O N T   O F   A black car at the edge of the woods. She's covered in mud, her hair a matted mess, and I can see the fear on her face from here as she talks to him. Reid starts to voice a plan when Brooks' hands jut out and close around her throat. The sight of her being physically harmed ignites a fire in me that I've never felt before.

All I see is red.

All I feel is pure rage.

I'm gonna fucking kill him.

Ivy continues to struggle, kicking and clawing at him, but the bastard holds her tight. Body on autopilot as adrenaline surges through my veins, I charge up behind him just as he releases his hold and she crumples to the ground. Every fiber of my being is hyper-focused on protecting her. There's no room for hesitation or fear, only the overwhelming need to shield her from pain. I hook my arm around his neck and bend backward, arching him and cutting off his airway. I throw my fist rapidly into his side before he starts to fight back. He's about my size, but I've got adrenaline and anger on my side. He hurt my baby and fuck if I'll let him get that opportunity ever again.

reid

S AWYER GRAPPLES WITH THE MAN AND I RUN STRAIGHT for Ivy. I need to know that she's okay, that we got here in time. She collapsed to the ground when he let go of her, but she's coughing so I know she's breathing. That's a good sign. I scoop her up into my arms and move her to the back of the vehicle, shielding her from Sawyer and her ex as they fight on the ground.

"You're safe, you're okay, sweetheart. We're here." I whisper to her, pushing her soaked, wild hair out of her face and moving her hands out of the way so I can check for external damage on her throat. There's no telling how hard he squeezed and if any harm came to her throat or vocal cords. The skin is bright red and angry. "The police are on their way, sweetheart. Just hang on. You're going to be okay. We're here." I do my best to reassure her.

"Gun. He's. Got. A. Gun." Her voice is thick and raspy and my heart bottoms out in concern when her words finally register. "Stay here. Don't move." I look over the trunk of the car and find Sawyer straddling him, throwing punch after punch into his face. I get to my feet quickly and run to their spot. The man's still conscious but not fighting back, and laying limp, his arms splayed out at his sides. His face is disfigured, already swollen, and starting to bruise. He's covered in blood. Sawyer keeps landing blow after blow. I grab him under his arms with my forearms and yank him off. I fall on my ass and pull him with me as I go. "Sawyer, It's me. It's me. You're gonna kill him, brother. You can't have that on you. You've gotta stop. Ivy needs you. She needs you."

"Ivy."

"Yeah, brother, Ivy needs you. The police are on their way. I gotta get them our location. Get to Ivy. I'll take care of this. He'll never hurt her again, I promise you."

Sawyer jumps up and rushes to the car looking for her. I pat down the asshole and find his gun, pulling it free of his pants and tossing it on the ground near us. I pull out my phone to call Dallas and he answers immediately.

"Where the fuck are you guys?"

"We're about a mile into the woods behind Ivy's house, about a quarter of a mile off of the highway from the other direction. Get here. Tell the police we need an ambulance. I don't know if he's going to make it."

"Who's not going to make it?" Dallas bellows into the phone.

"The ex! Sawyer's with Ivy."

"Fuck, Reid! Start with that next time! Stay put, we'll find you."

I hang up and go check the motherfucker's pulse with my fingers. It's weak, but it's there. I kneel down on the sodden ground next to him as rage fills me, blinding me from everything else. I do my best to separate my past from the present, but he hurt her, and a haze fills my vision until all I see is her lifeless body. I can't change my past failures, they'll haunt me for the rest of my life, but I can make sure that Ivy never sees the same fate. I lean down and brace my forearm on his throat, placing all my weight into it until his breathing stops altogether.

"You'll never hurt another woman. Scum like you shouldn't be allowed to walk the earth." I stand and push my drenched hair out of my face, staring down at his corpse and not feeling an ounce of regret. "And now you won't."

CHAPTER 49

Sawyer

I ROUND THE BACK OF THE CAR AND FIND IVY IN THE fetal position on the cold, wet ground. I crouch down at her side, not wanting to scare her. I'd fucking die if she jerked away from me in fear right now. "Baby. It's me. I'm here."

"Sawyer," she croaks, her precious voice cracking. She scrambles into my arms and I hold her tightly against my chest, leaning back against the bumper of the car and keeping her wrapped up on me. Her arms loop around her waist, holding herself just as tightly as I'm holding her, and my heart breaks. How the fuck did this happen?

"You're going to be okay. I've got you and for as long as you want me, I'm never letting you go. You're safe, baby. He'll never hurt you again."

"I love you. I thought I'd never see you again. I was so scared," she confesses, and my heart aches painfully imagining what she just went through. Her voice sounds clearer, but I know I need to get her some water and get her checked out by a doctor. The sirens are closer now, but I don't know how long it'll be before they find us here in the woods.

"I love you too. You have nothing to fear anymore, it's over. We're gonna start that life we talked about. You and me, baby.

We've got this." She nods her head in agreement and relaxes into me. I'm so fucking proud of her. She survived. I anticipated finding her having a full panic attack, but as she sinks into my chest and her breathing steadies, I realize how much she's healed, she'll heal from this too. I'll make damn sure of it. She's so goddamn strong. No woman should ever have to go through what she just did, and the fact that it's a reality for so many rips me apart. I was so close to losing her, if we had gotten here moments later. Fuck. I can't let myself go there. She's breathing. She's alive. She's going to be okay.

Sitting next to Ivy's hospital bed waiting for her to wake up is fucking torture. She managed to stay awake through the ride in the ambulance, but crashed immediately after the doctor did his exam once we were at the hospital. Her throat is going to be okay, just minor swelling, and will heal with ibuprofen and warm liquids. Her neck and cheek are slightly bruised and the cut on her lip has been cleaned. It fucking kills me to see her like this. Physically, she'll bounce back. It's the emotional, mental part that has my stomach in knots. I'm prepared to support her in whatever she needs.

I gently stroke her hair and watch her sleep, my beautiful, perfect butterfly. My heart aches painfully as I look over her face, her eyes closed in peaceful sleep, the thin, gold chain of her lion necklace resting around her collarbone. I put it back on her while she was sleeping, hopefully giving her the reminder she needs that she can face anything and come out on top.

I pull out my phone to update my family, not bothering to read the dozens of missed texts and phone calls.

Me: She's resting. Doctor said she'll be discharged once she wakes up.

Liam: What can we do? What do you need?

Dallas: Let us know once you're home and settled

Carter: Glad she's going to be okay

Kins: Thank fuck. How is she?

Me: She's going to be okay physically. Time will tell about the rest.

Me: I don't know what to fucking do. I've never felt like this before. What if this fucked her up so bad she runs? I won't fucking survive it.

Carter: You sure as shit don't lay down and wallow. You two are meant to be together. I see that now. So get your shit together and be there for her. She won't run so don't even go there.

Liam: Wow. Was not expecting that from him

Dallas: Yeah. Damn man. Where you been hiding?

Kins: Carter's right. Don't go there. You two will get through this. She's not going to leave you. She's going to need you so buck up

Liam: I'll text Mom and Dad and update them. You've got this.

I wipe a stray tear from my eye and look over at Reid, who's lying sprawled out on the tiny couch in her room. Once the ambulance arrived, they checked out Ivy and put her on a stretcher to transport her to the hospital. Reid stayed and handled the police. Once we got Ivy into her own room, Reid showed up. He patted me on the back, looked Ivy over, and then laid down on the couch and closed his eyes, essentially giving us privacy without giving us privacy. He wakes, sits up, and looks me over, taking in my shitty appearance and the agony that's written all over my face.

"He's dead. You didn't kill him. Just move on and take care of her. Got it?"

I don't ask for further explanation. None is needed. I know him and I get it. If the tables were turned and I had his history, I'd have done the same thing.

We are discharged shortly after Ivy wakes up. Reid walks with us into the parking garage and it occurs to me I don't know how the hell I'm getting her home.

"Here." Reid holds out the keys to my truck. "Your brothers." I reach out and take the keys from him. We stand in front of his motorcycle and my truck and I don't know what to say.

"Thank you doesn't seem like a strong enough thing to say. But it's all I can come up with right now. I'll never forget it."

"Just like I've never forgotten the shit you've gotten me out of. It's what brothers do," he says. I lean in and we give each other a big hug, then he turns to face Ivy.

"Thanks, Drogo. For all of it. Just, thank you for being there." He glances at me and I know he's silently asking for my permission, as if I have any worry about his loyalty to me, and feeling like an ass for ever questioning it. I give him a nod anyway and he takes a step forward to pull my girl into a big hug. She returns it, and instead of jealousy, I just feel fucking grateful. Grateful she's got people who love her, that she's alive, and safe, and grateful that now, she's finally free.

We part ways with Reid and I drive us home with Ivy in the middle, resting her head on my shoulder, the stick shift between her spread legs. I told her she'd be uncomfortable, but she said she just needed to be close to me. I get us home and park out front, pulling her out of the truck and setting her on her feet. Clasping her hand in mine, we walk together into the house, the smell of warm apples and cinnamon immediately assaulting my nose.

"Mmm. Muffins," she says as she releases my hand and walks

through the entryway and into the kitchen. There she finds a tray filled with warm apple cinnamon muffins, a case of Elysian Bifrost, and bouquets of flowers on almost every surface of the living space.

"Who did all of this?" she asks me.

"Fuck if I know," I answer honestly.

She walks to each bouquet and pulls off the cards, reading them aloud as she goes.

"Dallas. Hannah, Charlie, and Ms. Nettie. Your parents. Kinsey. Luna. Barrel House family. Carter. Liam. Dom. Zoe . . . Zoe's says, 'The only reason I'm not there is because Dallas assured me you were okay and that you just needed sleep, but if you don't call me within twenty-four hours, I'm showing up.'" She laughs before looking around at all the flowers and then down at her little pile of cards. "Sawyer. This. I don't. Wow." I laugh at her lack of ability to form a complete thought.

"I told you you were loved, baby. Believe me now?"

"I guess I have to."

She walks up to me and wraps her arms around my waist, resting her head on my chest. I rub her upper arms, careful not to press too hard around the finger bruises from where she was hurt. "Shower with me? Please," she asks me.

I bend down and scoop her into my arms bridal style and carry her down the hall to the master bathroom before setting her down gently while I turn the water on and let it heat up. I undress her slowly, pulling her shirt over her head and watching as her hair lifts and falls back down onto her body. She watches as I unclasp her bra and drop it to the floor. I move to pull her leggings down next, hooking my fingers into the waist and drag-ging them down her legs. I squat in front of her as she lifts each foot while I free her from their confines. Then I undress myself, reaching back and pulling my shirt off, I quickly drop my pants and kick them to the pile of our clothes on the floor. Placing my hand under the stream of water and testing the temperature before I step in, I pull her by the hand to join me. I line her up so that the shower beats down on her back and wrap my arms around her waist.

"I love you, baby."

"I love you too," she responds.

"Lean back, let me get your hair wet." She tilts her head back into the spray and I use my hands to move her hair around, letting the water soak it. I turn her to face the water while I lather her hair in shampoo, massaging her scalp and taking my time before rinsing her and repeating with the conditioner. I squirt her body wash into her loofah before working it into a bubbly lather and slowly washing her body, rubbing over each of her shoulders and down her arms, under them and down her sides, curving over her hips. I kneel at her feet and wash each of her legs, lifting them to clean her feet. I stand and rinse out the loofah before running my hands over her body and rinsing the soap from her. She hums her appreciation the entire time, but otherwise we stay silent. I quickly run some soap over my body and rinse before taking her back in my arms and letting the hot water hit her until it starts to run cold. I flip the water off and reach out to grab a towel before wrapping her in it and then myself. Grabbing her brush in one hand, I lead her to the bedroom where I sit her between my legs and brush through her long locks, being careful to start from the bottom and work my way up so that I don't hurt her. We sit in comfortable silence, neither of us feeling the need to speak. Once done, I remove both of our towels and pull back the sheet and blanket and we climb under them. Pulling her into me, I hold her until we both fall fast asleep. Content, relieved, and happy to have her with me, breathing and living.

ivy

SAWYER ENCOURAGED ME TO TAKE THE WEEK OFF OF work, and even though I haven't been there long, everyone understood. He's been working from home and been by my side since we left the hospital. It's been three days since everything blew up at my parents' house. My throat feels a million times better, thanks to all the tea and ibuprofen. My bruises are a nasty purple-green that Sawyer gently kisses every chance he gets. That night is a memory I'd much rather forget. Luckily, and I use that term loosely, neither Sawyer nor Reid were charged with Brooks' death. It was deemed self-defense and really couldn't be disputed with the attempted kidnapping with a deadly weapon, as well as the bruises on both Sawyer and myself. It was all surprisingly hush-hush. I haven't asked for details. I do my best not to give what happened to me thought or I'll spiral. The reality of how close I came to almost losing everything rocks me to my core. But the events really set in stone what I want in life. I had already known I could never leave Sawyer again after being back and feeling the peace that came along with it. After spending so many years holding it together, the last thing I want is space from Sawyer.

It took me ten long years of fear, a controlling, abusive ex-boyfriend, and my life falling apart, but I found my way back and now I can focus on creating the life I always wanted. Living for myself without considering the expectations placed on me by anyone else is new, and I'm learning, but Sawyer helps. He encourages me to do what will make me happy, whatever that may be, as long as it's my choice. Working as the executive chef and running my own kitchen at Barrel House has given me more purpose. The noise of the controlled kitchen chaos, sizzling pans, and clattering utensils used to drown out the fear and pain. Now it fills me with peace and excitement. It's been a long road to get to where I am, living a life for myself and chasing dreams that make me happy. I'm just grateful to be here. Any lingering hesitations or anxiety I felt over being back in Aspen Ridge disappeared when Brooks attempted to kidnap me and take me from it.

"Hey, butterfly," Sawyer says next to me, holding my phone out in his hand. "It's Zoe. You ready to talk? I can't hold her back much longer."

"Shit. Yeah, hand it here." I take the buzzing phone from him with a grateful smile.

"I'll give you two some time to talk. I love you." He leans down and kisses my forehead and then my cheek before leaving and closing the door behind him. I swipe up to answer her video call.

"Since when do we ignore each other? I don't care what is going on, you do not ignore me, Ivy Paige! Oh, baby, look at your face! That son of a bitch, if he wasn't already dead I swear I'd fuckin' kill him myself!"

"Breathe, psycho. I'm sorry. I've been sleeping a lot."

"Sawyer has been sending me proof of life, I forgive you. I still can't believe everything that happened. Are you okay?"

"Getting better every day."

"Good. That man of yours is probably helping and mother-henning the shit out of you."

"You have no idea. He was protective before Brooks tried to kidnap and hurt me, but now? Fuck. I have to fight him out of the bathroom just so I can pee alone. I'm surprised he left the room to let us talk."

"But damn if he doesn't love you fiercely, babe."

"He really does. When can I see you again?"

"Ugh. Soon! But not soon enough. Work is ridiculous this time of year but I'll be up next weekend."

"Good. I love you, ZoZo."

"I love you too!"

The rest of the week passes in a blur. We settle into a routine like two people who've known and loved each other all their lives. It's easy and I'm thriving. We eat enough apple cinnamon muffins to make up for the time I lost. When I asked him why he still chooses to eat them, he gave me the same answer as the first time I asked. "It's a part of you that I can have whenever I want."

I'm having coffee on the outdoor couch with my feet in Sawyer's lap, our simple morning routine that I've come to love so much. It's mid-October and the chill in the air is present. Fog stretches across the land in front of us, blocking our view of the mountains that rest off in the distance. Sawyer reaches forward and sets his mug down on the table.

"Iv. We haven't really decided how to move forward, and I just want to make sure we're on the same page. You've been staying here since you got back in town, but I need to hear what that means for you and for us. I haven't wanted to put pressure on you, baby, but I need to know. With words."

He hides his insecurities so well, but I should know better. I should know to give him more reassurance and I've been so blinded by everything else going on around me that I've failed him in that way.

"I'm staying in Aspen Ridge if that's what you're asking." He sighs and there's no mistaking the relief written all over his face.

"That's good. But what about everything else? I want you here, Ivy. In our house. In our bed. I want all of this"—he motions around in front of us—"to be ours. I told you, I'm all in. I need to know where you're at. Are you going to find your own place?"

I smile so big that it hurts my cheeks before responding.

"This"—I copy his motion of pointing everything out around us—"is what I want. I'm sorry for assuming and not talking about it. I want a life with you, it's what I've always wanted, and nothing is going to get in our way this time."

"Fuck yes, Ivy. I needed to hear you say that," he says.

"Like you said, this thing between us is real. We both feel it. We've always felt it and there's no point in ever trying to fight it. I wouldn't want to anyway."

"God, I love you."

"I stopped taking my birth control," I confess.

His eyes shoot up to me. "When?"

"The night we had sex again for the first time. You asked me to be all in. I'm all in."

He moves so fast it catches me off guard. He pulls my coffee mug from my hand and sets it roughly on the table, sloshing coffee everywhere, before yanking the blankets off of me and roughly pulling my panties down my legs.

"Sawyer!" I yelp. "Shit, I think you might have a breeding kink." He leans forward, kissing my neck and palming my breast as he drags my ass to the edge of the couch and pulls down his sweatpants, freeing his already hard dick. He pushes two fingers into my core and I moan in response.

"Does that mean I want to pump you so full of my cum that there's no chance you won't get pregnant?"

"Yeah, kinda."

"Then yeah, sounds like I do." He continues to fuck me with his fingers, pushing them in deep and curling them up, making my head spin. "So wet. So perfect. Now relax and let me put a baby in you."

I laugh at him as he lines himself up and sinks into me. The world around us melts away just as it always has when we're together.

"Hi, butterfly." I look up from my Kindle to find Sawyer standing in the doorway of our bedroom, his arms straining against the fabric of his button-up shirt. He's so handsome and my heart beats rapidly at the sight.

"Hi."

"How about a ride on the bike?"

"Yes, please." I toss off the blankets and close my Kindle.

I climb onto the back of the bike, wrapping my arms right around his waist and feeling the rumble of the engine come to life underneath us. We ride casually through Aspen Ridge, the wind in our faces and the scenery blurring past. As he pulls into the small parking lot of Grace Beach, complete peace washes over me. This place has always held a special place in my heart, and being here with Sawyer always makes it that much more magical and serene. We get off and rest our helmets on the bike before walking across the rocky coastal beach, the twigs and rocks crunching under our boots. The cloud coverage is sparse, the sun doing its best to peek through them. I close my eyes, taking a deep breath of the fresh salty sea air, and truly feel free. In this moment, nothing else matters except the sound of the waves crashing against the rocky shore and the warmth of his body against mine. Sawyer releases me and I hear him take a step back. I open my eyes to reach for him and find him down on one knee with a small black velvet box in his hands. My knees immediately drop to the ground to look at his gorgeous face straight on.

"You are the only girl I have ever and will ever love. From the moment you walked into our classroom on the first day of sixth grade, I knew I had found my person. We didn't know it then, but I handed over my heart that day and I've been wholly yours ever since. No amount of time could ever change what's between us and I'd like the rest of our lives to prove it to you. Baby, I love you so much. Will you marry me?"

"Yes! Yes. Always yes." I grab his face in my hands, his skin cold from the chilly weather, his stubble rough on my palms, and pull his face to meet mine. I kiss him hard, our tongues racing to meet. There's no finesse, just that passion between us that goes from zero to sixty in a moment. He releases me much too soon and grabs my left hand, sliding the ring onto my finger. I look down at the beautiful oval solitaire diamond sitting on a simple, thin, yellow gold band and my mouth drops open at the stunning simplicity of it. It's breathtaking.

"Sawyer, this is the most gorgeous thing I've ever seen."

"I'm so glad you love it, baby," he says as I look up from my ring to find him staring at me.

Overcome with emotion, I kiss him again, both of us kneeling on the cold ground in my favorite place in the world. I kiss him like I always have, like he's the only person in the world who's ever known and loved all of me.

"Take me home."

CHAPTER 51

Sawyer

We shuffle to the bedroom without losing physical contact with each other, my hands rubbing over Ivy's bare skin. I plan to lick every fucking inch of this woman every day for the rest of my life.

"Clothes. Off," she says, eyes already heavy-lidded.

I reach behind my head to pull my shirt off and watch as Ivy peels her skinny jeans off her toned legs. I move toward her, and she immediately drags her fingers down my chest until she reaches the top of my jeans. She starts to unbutton them, pushing them down over my hips with my briefs at the same time. My cock springs free, bobbing upward, thick and hard as steel. Ivy swipes her tongue across her lips as she stares down at me. Placing my hand on the center of her chest, I push her back to sit on the bed as I kick off my shoes and work my jeans the rest of the way off. Hands finally free, I brace myself over her before taking her lips again, she immediately opens for me, her tongue meeting mine in an eager tangle while my hands rove over her perky tits and pinch each of her nipples.

"Yesss," Ivy moans against my mouth. I push off the bed to stand back up and take a moment to look at my sexy fiancé spread out in front of me on our bed. It doesn't feel like that long ago that I was picturing this very scene playing out in my head. I'm the luckiest man in the world to get a second chance with her. Remembering that night in my shower, jerking myself off to the image of her just like this, wishing for any miracle to bring her back to me. I drop to my knees at the edge of the bed and pull one of her legs over my shoulder, spreading her wide. I shower her inner thighs with kisses as I work my way up to her sweet, pretty pussy. She's already glistening and dripping wet. I take one long, torturously slow lick with the flat of my tongue up her drenched center. Fuck, she always tastes so fucking good. I'm so addicted to everything about this woman.

"Ohh. Yes. Sawyer. Yes. More!" Her moans urge me on, but I don't give her what she wants.

I drag my nose through her slit, inhaling her heady, sweet scent before continuing with long, slow licks, stopping at her clit to make small circles. Then I work my way back down and repeat the actions over and over. Her hips take on a life of their own, gyrating and fucking my face. Going down on her is fucking bliss. I gently circle her entrance with my finger and then drive it home, pumping twice before adding a second, pressing into her, and curling them upward toward her belly. Ivy bucks into my face and lets out the sexiest fucking noises. I reward her by sealing my mouth around her pussy, sucking her clit in little pulses. She continues to writhe underneath me, pushing her pussy further into my face, doing whatever she can to chase her release. Her hands thread through my hair, trying to force me closer to her. She's so responsive, so wet that she's dripping down my chin. I love every moment of being between my women's legs.

Another swipe and a light bite and Ivy's walls clench tightly around my fingers, her clit swelling and throbbing against my tongue.

"Fuuuuuuuuck. Yesssss," Ivy screams as she comes on my tongue and fingers, her legs trembling and body convulsing. I don't let up until I've squeezed every bit of pleasure from her. I let her come down from her orgasm and lay her foot back on the ground to sit back on my heels.

Taking a moment to look down at Ivy's legs still spread open in front of me, her pussy dripping, I swipe two fingers through her wet folds, pushing them deep into her slickness before withdrawing completely. I hold them out to her, curious to see what she'll do. She opens for me and sucks my fingers into her mouth, swirling her tongue around them, cleaning them off before releasing them with a pop. And fuck if the sight and feel of that didn't make my cock ache for attention. I let Ivy catch her breath before I stand and climb onto the bed, grabbing her hips and rolling her gently so I can straddle her legs. I brush the hair from her beautiful face with my hand as she moves, and look down at her.

"You're so fucking perfect."

ivy

I DO MY BEST TO MOVE MY SATED BODY ONTO MY stomach. Sawyer rubs his hands over the dip of my lower back, moving down to grip and massage my ass cheeks. "This ass, Ivy. Fuck. We're not done tonight. I thought I lost you again and I refuse to have any more regrets. I want everything with you, baby. Trust me?"

"Sawyer," I whisper.

"I need to hear you say it, butterfly. Do you trust me?"

"Yes. You know I do," I pant, pushing my ass back into him, desperate for him to enter me.

"Relax for me."

I stretch my hands out in front of me and he leans forward, peppering kisses along my neck, sucking and nibbling as he goes.

"I need a safeword," he whispers, "any word will do. I know your body well enough if something is wrong, but it's for you to use if at any point you want me to stop, just say that word and I will."

Pineapple. Why the fuck is that the first word that comes to my mind? Get it together, Ivy. Banana? God that's dumb too. Apple? Fuuuck. I'm such a mess. Why am I only thinking of fruit right now?

"Red. Red means stop."

Chuckling under his breath, he sits up, straddling my thighs and rubbing his hands up and down my back. Leaning back down over me, he pulls my chin further to the side so he can kiss me. I can taste myself on his tongue and feel the wetness pool further between my legs. Just as fast as it started, it's over, and Sawyer is climbing off of me, walking over to the end table and grabbing a bottle of lube. Butterflies take flight in my stomach.

I'll never tire of seeing this man naked. His thick cock bobs up toward his belly, the head red and angry, I find myself salivating to taste him. He walks back over to the bed, clearly reading my mind. He grasps his hard length in his hand and taps it on my lips.

"Open for me."

I do my best to open wide at the angle I'm at on my stomach, with my head turned toward him. He runs his hands through my hair, fisting it and pushing his big cock into my mouth, hitting the back of my throat. I involuntarily gag around his thick length and tears fill my eyes. I remember to breathe the best that I can through my nose and relax my jaw and throat while he moves in and out of my mouth.

"That's my good girl. I love your mouth, baby. But this isn't what we're doing tonight."

Pulling his length from me with a sudden pop, he climbs back on top of me and spreads my legs to find my pussy ready and waiting for him to fuck. He takes his time with me, rubbing the crown of his dick from my entrance to my clit. I eagerly lift my hips off the bed, pushing myself into him in search of more.

"I want all of you, Ivy. Every piece of you. I don't want there to be anything left of you that I haven't touched. Do you understand?"

"Yes," I choke out, my heart pounding out of my chest.

He gives my ass a powerful squeeze and slides his hand slowly upward from the base of my spine to the middle of my back and down again while continuing to rub his cock through my slick folds, coating himself in my moisture. I love the feel of his hands on me. The feel of his silky-smooth cock sliding through me. I can't get enough.

His grip around my hips tightens as he lines up with my entrance and in one powerful thrust, drives his cock balls deep inside of me. The moan that rumbles through his body is what dreams are made of. I grip the blankets in tight fists and push back against the onslaught of his length pounding in and out of my body, each thrust hitting his hilt and sending shockwaves through me. In one quick move, he pulls my hips up so that I'm on my knees, head pressed down into the mattress, and my ass further in the air. Sawyer's hands sweep over every inch of my ass, his fingers stopping at my puckered hole and rubbing gentle, firm circles. He's never touched me there before and I've certainly never let anyone else come close. My mind spirals with an intense array of emotions all at once.

It feels so taboo.

So dirty.

So wrong.

Yet I've never been more turned on, I've never wanted anything or anyone more than I do at this moment. Pulling his cock out far enough to swipe up some of my wetness with his fingers, he returns to that forbidden hole and slowly presses the tip of his finger inside while rubbing my lower back with his other hand.

The moan that escapes me sounds like it came from someone else. My body tightens around the intrusion, but I want more. I need more.

"More. Please. Sawyer," I pant, desperate to get all of this man.

"Fuck, Ivy," he says through clenched teeth.

While he continues to relentlessly fuck my pussy, he slides his finger all the way in and starts pulsing it in time with the thrusts of his hips.

"You like that, baby? My dirty girl."

"Yes. More. Sawyer!"

I feel the pressure of him adding a second finger. He slowly works his way in, stretching me around him.

I feel the walls of my pussy clenching around his hardness and the signs of another orgasm building within me. My knees begin to shake, and I continue to pull and tug at the blankets under me, looking for purchase. Sawyer withdraws completely and I moan in protest. I hear the squirt before I feel the cold gel on my ass, coating me. Sawyer rubs his wet cock over my tight little hole while rubbing my lower back.

"Safeword, Ivy. What is it?"

"Red," I practically moan.

"Good girl."

My heart is racing so fast and hard I fear it will beat right out of my fucking chest. The anticipation of what he's about to do is driving me absolutely mad with lust. Desire has taken hold of every logical thought, all I see is Sawyer, and he equals pleasure and primal need.

He lines himself up and slowly pushes forward. The immediate sensation is making my head scream "NO!" as I clench up and struggle to breathe. He is much bigger than two damn fingers. "Fuck!" I yell.

"Take a deep breath, baby. Breathe for me. I need you to relax and let me in. Let the lube do its job," he lulls.

Trusting him, I take a deep breath and unclench my body. I let myself relax and just feel. Feel his strong, rough hands as they caress my body, feel his cock that's so hard for me slowly pressing further into my body, listening to his jagged breathing. I calm down and let all of myself go to this man.

"Fuck, you're so tight. Fuck, Ivy."

Sawyer bottoms out and stops, continuing to rub his hands over my body, allowing me time to adjust to him. I continue to breathe and relax until the stillness becomes too much. My body is practically vibrating with need. I'm a desperate mess for him to move within me, so I push back against him and let out a breathy moan. Finally, finally he starts to withdraw. He continues the motion slowly as I get used to his size, letting him stretch me fully and adjust to the foreign sensation. The slow pace only heightens my desire for him, the build-up already forming in the pit of my stomach.

Reaching under me, Sawyer begins to stroke my clit in circles, applying the perfect amount of pressure as he picks up the pace of his thrusts. Holding my hip roughly to keep my body where he wants me, he continues working my ass and my clit simultaneously until I start to unravel.

"So good, Ivy. You take me so fucking well, baby."

He fucks me hard and deep. He never stops whispering filthy words of praise and appreciation.

"Come for me, Ivy. Come around my fingers while my cock is deep in your perfect ass. Come for me. Right. Fucking. Now."

"God. Sawyer. Yes. Yes. YES," screaming, I explode. The orgasm is euphoric. I feel it everywhere. From the tips of my curled toes, pulsing through my entire body. I involuntarily jerk, my pussy spasming, my eyes squeezing shut as they leak tears, as I gasp for air and continue to scream his name. Over and over and over again.

Sawyer follows right behind me. He arches over my back and places his forehead along my spine, his cock jerking in my ass as he fills me with his cum, my name releasing between his moans.

We stay like that for a moment, with his arms wrapped tightly around my waist, his body bent over mine. When he sits up, he pulls himself slowly from me, lays me down gently, and wipes the tears away from under my eyes, kissing them each tenderly. Rolling me over, he pulls me to his chest and cups my face, pushing my wild hair out of the way.

"Are you okay?" he asks, concern etched into his strong features.

"I'm perfect. I've never been better." He reaches for my left hand and brings it up between us, kissing the ring that sits on my finger.

"It's always been you, Ivy. Only ever you."

IVY

I WALK THROUGH THE GRAVEYARD LOOKING FOR THE location Sawyer told me my parents were buried. The sky is perfectly overcast, the rain ready to give at any moment.

I welcome it. I walk past peoples' loved ones' final resting spots until I come up to my mom's. I take a seat on the ground in front of her tombstone, choosing to ignore my father's, who is placed next to her.

"Hi, Momma. I should have come to see you before now, but I honestly didn't know what to say. I've had a lot to work through. I'm back home. And I know that's not what you wanted for me, but it's what I've always wanted for myself. I found my way back to Sawyer. He waited for me, Mom. All he's ever asked of me is to just keep breathing and for my heart to keep beating. I'm happy now. I'd like to think you'd be happy to see my life fulfilled, even if it's different from what you wanted for me."

I wipe my tears away as the rain starts to escape from the heavy clouds above. It cascades down my body in the comforting caress it always has.

"I forgive you, Mom. I understand that you did what you thought was best, to mother me the only way you knew. So, I

329

forgive you. I don't hurt anymore. I'm not scared anymore. Most of all? I'm not forced to hold it together anymore. I get to just *be*."

I tip my head back to face the sky, close my eyes, and let the rain wash over me. I rub my palm over my belly and smile.

"I'm going to be a mom. Sawyer doesn't know yet, but nothing is going to make him happier. We lost enough time, and we aren't wasting anymore. I just. I wanted you to know. I love you, Momma. I hope you're out there somewhere, exploring and finally free, because I am now. Finally free."

I stand and dust off my pants before walking to my jeep. I've let everything go, it's time to focus on the life ahead of me, with the only man who's ever known and loved all of me.

epiloque

SAWYER

I RETURNED HOME AFTER A LONG DAY AT THE distillery to find Ivy reading her Kindle in our bed. I lean against the door frame and take in my future wife. Her back is resting on the headboard, her long black hair cascading down one of her shoulders, her white robe falling off the other, exposing her smooth skin and the top of her breast. She's so fucking beautiful it hurts.

"Hi, butterfly."

She drops her Kindle to the bed and I get to watch as her eyes light up and her lips turn into a huge smile.

"Hi."

I start to unbutton my crisp white button-up that she loves to see me in so much. Button by button, her eyes never leave my chest as more and more skin is exposed. I let my shirt drop from my shoulders, piling it on the floor before pulling off my belt and dropping it on top of my shirt. I take slow, measured steps toward the edge of the bed. Her chest rises and falls in deep breaths. I know if I had her spread her long legs for me right now that I'd find her pussy wet and ready for me. I unbutton my pants and push them down with my briefs before kicking them off. Ivy swipes her tongue between her lush lips as she stares at my hard

331

cock jutting up toward my navel. Not able to wait a minute longer, I crawl onto our bed until I've reached where her knees are bent upward, feet planted on the mattress. I rub my hands up from her ankles, over her shins, and knees before pushing them open to make room for me.

"Let me in, baby."

She spreads her legs for me, and I reach down to untie her robe, pushing it open and exposing her perfect naked body to me. Her breasts are full, nipples straining and hard already, begging for my mouth.

I kneel between her legs and look at her beautiful green eyes before she reaches for my hands.

"I love you, Sawyer."

My heart, beating again in my chest, pounds against my ribcage. I'll never tire of hearing her say that.

She takes both of my hands and turns them palms down before placing them on the bottom of her tiny stomach. I watch her face as her eyes glass over and then look down at where our hands rest on her body, her thumb rubbing aimlessly over the top of mine.

"Ivy?"

I meet her eyes again, her tears falling over her long eyelashes and cascading down her sweet face. She nods her head slightly a few times, a huge smile taking over.

"Our baby is inside you?"

"You're going to be a daddy."

I close my eyes and take a deep breath before climbing completely on top of her and cradling her face in my hands.

"A baby? Ivy, we're having a baby?" My voice cracks with emotion.

She laughs through her tears, my own falling freely down my face. She reaches between us, wiping them off of my cheeks.

"We made a baby."

"Thank you for coming back to me, butterfly."

I take her lips then, kissing her deeply and passionately. This woman is everything. My heart is wholly connected to hers, two halves of a whole, soulmates made just for each other. I fold her little body beneath mine and slowly thrust inside her, filling her completely.

"I love you." I kiss her forehead and down her nose.

"I love you." I kiss both of her eyes as I start to pull out slowly and push back in.

"I love you." I kiss her cheeks, and down her jaw. Pushing myself in deeply, she runs her hands up and down my back, holding me close.

I take her slowly, showing her with body and my words just how much I've always and will always love her.

Please consider leaving a review! As an indie author, reviews are so important! Thank you so much for your support.

Dallas' story, book two in the Aspen Ridge series, is next! Find out how our brooding Hayes brother finds love with the newest distillery employee in Crave Me.

also by jenn plummer

Aspen Ridge Series

Crave Me

Love Me

Wreck Me

Complete Me

Aspen Ridge Holiday Novellas

Ready or Not

Sweet Girl

Daddy Issues

acknowledgments

Wow! I did it! I actually wrote and published a book! Since before I was ready to, I've been focused on raising a family and being a supportive military spouse. I never learned to prioritize myself and my dreams until now. This accomplishment is so deeply personal and life-changing for me. I wouldn't be here today without the support and love I've been shown. Thank you all for helping make my dreams come true!

My husband, Michael,

Your wife is an author, baby! This wouldn't be possible without your support. Thank you for pushing me to chase my dream, for believing in me so fiercely, for showering me with encouragement, giving me the time to focus, and loving me like no one else ever has. You've only ever asked me to do what will make me happy, whatever that may be, and I'm finally doing it. You're my home, my safe place, my comfort, the only thing I want when life gets hard. I love you and I'll be obsessed with you until my very last breath.

My four incredible children,

Thank you for your endless patience, your support, and encouragement while I gave every free moment to this book. You are saints for picking up all the slack and I love you all. All of your notes and reminders to keep going mean the world to me. I hope I've made you all proud and shown you to NEVER give up on your dreams.

Mumma,

I did it! I'm a published author! I finally straightened my crown and made my dreams happen. Thank you for the support and love you've given me and for always believing that I could do something with my writing. You've been telling me since I was little to write and here I am! Thank you for being my biggest cheerleader. I fucking did it!! I love you.

Katie, my editor and friend,

I truly could not have done this without you, nor would I want to. I'm sure this will be riddled with grammatical errors and missing an obscene amount of commas but it was important to me that you didn't edit my acknowledgement to you. It has been the time of my life working on this project with you and I'm so thankful to have you in my corner. I can't wait for everything else to come. Thank you for your patience, your advice, your invaluable input, for teaching me along the way (even if I still have no idea how to correctly use commas) and for being the best human. This story and these characters wouldn't be the same without you. Thank you for all of your hard work on this. I'm obsessed with you and I'm so glad we get to continue to work together. I love you!

My alpha readers,

You each have put in the time, the sweat, dealt with my endless need for reassurance, given me incredible feedback, kept me on track, adjusted to my crazy writing out of order process, spent hours scrolling through photos for cover ideas and reading and re-reading all of my work for the last four months. You are embedded deeply into the creation of this book and words will never be able to express my gratitude.

Laura S.,

When I felt like my world was falling apart at the seams, you pushed me to keep at it and start over. Your love, encouragement, strength, and unwavering support is a huge reason this book is out in the world and that I wrote it to begin with. Your help, feedback, plotting sessions, and everything in between was huge! I am so thankful I accidentally sent that filthy review of a super smutty book to the wrong group chat that day because I got you out of it. I would be lost without you. I love you so much!

Lauren R.,

You have put in the time, energy, research, and love into this book. You've lost sleep, read every line so many times your eyes hurt, given hours of thoughtful feedback, you've been my sounding board, and helped with every single aspect of this book from creation to publication. Unravel Me wouldn't be what it is without your help. Thank you for answering my post looking for an alpha reader. I not only got an incredible partner to help and support me, but I got a lifelong friend in the process. I love you. I'm thankful for you and I cannot wait to be able to squeeze you in a hug some day.

Dylan O.,

Who knew that those wild preteen friends would eventually grow up and work on a book together? I'm sure everyone who knows us is just as shocked as we are. Thank you for helping me bring Sawyer to life. You saved him from a fate of lackluster character traits and being a man who was unable to ride the motorcycle he loves so much. I hope a little piece of him is carried with you forever. Thank you for answering all of my questions, no matter how ridiculous, and for giving me and my book your time, care, and attention.

Dani & Nouha,

Would this even exist if it weren't for you two holding my hand? I can't begin to thank you two for being there for me with open arms, love, and support while I lost my shit over how to publish a book. It was the welcome I needed into this world and I'm so thankful. Thank you for loving and supporting me! I love you my queens!

Rose,

I did it! Thank you for loving me, for manifesting our dreams with me, for being my biggest cheerleader. Your support and encouragement, check-ins, and hilarious brainstorming sessions have kept me going. But most of all, thank you for always dropping everything to be there for me when my mental health tanks. We've lost countless days getting lost in our favorite books together and those breaks from life was the support I've needed most. We are so in-sync with each other, you always just know and are always there. I love you. You're next!!

Najla and the team at Qamber Designs,

Thank you for your hard work on these covers and for bringing Sawyer and Ivy to life. Working with you has been a dream and I'm so proud of the finished product. I can't thank you enough!

Lemmy at Luna Literary Management,

I love you! Thank you for cheering me on, for everything you do for me, and for every bit of encouragement, and support you've given me. I'm so grateful for all your hard work!

To all of my family and friends,

Thank you for your love and support! It means the world to me!

To every ARC reader, reviewer, and bookstagrammer,

Thank you for taking a chance on this indie author's debut novel! Your support is everything and I appreciate every single one of you!

To every reader who picked up my book and took a chance on me,
Thank you! You have made my dreams come true.

about the author

Author, wife, mother, lover of reading, overcast skies, chilly
weather, and hockey.

A romantic at heart, Jenn has always been a lover of books and is
constantly dreaming up heart-wrenching stories that will have you
reaching for tissues and make you blush.

When Jenn's not writing, she can be found reading a spicy
romance novel, watching scary movies, and enjoying her quiet life
in New England, living out her real-life romance story.

Follow along for updates on new releases and book news.

www.jennplummer.com
Instagram @authorjennplummer
Goodreads @jennplummer
Amazon @jennplummer
Threads @authorjennplummer